PRAISE FOR TIM WAGGONER!

"*Pandora Dri*... ...s ahead in linear fashion... ...ll have to go back and ... ...ear's *Like Death*."

—Tale Bones

"Reading something like a cross between Edward Lee and Lewis Carroll, *Pandora Drive* simply has to be read to be believed. Hop onto Tim Waggoner's magic carpet and hang on tight as *Pandora Drive* gleefully unravels."

—Hellnotes

"Waggoner is in possession of a talent that should be taken seriously, and I can't wait for his next book."

—Dread Central

LIKE DEATH

"The plot is compelling... [*Like Death*] is the best novel of 2005."

—Cemetery Dance

"A well-written, fast-paced, horrifically gory novel... incredibly unique."

—The Horror Channel

An "unusual, atmospheric horror novel... Waggoner does a very good job with his characters and an even better one in creating bizarre images and landscapes through which to conduct his readers."

—Chronicle

"Tim Waggoner works some mojo!"

—Douglas E. Winter, Author of *Run*

FAR WORSE THAN DEATH

From her current vantage point, Ricia couldn't see where they were going, but she didn't need to. She knew they were heading for the barn. She could see the fluorescent glowing on the ground, see the liquid black shadows of her captors sliding along behind them.

Riding over the bald man's shoulder and looking downward, Ricia saw gravel give way to bare earthen floor. The light changed, too, from blue-white fluorescence to a glaring bright yellow, as if work lights had been strung up in the barn. She took a breath and nearly gagged.

"Well, we finally made it," the bald man said. He removed his hand from Ricia's back and leaned forward. Ricia slid off his shoulder and flopped onto the ground. Her broken ribs screamed in agony, but no sound came out of her mouth. Why bother? She was already as good as dead.

The bald man squatted down on his haunches so he could look her in the face. He gestured, then spoke in a hushed, reverent voice. "Behold the Tapestry."

She didn't want to look, knew that she'd regret it more than anything else she'd ever done in her life, but she couldn't help herself. She slowly turned her head and gazed in the direction the bald man indicated.

She saw the Tapestry, and she realized then that there were worse things than death. Infinitely worse. She screamed then, and she was still screaming several hours later when she became the Tapestry's latest addition....

Other *Leisure* books by Tim Waggoner:

PANDORA DRIVE
LIKE DEATH

TIM WAGGONER

DARKNESS WAKES

LEISURE BOOKS NEW YORK CITY

A LEISURE BOOK®

December 2006

Published by

Dorchester Publishing Co., Inc.
200 Madison Avenue
New York, NY 10016

ISBN 0-8439-5794-8

Printed in the United States of America.

Visit us on the web at www.dorchesterpub.com.

DARKNESS WAKES

CHAPTER ONE

The unmarked metal door banged open, and a short potbellied man stumbled out into the night. Eyes wild with fear, breath coming in ragged, phlegmy gasps, he wore a red polo shirt stretched tight over his protruding stomach and khaki shorts from which emerged a pair of surprisingly bony legs. Sweat streamed from the man's body as if his pores were weeping, and his damp clothes stuck to him like a second sodden skin.

He hurried across the sidewalk in front of the businesses in the shopping center and ran into the parking lot, sandaled feet slapping against the blacktop. He was in his midfifties, and though he'd gotten a clean bill of health during his last checkup, heart disease ran in his family. He could hear his heart pounding rapidly, could feel it slamming against his chest wall as if it were a terrified caged animal desperate to break free. He feared that his heart might burst before he could escape, but given how likely that was, maybe he'd be better off if his heart did pack it in. He was certain it would be a painful, awful way to die, but he was also sure it would be preferable to what his pursuers would do to him if they caught him.

It was after midnight, but the absence of sunlight didn't do much to make the late July air any cooler. If anything, it seemed hotter and more humid than during the day. Breathing was like sucking in the air from a blast furnace, and he imagined it searing his throat and lungs, cooking him from the inside out.

Stop it! he told himself. *Keep thinking like that and you'll talk yourself into having a heart attack!*

All he had to do was reach his SUV. Once he was behind the wheel of his Suburban Uber Vehicle, as he thought of it, he'd be safe. He'd drive straight out of town, not bothering to stop at his condo and pack. He had an old college buddy in Kentucky whom he went fishing with now and again. He'd head for Stan's place—none of *them* knew about it, so *they* wouldn't be able to find him there. He'd hole up there for a few days, maybe a week or two at the most until he could get his shit together and decide what to do next.

There weren't many vehicles in the parking lot at this time of night, and he'd left his SUV—with vanity plates that read FOOTZEE—beneath a fluorescent light pole, so he had no trouble finding it in his panicked state. He headed straight for it, wishing that he'd spent more time in his life exercising than sitting on his fat ass watching TV or surfing the Net. Hell, right now he wished he'd trained to be a goddamned Olympic sprinter!

He hated to leave, though he wouldn't miss Ptolemy. The town was little more than a stain on the southwest corner of the Ohio state map. And while he regretted abandoning his podiatry practice, the truth was he'd long ago gotten sick of treating ingrown toenails and bunions. He had no family and no real friends here, save for those he now fled from. The only thing he would regret leaving was Penumbra, and the dark ecstasy that he had found within its walls. The very thought of going without its fell bliss nauseated him, and he imagined he could already feel the first faint pangs of withdrawal.

He reached his SUV and jammed a pudgy hand into his shorts pockets in search of his keys. At first he couldn't find them, and an icicle of fear pierced his gut. Had he lost his keys earlier in the club? Or had the others, somehow anticipating his failure tonight, stolen them from him? He didn't see how the latter was possible, but that didn't mean it was *not* possible. Not for *them.*

But he dug a little deeper and found his keys right where they were supposed to be. He pulled them out and fumbled for the car remote. He unlocked the car, gripped the handle, and threw the driver's-side door open. But before he could climb up into the seat, he felt a hand clamp down on his left shoulder. A tiny screech escaped his throat, a sound like a frightened little girl might make. His keys slipped from his fingers as he was turned around, and they hit the ground with a jingle. Excuses began to dribble from his lips like an idiot's drool.

"I didn't know she was strung out, I swear to Christ! If I had, I never would've brought her, never!"

"You should've checked her out before you brought her to Penumbra, Morgan." Caroline's voice was cold and without pity. She was the only one who had caught up to him so far, but though she must've run fast to catch him, he hadn't heard her and she wasn't breathing hard.

"What was I supposed to do? Take her to a clinic for a blood test?" He surprised himself by how calm he sounded, as if the fault for what had happened was theirs instead of his.

"If you weren't certain, you shouldn't have brought her. You know the rules."

Morgan detected movement out of the corner of his eye. He glanced toward the open doorway that was the entrance to Penumbra and saw the others were filtering out one by one to join them. They didn't run, didn't even walk fast. They simply walked out of the club and into the parking lot as if nothing out of the ordinary was happening. Somehow, that was even more frightening to Morgan than if they had run. It meant they weren't concerned about his escaping, that they'd never even considered it a serious possibility.

"But I couldn't find anyone else, and it was my turn tonight." He hated how whiny and pathetic his voice sounded, like a little boy trying to talk his way out of being punished. But he couldn't help it. "I didn't want to come empty-handed. Didn't want to go without any longer. I . . . *needed* it."

The others were coming closer. They were all there—Wyatt, Gillian, Trevor, Shari, Spencer, and Caroline's husband, Phillip—and they all shared the same grim expression on their faces.

"We all need it," Caroline said. "Just as badly as you do. But the difference between us is that we're *still* going to get it." She stepped closer, smiled, and touched her index finger to his pudgy dry lips. "And *you're* going to give it to us."

Morgan cried out in terror and shoved her away. He knelt down to search for his keys. He saw them lying on the ground, reached for them, but Caroline kicked out and knocked them under his SUV with the side of her flip-flop. Morgan swore, crouched lower, stretched his hand under the car, fingers scrabbling frantically as he tried to grab hold of his keys. But even as he reached for them, he knew it was too late. Even if he managed to get hold of them, he'd never be able to get into his SUV in time, let alone shut the door and start the engine.

He heard footsteps on the blacktop draw closer, then stop. He turned his head and saw the feet and legs of his friends and fellow addicts. He knew he should stand up and accept his fate like a man, but instead he collapsed to the ground and began to sob. Someone—Phillip and Trevor, he guessed, though he couldn't tell through the tears in his eyes—grabbed hold of his fleshy upper arms and hauled him to his feet. And then they began escorting him back to Penumbra, walking on either side of him, holding tight to his arms so he couldn't escape. He considered letting his body go limp, becoming deadweight. He was heavy enough that they would have trouble getting him back inside if he didn't help them. If he could delay them long enough for someone else to enter the parking lot, perhaps a patrolling police car . . .

But Morgan didn't do it. For with each step he took back toward the open doorway, his fear slowly receded to be replaced with the first faint stirrings of desire, and he was surprised to find himself starting to become erect. He knew he was going to die this night, and in a way far more horrible than most people could imagine. And yet, at least he'd get to be in *its* presence one more time, feel its cold loving touch . . .

Maybe it won't be so bad, he thought. *Maybe it'll even feel good . . . better than ever before.*

And so by the time Dr. Morgan Pierson, DPM, was escorted across the threshold and back into Penumbra, his fear had given way to anticipation. The last person to return to the club shut and locked the door behind him. And though no one outside could hear because of Penumbra's soundproofed walls, several moments later, Morgan began to scream.

He'd been wrong; it didn't feel good. Not for him, anyway.

CHAPTER TWO

Aaron pulled into the parking lot of the Valley View Shopping Center at 11:48 P.M. with eleven minutes to spare.

He parked in a handicapped space in front of Starbrite Movie and Game Rentals, put his Lexus in park, and cut the engine. Normally he wouldn't have taken the space, but it was almost midnight, and he was only going to be here a minute. He'd had his Lexus for two weeks, but he still hadn't gotten over his boyish glee at driving it. That was the real reason he'd gone out this late to return the DVDs he'd rented. He didn't give a damn about late fees; he just wanted any excuse he could get to climb behind the wheel of his new toy and drive. And none of this certified preowned shit for him, either. He'd bought this baby brand-new. Of course, he'd waited until an inventory-reduction sale at the dealer, but new was new, right?

Doesn't really count unless you can afford to walk in the very first day, hell, the very first minute *the new*

*models go on sale and plunk down the full amount on
the counter—cash money.*

The thought was his, but the voice he heard it in
wasn't.

He grabbed the three DVDs off the passenger seat—
two chick flicks for Kristen, and an old eighties slobs
vs. snobs comedy for him and the kids—and got out of
the car. He locked it with the key remote and headed
for the store entrance. As he stepped onto the sidewalk
in front of Starbrite, he passed a blue metal return box,
but he didn't even consider dropping the movies inside. The last time he'd done that, the tattooed and
pierced teenager behind the counter had insisted he'd
returned them late the next time he rented movies, and
no amount of arguing could dissuade the little prick. *It
says so right here on the store computer, sir.* Aaron had
wanted to say, *Fuck your computer! I say I returned
those goddamned movies on time!* But he hadn't bothered. Kids from Metalface's generation didn't believe
anything unless they saw it on a screen. Ever since
then Aaron had taken his DVDs back inside himself,
regardless of what time it was or how much of a hurry
he was in.

The bell above the glass door tinkled as Aaron went
inside, and he was glad to see that Metalface wasn't
working tonight. Instead, a cute little blonde stood behind the counter. She had long straight hair, a heart-
shaped face, and too much eye shadow and lipstick,
but Aaron figured, what the hell? He'd always liked the
bubblegum whore look. He smiled as he handed her
the DVDs, but her eyes didn't even meet his as she

took the movies and tossed them down on the back counter.

"Thankshaveanicenight," she mumbled.

"Yeah, you too." Aaron turned and left the store, ego stinging. Sure, he was forty-five, but he took care of himself, ate right, exercised regularly . . . well, regularly enough. He was starting to go gray at the temples, but he thought it made him look distinguished. But the blond clerk had acted like he was invisible, as if he wasn't male but rather some third gender: neuter-guy. When he'd been younger, he could've chatted little Miss Blondie up and gotten her phone number within a couple of minutes. They'd be out on a date the next night, and there'd be a good chance he'd get to bang her before the evening ended.

When he was younger.

Don't kid yourself, Aaron. You never were that *good with the ladies. Nothing like your old man.*

Aaron did his best to ignore the thought as he walked across the lot. Though he hadn't noticed it crossing from his car to the store, the night air was humid and thick. Breathing was like trying to suck air through a mouthful of wet cotton. Not unusual weather for late July in Ohio, but for some reason, he'd thought it'd be cooler when he left the house. Now he wished he'd worn a T-shirt and shorts instead of a polo shirt and jeans. Maybe if the blonde had gotten a look at his tanned, toned legs . . .

As Aaron walked back to his car, he noticed swarms of small insects darting around the fluorescent lights that illuminated the lot. Aaron was no entomologist, but he was a veterinarian and had always had an interest in animals of every sort. He remembered reading once that the reason nocturnal insects such as moths were drawn to artificial light was that they navigated by moonlight and were disoriented by other light sources. He supposed their mindless compulsion was pathetic, especially since it so often led to their destruction from heat or simply smacking into a bulb until they died. But he envied them a little, too. What would it be like to feel such total, all-consuming passion for something? Aaron couldn't remember the last time he'd experienced such intensity of emotion, if he ever had. To know such passion, even if only for the briefest of moments before the heat of that passion burned you to a crisp . . . wouldn't that be worth the price? Any price?

As he drew near his Lexus, he thumbed the key remote again and the door locks snicked open. He got inside, closed the door, put the key into the ignition, and was about to turn it when headlights washed over his windshield. He squinted but didn't turn away from the light, and then the car moved past him and pulled into a space two rows over from where he was parked. Aaron wondered who it was and what he or she was doing here this time of night. Not returning movies, not unless whoever it was hadn't paid attention to where they parked. But Starbrite was the only business still open; unless you counted the bar at the eastern end of the shopping center. From west to east, there were nine businesses: an insurance agency, Suds-o-Rama (a laundry); Lose It and Use It (a weight-loss clinic); Around and Around (a secondhand kids' clothing store); I'd Buy That For a Dollar (where everything cost a buck or less); Starbrite Movie and Game Rentals; the Hobby Horse (a hobby shop); Earl's Carpets; and Deja Brew—the bar. There were only a handful of cars in the Valley View Shopping Center's lot, and most of them were parked down by the bar. But the recent arrival had parked down by the dollar store, directly under a light pole. The vehicle was a white Infiniti, and for some reason it struck Aaron as familiar. He understood why a second later when the driver got out. It was Caroline Langdon.

Tall, thin, with short, straight black hair and the beautiful but cold features of a European model. She wore a white top with long sleeves, black capri pants, and stylish black sandals with thin crisscrossing straps. Aaron noticed she was empty-handed, no purse and certainly no DVDs to return to Starbrite.

He considered getting out of the car to say hello, or at least rolling down the window and sticking his head out. Caroline and her husband, Phillip, lived on the same street as Aaron, and though they were hardly best friends, they knew each other well enough to wave if either was out working in the yard as the other passed. Besides, Caroline was exotic and sexy, almost the polar opposite of his wife, Kristen. Aaron had never made a play for Caroline—masturbatory fantasies excluded, of course—but he loved being near her. He loved inhaling the faint, subtle odor of her perfume, loved watching the way her thin lips moved as she talked (while imaging those lips forming an airtight seal around his cock). Most of all, he loved the way her large brown eyes focused so intently on whoever she spoke to, as if at that moment he or she was the most important and fascinating person on the planet.

Just a quick hello, he told himself. So he could look into those eyes, inhale her scent before he had to go home to his wife.

Forget it, kid. Even if you weren't a married man, that one's way out of your league.

Aaron reached for the door handle, but before he could get out, the Infiniti's passenger door opened, and a man got out of the car.

"Fuck," he muttered. Caroline wasn't alone; Phillip had come with her. Not that it made any real difference, Aaron supposed. It wasn't like he intended to hit on her. But now he wouldn't be able to say hi to Caroline alone; he'd have to talk to Phillip, too. And Phillip's presence would be a definite buzz-kill in the fantasy department. But then Aaron got his first good look at the man who'd climbed out of the Infiniti and realized that he wasn't Phillip Langdon. In fact, he wasn't anyone Aaron had ever seen before.

The man was younger than Caroline by about five years, Aaron guessed, which would put him in his early thirties, maybe late twenties at the youngest. He was thin with curly black hair and a thin mustache. He wore a white shirt with horizontal stripes—blue or purple, it was hard to tell in the fluorescent light—untucked, sleeves down but the cuffs unbuttoned. Long khaki pants and black running shoes completed his outfit. He looked as if he'd dressed for a night of clubbing, but there were no clubs in Ptolemy. There were a few in Ash Creek, but the closest city with any real nightlife was Cincinnati, about a forty-minute drive away. One thing Aaron was sure of, however: There wasn't any club in the Valley View Shopping Center. And they obviously weren't headed for the bar, since they began walking in the opposite direction, toward Starbrite video.

As they walked, Caroline stepped closer to the young man and put her arm around his trim waist. He gave her a smile and reciprocated by putting his arm over her shoulders.

I'll be damned, Aaron thought. *She's cheating on Phillip.* He felt a mixture of disappointment, jealousy, and envy that she wasn't cheating with *him.*

He sure as shit wasn't going to get out and say hi to her now, but he made no move to start his car, either. He didn't want to draw her attention, for one thing. Though he'd secretly lusted for her in his heart for years, it wasn't his business who she walked with across a parking lot at midnight. Plus, he didn't want to embarrass her by letting her know that she'd been caught by one of her neighbors. Not that he'd do anything with the knowledge. He knew Phillip well enough to say hi and bitch about how poorly their lawns were faring this summer, but they were far from friends.

But there was another reason Aaron just sat there behind the wheel of his Lexus. He wanted to watch and see what Caroline and her stripe-shirted beau did next. Circumstance had made him privy to a secret aspect of Caroline's life, a hidden intimacy that she'd unknowingly revealed to him, as if she'd been undressing in front of an open window without realizing Aaron was standing on the sidewalk outside, watching. He couldn't turn away if he wanted to. He *had* to watch.

As Caroline and her "companion" stepped onto the sidewalk that fronted the strip mall, Aaron saw that they weren't headed for the video store. Which was good, since the girl inside—perhaps worried by the seeming approach of two last-minute customers—chose that precise moment to turn off the neon sign over Starbrite's door. But Caroline and Mr. Striped Shirt moved quickly past the video store, past a row of vending units that contained copies of a free alternative paper, booklets of apartment listings, and the like. Aaron assumed they would continue on past the next shop, I'd Buy That For a Dollar, but they stopped in front of a featureless gray metal door between the freebie vending machines and the dollar store.

Aaron frowned. He couldn't remember ever seeing that door before tonight, but he supposed he must have. After all, it wasn't as if the door had suddenly appeared in the strip mall overnight . . . He assumed the door led to a storage space or perhaps a maintenance room where the controls for the entire building's electrical system were housed, and probably the heating and cooling controls, too. There was no neon sign above the door, and no windows on either side. Just plain redbrick. But if the door didn't really lead anywhere—at least anywhere interesting—then why had Caroline and her young lover stopped in front of it?

Caroline let go of Mr. Striped Shirt's waist and reached into her purse. She withdrew a key—not a set of keys, just a single key that wasn't attached to anything else—and inserted it into the lock above the door's chrome metal knob. She gave the key a twist, then gripped the knob and turned it.

The door opened inward.

Caroline removed the key from the lock and tucked it back into her purse. She then smiled her at companion—a somewhat lascivious smile, Aaron thought, one that he wished was directed at him—and gestured for Mr. Striped Shirt to enter. The man hesitated for a moment, and Aaron began to think that maybe he was going to chicken out. But then he returned Caroline's smile and stepped inside. Caroline followed, pulling the door closed behind her.

There was no way Aaron could hear it from where he sat, but he imagined the door shut with a soft metallic *click*!

Aaron sat for a moment, trying to understand what he'd just witnessed. And then it came to him. Caroline had taken her lover to a sex club. He'd heard of such places, though he'd never visited one himself. Clubs where men and woman, singles and couples would go to indulge in all sorts of sexual behavior— partner swapping, group sex, role-playing, S&M, B&D, and who knew how many other combinations of the alphabet? Such businesses weren't exactly the kind chambers of commerce lauded on promotional pamphlets and Web sites, so these clubs often refrained from displaying any outward signs of their existence, preferring to advertise by word of mouth alone. Aaron wondered how many people walked past that door every day without realizing what went on behind it at night. Even the employees of the businesses on either side might not know, depending on how discreet the club's clientele was. Aaron couldn't believe it. A sex club, right there in little old Ptolemy,

Ohio. And it seemed that Caroline Langdon was a member.

This cast the situation in a whole new light for Aaron. Maybe Caroline wasn't cheating on Phillip. Maybe they had an open marriage, maybe they were swingers, maybe Phillip was a member, too. He might already be inside getting it on with someone else. Or maybe waiting for his wife to bring Mr. Striped Shirt by for a threesome. Aaron pictured Caroline, Phillip, and Mr. Striped Shirt naked: one of the men lying on the floor, Caroline on top of him, the other on his knees behind her, all three fucking the shit out of each other like rabid weasels. Which would be the backdoor man, Aaron wondered, Phillip or Striped Shirt? Maybe they'd take turns. Pornographic images passed through Aaron's mind of every possible sex act three people could indulge in—and several impossible ones as well. He felt his penis begin to stiffen, and he was tempted to undo his zipper, free his cock, and start stroking, but he was a little old to be jacking off in parking lots. Besides, there was no way he was going to get cum stains on his Lexus's upholstery.

Aaron watched the door for several more minutes, but no one came out; and no new cars pulled into the parking lot. Unless he was prepared to sit here for a while—and how would he explain his delay in returning home to his wife?—it looked like the show was over, at least for him. He gave the door one last look and sighed. He was glad someone he knew was having fun tonight, living on the edge, experiencing real *passion*. All that lay before him was a boring drive home to a wife who was probably already asleep. And even if he woke her up and told her he wanted to make love, she'd say she was too tired, they both had work in the morning. And in the unlikely event that she said yes, the sex would be vanilla at best. Kristen would climax—she almost always did—as would he, but he would barely feel his orgasm. He certainly wouldn't be satisfied with it. Hell, he wasn't sure if he'd ever truly been satisfied in any meaningful sense of the word in his entire life.

He started his Lexus, got so far as putting the car in drive, and then a little voice whispered in his mind.

Why don't you go see if the door's still unlocked, kid? Maybe it is, maybe you can open it, and go in. Maybe you can join in with Caroline, Phillip, and Striped Shirt, make the threesome a foursome. After all, she's got three holes to fill, right? A pause. *That is, if you got the stones.*

Aaron gazed through his windshield at the gray metal door. He sat there, staring at it for almost a full minute before putting the Lexus back in park, turning the engine off, and getting out.

As he walked across the parking lot, he became aware of his pulse pounding in his ears, felt a line of sweat trickling from his right armpit and down his side. His footsteps seemed muffled, as if the black asphalt was somehow absorbing the sound of his passage. He experienced a crawly-tickly feeling on the back of his neck, and he quickly glanced around to see if anyone was watching him, just as he had watched Caroline a few moments earlier. He saw no one, but that didn't mean he wasn't being watched. Anyone could be out there in the darkness, watching hidden and unseen. Wouldn't it be ironic if a friend or neighbor was watching him, someone who'd report back to Kristen that her husband had been seen approaching the notorious Valley View Shopping Center sex club? He wondered how Kristen would react to such news. It would almost be worth getting caught just to see the expression on her face as she learned her husband—good old reliable, dependable Aaron—had taken himself a little walk on the wild side. Would she be horrified? Dismayed? Unbelieving? Or would she be surprised and perhaps even a little intrigued by the revelation that her husband of nearly twenty years had a hidden dark side?

The feeling of being watched didn't go away, but he forced himself to ignore it. Even if someone was watching, what were the odds that they'd recognize him?

You recognized Caroline.

That was different. She was a neighbor, and he'd secretly had the hots for her for years. Most of his other neighbors were either couples with very young children or old folks on the verge of moving to assisted-living facilities. None of them likely to be here at this hour. He supposed one of his clients might be out and about this late, but a vet wasn't like an MD. People didn't see him the same way, didn't really see him at all sometimes. They were usually too worried about little Puffball's fleas or lack of appetite. To most of his clients, he was just the guy that wrote prescriptions for their pets.

He reached the sidewalk and stepped up onto it, then walked over to the gray metal door that Caroline had unlocked for her stripe-shirted friend. He stopped two feet from the door and examined it. Its gray paint flaked around the edges, revealing reddish brown scales of rust beneath. The surface was otherwise smooth and featureless, save for where someone— some teenager who fancied himself a daring wit, Aaron guessed—had tried to carve the word *fuck* onto the door using a pocketknife, or perhaps the tip of a car key. But either the kid was a lousy speller or, more likely, had been interrupted during his act of minor vandalism, for the last letter wasn't quite complete, looking more like an L than a K, making *fucl*.

"Fuckle," Aaron whispered, the word sounding at once silly and sinister at it spilled past his lips.

He stepped closer to the door until he stood only inches from its surface, *fucl* almost even with the tip of his nose. He turned his right ear toward the door and listened. He didn't know what he hoped to hear. Music, conversation, laughter, moaning and groaning, the wet smack of sweat-slathered bodies pounding against each other . . . But he heard nothing. He was tempted to put his ear to the door. Metal conducted vibrations well, didn't it? He'd be bound to hear something. But he couldn't bring himself to do it. Maybe because it seemed too juvenile, or maybe because he could just see someone inside opening the door while he stood there, throwing him off balance and causing him to fall inward flat on his face, like some hapless sitcom character. He had more dignity than that. Not that there was all that much dignity in sneaking up to the door of a sex club after seeing your neighbor go inside with her lover, but hey, a guy's gotta have some standards, low as they might be.

Aaron looked down at the doorknob. He'd noticed earlier that it was chrome, but what he hadn't been able to see from behind the wheel of his Lexus was that half of the metal was faded, exactly where a person's hand would grasp it. This knob had been here for a long time and had seen a lot of use.

This is stupid. Even if it's unlocked, what are you going to do? Walk in and shout, "Here's my dick, where's the party?" It's one thing to fantasize about stuff like that, kid, but it's another thing to go ahead and actually do it.

He looked again at the doorknob, noted how it seemed to glow bluish white in the reflected glow of the parking lot lights. A color like that made him think it would be cold to the touch—damned cold.

He almost turned around and walked back toward his Lexus, but he didn't. Instead, he reached out and wrapped his fingers around the knob, steeling himself against the anticipated sensation of cold. But the metal wasn't even cool. It was warm, moist, and despite being molded from metal, almost pliant. It reminded Aaron of shaking hands with a fat, sweaty person, a sensation he found far from pleasant. But he didn't let go, even when he thought he felt the knob shift in his grip slightly, as if it were trying to get comfortable. Without squeezing any harder—primarily because he didn't want to, was afraid that the knob might explode in his hand like a rotten tomato—Aaron turned it. Despite its worn exterior, the knob turned smoothly, as if recently oiled. He imagined the knob turning all the way, the door opening wide to reveal whatever secrets lay behind it. But the knob barely turned at all before stopping with a soft click. It was locked.

Of course it is, Aaron thought, remembering Caroline's key. This club was Members Only, it appeared. He thought of Striped Shirt then. Okay, Members and *Guests* Only.

So, what are you going to do now? You can't just stand here like an idiot and wait for someone to come out.

Aaron supposed that there really wasn't much else he could do, not unless he chose to knock. And how lame would that be?

Hi, sorry to bother you, but I happened to notice my neighbor come in here with a young lover a little while ago. Would it be okay if I come in—just for a little while—and watch her get the shit fucked out of her? I promise to be quiet and not bother anyone.

Extremely lame.

It seemed his walk on the wild side had been more of a stroll, and it had come to an end. With nothing else to do, and beginning to feel like a prize asshole for standing here in front of a locked door, he turned away from the gray door with the word *fucl* scratched into the metal and began heading into the parking lot.

Somewhere out in the night's darkness, a pair of eyes watched Aaron get into his Lexus, shut the door, start the engine, and flip on the headlights. These eyes continued to watch as Aaron put the car in gear and pulled out of his space. Since the parking lot was almost completely empty, Aaron was able to pull his car forward instead of backing up. The owner of the eyes thought

Aaron would whip his Lexus around and squeal his tires as he accelerated toward the shopping center's exit, using his car as an outlet for the emotions that had built up as he'd stood in front of the entrance to Penumbra. But Aaron drove slowly and calmly toward the exit, stopping and even activating his turn signal before pulling out onto the road. Even then he didn't gun the engine, just continued driving slowly, doing at least five miles per hour less than the speed limit.

The watcher narrowed his eyes. Interesting. Most people couldn't contain their emotions after being so close to Penumbra and being denied entrance, even if they didn't know what went on behind its steel door. *Especially* if they didn't know. But the owner of the Lexus had maintained control. He would bear continued watching. He might prove useful in the war to come.

The watcher started his blue Volkswagen Bug—robin's-egg blue, though it looked bone white in the fluorescent wash of the parking lot lights. He turned on his headlights and followed after Aaron, his dome light flickering erratically, nervously rubbing the uneven stubble atop his shaved head and muttering softly to himself as he drove.

CHAPTER THREE

Saturday afternoon in early September, a glorious time that's not quite summer but not yet fall. Warm and sunny, but not hot and sweltering. A touch of coolness in the breeze, but not even a hint of winter's coming chill. A good time being out in the backyard with your dad, playing catch.

Aaron is nine and average in far too many ways. Average height, average build, average dexterity, reflexes, and speed . . . He played Little League ball for the first time this summer, and he spent most of the time polishing the bench with his ass. His father played baseball throughout his school years, on into high school and even college. He stopped playing when he went to law school, though.

I had more important things to do in law school than play games, *he always says.*

He's still a big baseball fan, hardly ever misses a game on TV—especially if the Reds are playing. Aaron wishes he could say the same about his Little League games, but his dad is busy working most of the time, and he rarely makes it to see Aaron play. And even if he does get to a game, he usually arrives late and leaves early. But Aaron's trying not to think about that now. He's thinking about what a great day it is and how lucky he is that his dad doesn't have to work this afternoon. Today, it seems time is standing still, that the outer world has ceased to exist, and it's just Aaron, his dad, two baseball gloves, and a fresh white ball that's just been taken out of its packaging. If this isn't heaven, it's close enough for Aaron.

"Throw me one, kid! Nice and hard!"

Aaron does so, his right arm flapping out to his side like a chicken wing as he releases the ball. It goes wide, but his dad steps deftly to the side and plucks the ball out of the air with his bare hand as easily as if the ball were a piece of slowly drifting dandelion fluff.

"That's no way to throw, Aaron." Dad comes toward him, brow knitted in a frown, lips tight with disapproval. "You're side-arming it."

When he reaches Aaron, Dad puts the ball in his hand and positions his son's first three fingers over the top of the ball. He steps back and says, "Hold it like that and next time throw it overhand, like this." He demonstrates by pretending to throw an invisible ball in slow motion.

Aaron watches close, takes it all in. When Dad's finished, he nods. "Got it."

Dad looks skeptical, but he says, "Okay, let's see you give it a try." He walks back to his previous position on the grass, then as if thinking better of it, takes two steps forward. Aaron tries not to let this bother him.

He concentrates on holding the ball just right and throwing it overhand instead of side-arming it. The ball flies fast and true and strikes the middle of Dad's glove with a satisfying thwack!

Dad smiles and nods approvingly. "Better."

It's not much, but it's the most praise Aaron can ever remember getting from his father, and it makes the boy nearly giddy to hear it.

"All right, let's see you how catch."

Aaron expects Dad to throw a fastball toward him, but instead he hurls the baseball almost straight up, so high it seems to dwindle to a speck, lost in the clouds. Aaron looks up, glove ready. But the sun is bright and shining in his eyes, and he can't find the baseball in the sky. But that's all right, because a few seconds later the ball finds him. It smashes into the right side of his head, and pain explodes in his ear. The impact and the pain cause his legs to fold beneath him, and he falls to the ground. He shakes off his glove, sobbing, and reaches up to touch his ear, which blazes with so much pain it feels like it's on fire.

Please don't let there be blood, please don't let there be blood . . .

Terrified, Aaron looks to his dad. He's just standing there, a look of disgust frozen on his face. Finally, still wearing a mask of disappointment, Dad starts walking toward him. Aaron wishes he would stay away, because the expression on his father's face makes him feel ashamed, makes him feel as if he's not good enough for his dad . . . not good enough for anything.

* * *

"You're really something, kid."

Aaron tore his gaze from the gray metal door and turned toward the man sitting in the passenger seat.

"Why's that, Dad?" Aaron tried to keep his tone neutral, but he couldn't keep the weariness he felt out of his voice.

"You're forty-five years old, but you're acting like a teenager with a twenty-four-hour-a-day hard-on."

Martin Rittinger—Marty to his friends, of which there were precious few—looked just like Aaron remembered him: a thin man in his seventies with an unruly thicket of white hair dressed in a gray cardigan, white shirt, khaki slacks, and brown loafers. He looked more like a college professor than a bankruptcy lawyer.

"It's just a fantasy, Dad. It's not like I'd really do anything."

Aaron hated trying to explain anything to his father. No matter what he did, no matter his motivation for doing it, it was never good enough. Not for Martin Rittinger.

"Jesus Christ, listen to you!" Martin shook his head in disgust, a gesture Aaron had seen far too many times before the cancer that had devoured his father's prostate had claimed his life. "This is what I'm talking about, kid. A real man would make a commitment one way or the other: stay faithful to his wife or go after that sweet piece of ass behind Door Number One. Life's all about making choices, kid, and once you make them, you stick to them."

Aaron hated it when his father called him *kid*. He'd tried to explain once how the continued use of the childhood nickname made him feel as if Martin was belittling him. But all Martin had said was, *It shouldn't matter what anyone else calls you. You should be in control of your feelings. No one should be able to make you do anything—including feel.*

Before Aaron could reply to his father, he sensed movement from the direction of the shopping center. He looked away from Martin and saw that the gray door—the fuckle door—was starting to open.

Aaron spoke without looking at his father. "Listen, Dad, I'd like to stay and talk"—which was one of the biggest lies Aaron had ever told—"but I really need to go." He reached for the car door handle, but before he could open the door, his father grabbed hold of Aaron's upper arm.

"Not tonight, kid. You're not ready yet."

Someone was coming out of the open doorway, but Aaron couldn't tell who it was. His vision seemed to have blurred, and all he could make out was a shadowy silhouette that might or might not have been human, let alone Caroline. But if there was even a chance that it was her . . .

Aaron turned to his father. "Let go. And don't . . . call me . . . kid." Aaron's voice died away as he saw that Martin Rittinger no longer had eyes in his head. They'd been replaced by seething pools of inky blackness.

Martin smiled. "Time to wake up, kid."

And then darkness gushed forth from his father's skull to engulf Aaron. He opened his mouth to scream, but the sound was choked off as the blackness surged down his throat and filled every empty space inside him.

* * *

Aaron opened his eyes to find himself staring up into darkness. At first this didn't disturb him, but then he remembered his dream and cold fear washed through his guts. His bladder was full and aching, and for a moment he thought he might actually lose control for the first time since he was four and piss the bed. He felt a couple of drops of urine squeeze out from the tip of his penis to dampen his underwear—which was all Aaron ever slept in—but that was it. He felt relieved that he'd managed to hold back, but he felt irritated, too. It wasn't as if it had been *that* scary a dream. If his bladder hadn't been so damn full, he wouldn't have come so close to losing control. But he had to take a handful of cholesterol and triglyceride-lowering pills every night before he went to bed, and since he needed a lot of water to help him swallow pills, that meant he always had to pee at least once in the middle of the night. Ah, the joys of getting older.

Aaron sat up and looked over at Kristen. She was just a lump in the darkness, but she was still, her breathing deep and regular with just the faintest hint of a snore as she exhaled. Evidently he hadn't been thrashing about during his nightmare, or if he had, not enough to wake her. He slowly pushed the sheet off him. Even with the air-conditioning set to seventy-two degrees, it was still a bit too stuffy in here for him, though Kristen slept under a sheet and two other blankets. Aaron then got out of bed and walked across the bedroom as quietly as he could toward the master bathroom. He went inside, quietly shut the door, and without turning on the light, made his way to the toilet and sat down. He usually peed standing up, but he didn't want to wake Kristen by splashing too much. Sitting down, he could angle his urine stream so it would hit the inside of the bowl just above the water level and slide down with little noise. As he started to pee, he thought about why he didn't want to wake Kristen tonight. Normally it wasn't something that he worried about, since she never had trouble falling back to sleep.

Part of it was practicality. Kristen had been asleep when he'd gotten home, but he didn't know how long she'd been in bed. She might well have stayed up long enough to realize that he'd taken an awful lot of time to return a couple of movies, and he didn't feel like explaining himself right then. His brain felt too sludgy to provide a believable excuse. Another reason was undoubtedly guilt. Kristen was a good woman who loved him and was a great mother to their children. She deserved better than an emotionally and sexually restless husband, even if so far he hadn't done anything about it. While he was growing up, Aaron's parents hadn't been religious, but his maternal grandmother had been. Whenever the two of them were alone, even if it was only for a few minutes, his grandma would try to sneak in a little religious instruction, tell a quick Bible story or pass on a short quote from the gospels. And whenever she said good-bye to Aaron, she always added, *I love you and remember that Jesus loves you, too.* One of the lessons that she'd attempted to instill in him on several occasions was that sin was sin; there were no gradations to it.

Thinking an evil thought is just as bad as committing an evil act in the eyes of the Lord, she'd say.

When he'd been little, Aaron hadn't understood, but as he'd gotten a bit older, he began to wonder if there really was no difference between thought and deed. If God wasn't going to punish you more for one or the other, why not just go ahead and commit whatever evil act you were thinking about? The cost would be the same, and *doing* would be a hell of a lot more fun than *thinking*, wouldn't it? But young as he was, he'd known better than to share these thoughts with Grandma.

Aaron finished peeing, flushed, then washed his hands. He waited for the toilet tank to fill up and go silent once more before opening the bathroom door. Kristen was still asleep, though she'd shifted position and now the covers—instead of being drawn up to her chin as usual—were down around her waist. She wore blue silk pajamas, not that Aaron could see them in the dark, but he knew they were there. They always were. For years he'd tried to convince her to sleep naked, but though she'd tried, she always went back to her pajamas.

I'm sorry, sweetie. I just get so cold at night.

Aaron had resisted making a bitter joke then, though it hadn't been easy.

He stopped at the foot of the bed and listened to Kristen's soft night breathing. It seemed that Grandma's tutelage hadn't been entirely in vain. Why else would he be feeling guilty about tonight, even though he hadn't really *done* anything?

He considered crawling back into bed and caressing Kristen through her silk pajamas. He liked the way the silk slid softly over her skin, and he especially liked how her nipples felt through the fabric as they grew hard. He might be able to rouse her. It had been almost two weeks since they'd last made love. Maybe she was ready. Aaron subscribed to a number of magazines for his practice's waiting room, and though he didn't have time to read them all, he skimmed the more interesting-looking issues. Once he'd come across an article called "The Sexless Marriage." In it, the writer quoted a sex therapist as saying that a couple that has sex once a week or less was, for all intents and purposes, in a sex-less relationship. Aaron had been stunned. He couldn't remember a time when he and Kristen had made love once a week, let alone more often than that. Maybe when they'd first started dating. But by the time they'd gotten married, the frequency of their lovemaking had declined drastically. Hell, they'd gone on a two-week cruise for their honeymoon, and they'd only made love the first night. After that, Kristen was always "too tired."

He looked at his wife now. He'd been awake long enough for his eyes to adjust to the darkness some-what, and he could make out the rough shape of her face, his memory supplying the details that his vision couldn't. Fine, delicate features, large brown eyes, full lips, a dusting of freckles on her cheeks and nose, lush strawberry-blond hair. She was forty-two but looked younger, and though she wasn't a health and exercise fanatic, she took good care of herself. Her body was trim and her breasts, though on the small side, hadn't begun to sag yet. She dressed conservatively most of the time, but she still got plenty of looks from men when they were out. She'd always been attractive, but as the years passed, she'd gained a calm self-confidence that only added to her appeal. Aaron still lusted after her as much as he had when they'd first met in college. But the problem was she didn't lust him back. He doubted she'd ever experienced the emotion.

Feeling good and depressed now, as well as wide awake, Aaron walked out of their bedroom and softly shut the door behind him. As he walked down the hall, he stopped and looked in Lindsay's room. Her door was cracked open, just enough so that Aaron could get a glimpse of her huddled beneath her blue comforter that was covered with a pattern of bright yellow stars. She was definitely her mother's daughter when it came to how she felt about cold. Above her was a shelf displaying numerous stuffed animals that she'd outgrown sleeping with but hadn't quite outgrown enough to get rid of. She had the same strawberry-blond hair as Kristen, though hers was curlier, more like Aaron's mother's had been. Linsday was already pretty, and she'd no doubt be a heartbreaker in high school a few years hence.

Aaron then continued down the hall past Colin's room. As always, his door was shut, and if Aaron tried the knob he knew he'd find it locked. Colin was sixteen, and Aaron understood that the boy needed privacy. Hell, he'd always kept his door closed when he'd been a teenager—primarily to keep his dad from catching him looking at *Penthouse* and masturbating. But he'd never kept his door locked at night. Aaron had tried to point out to Colin that not only wasn't there any need to lock his door at night, but doing so was also a safety hazard. What if he became sick and needed help? Or what if there was a fire in the middle of the night? But whenever Aaron made these arguments, Colin just shrugged them off.

I sleep with my cell phone on my nightstand. If I ever got too sick to get to my door and too sick to yell for help—which I can't imagine—I'd just call you or Mom. And if there was a fire, I'd just open my window, knock out the screen, and climb through.

Aaron always wanted to argue the point. After all, Colin's room *was* on the second floor. But he never did. What good would it do? Besides, he didn't want to come off sounding too much like his own father. Always critical, always disapproving. But Aaron missed the days when Colin was young enough to sleep with his door open, missed being able to look in on him while he slept, listen to his gentle little boy breathing . . .

You're too soft on your kids. Always have been.

Aaron ignored the thought and continued down the hallway until he reached the stairs. He went down, turned, walked through the foyer and into the kitchen. They always left a light on over the sink, so Aaron didn't bother turning on any other lights. He went to the cupboard, took out a black mug with the words *Number One Dad* painted on it in white letters, then went to the refrigerator and poured some milk in it. He put the mug in the microwave and set it for two minutes. The microwave hummed to life, and the mug began turning in a slow circle as radiation agitated its molecules. Aaron didn't usually drink warm milk to help him sleep, would've preferred a double scotch instead. But—he glanced at the clock—it was 3:33 in the morning. He needed to get up at six and didn't want to risk oversleeping. So no scotch for him tonight. When the milk was done, he removed it from the microwave, walked into the dining room, sat down, and began sipping his milk. It was only lukewarm, but he didn't feel like going back to the kitchen to nuke it again. He'd make do with it as it was.

As he sipped his tepid milk, he thought about the dream that had awakened him.

He wasn't surprised that his father had been in it. He doubted he'd ever get Martin Rittinger out of his head. Everyone has a self-critical voice inside them, Aaron believed, though he imagined some folks' were louder than others. His had long ago assumed the tone and timbre of his father's voice, though it wasn't like he was mentally disturbed or anything. The thoughts expressed were always Aaron's. He'd asked a therapist about it once, years ago, after Colin was born but before Lindsay had been conceived. Aaron had originally sought out therapy to make sure he wouldn't be as critical of his young son as Martin Rittinger had been with his children. Aaron's older brother, Bryan, was a bachelor, a successful architect, and an alcoholic. His younger sister, Jeanne, had three kids, each by different fathers, and had a tendency to date jerks that smacked her around. Of the three Rittinger children, Aaron had turned out the most psychologically healthy, and now that he was a father, he wanted to make sure he stayed that way.

When he told his therapist about hearing critical thoughts in Martin's voice she'd said that his father's constant criticism—which had been so bad that it drove Aaron's mom away when he was six—had instilled in his children the feeling that nothing was good enough. Worse yet, that *they* weren't good enough. Because of this, Aaron would always struggle with a sense of pervasive dissatisfaction with himself and his life. And while he might temper this feeling of dissatisfaction and learn how to live with it, he'd never be able to escape it entirely. Aaron knew this was at least partially why he'd been so intrigued by Caroline tonight. Because of his constant sense of dissatisfaction with himself, the "I'm not worthy" syndrome, his therapist had called it, Aaron was driven to prove his self-worth. Not only did he want to be a good husband, a good father, and a good vet, but he wanted to be good enough to everyone in every way. That meant he wanted to be a good enough lover for Caroline, good enough to be chosen as her escort to whatever secret place lay behind the fuckle door. Whether he actually did it or not didn't matter as much as being good enough *to* do it, if he chose.

He realized then that from where he was sitting, he was facing the dining room window. The road they lived on, Kenyon Avenue, curved around so that Caroline's house lay in a straight line from Aaron's front yard, though there were two other houses between. Still, Caroline's house could be viewed from here, at least the southern corner of it. He got up, crossed over to the window, and drew open the curtains. The neighborhood was dark, save for streetlights and porch lights. He looked in the direction of the Langdons' house, but all he saw was blackness. It seemed they didn't have any lights on, at least not in the part of the house that Aaron could see. Caroline and Phillip were probably asleep. But then again, maybe they weren't home yet. Maybe they were still at their sex club fucking and being fucked in ways that most people could barely imagine.

But you can imagine, can't you, kid? The question is, can you do more than imagine? Are you good enough to do?

Aaron continued sipping his milk as he looked out his window into the darkness where Caroline's house should be.

Aaron didn't get sleepy again until 4:45. He considered just staying up, but Mondays were always busy with pet owners whose animals had gotten sick or injured over the weekend, and he was afraid he'd be too groggy in the afternoon if he didn't get in a little more sleep now. So he returned to bed, settled down next to Kristen, and closed his eyes. When he opened them again, he was alone and the digital alarm clock on his nightstand read 7:12. The realization that he'd overslept jolted him awake. He jumped out of bed and hurried down to the kitchen without bothering to put on his robe, dressed only in his underwear.

"Dad's naked!" Lindsay called out as Aaron made a beeline for the coffeemaker. His daughter sat at the breakfast nook table, a bowl of Honey Nut Cheerios in front of her. She wore a long nightshirt with a cartoon baby chicken on the front with the words *Chicks Rule* above it.

Aaron poured himself a cup of coffee. It was cold, but as long as it had caffeine in it, he didn't care. He gulped down half the cup's contents, then refilled it. He grabbed a peanut butter granola bar from the cupboard, tore off the wrapper, and took a large bite.

"What are you doing up so early?" he asked as he chewed, his words coming out in a sticky muffle.

"Soccer camp starts today. Eight thirty, bright and early. And don't talk with your mouth full." She smiled.

Aaron winced at Lindsay's good-natured rebuke. It reminded him too much of something he might say. Or his father.

"It's time for soccer camp already?"

Kristen was the keeper of the family's master schedule, and she wrote down all appointments, practices, lessons, and games on a calendar hanging on the wall next to the refrigerator. Aaron walked over and checked today's date. Sure enough, there—written in Kristen's precise handwriting in red ink—was *L-SC-8.5*. Beneath that was *C-LG-9*. C was Colin, and 9 was 9:00 a.m.

He turned to Lindsay. "What's LG?"

Lindsay was in the middle of chewing a mouthful of cereal, and she waited until she'd swallowed to answer. "Lifeguard. Today's the day Colin starts work at the rec center, remember?"

"Oh. Right." Aaron took another large gulp of coffee. Colin was on the high school swim team, but he'd only just finished his lifeguard training a few weeks ago, and even then he'd only completed it because Aaron had insisted he get some sort of job over the summer. Now summer was half over, and the boy was only just beginning his job. Still, he *had* finished his training, and next summer he could get started right away.

"Is he up yet?" Aaron had been so desperate for a cup of coffee that he hadn't noticed if Colin's door had been open when he'd passed on his way to the kitchen.

"I don't know. He hasn't come downstairs." Lindsay put her spoon inside her bowl, got up from the table, and carried her dishes to the sink. She removed the spoon, poured out what was left of the milk, rinsed both spoon and bowl, and then put them in the dishwasher.

Watching her, Aaron was both proud and sad. In many ways, she was so grown up, but it seemed like just yesterday that she'd been sitting on a booster seat and he'd been spoon-feeding Cheerios to her. He started to take another bite of his granola bar, but then he remembered Lindsay's rebuke and didn't.

"Where's your mom?"

"Outside puttering."

Puttering was Kristen's all-purpose phrase for any yard work she might do. Watering, weeding, mulching . . . if it was outdoors and involved some sort of plant life, it counted as puttering.

"I'm gonna go into the den and play some video games before I get dressed, okay?"

Lindsay left the kitchen without waiting for Aaron to grant her permission, but he barely noticed. He was angry with Kristen for not waking him up. He assumed the clock radio had gone off and he hadn't heard it. That happened sometimes when he was really tired. But Kristen *knew* he needed to get to work by seven thirty every day—*especially* on Mondays.

He drank the rest of his coffee and put the cup in the sink without bothering to rinse it. They kept a portable phone mounted on the wall next to the calendar—all the better for Kristen to make, change, and cancel appointments on the master schedule. Aaron walked over to the phone, called his office, and left a message for Diane, his receptionist—though she preferred the term *office manager*—letting her know that he'd be coming in a little late today. He hung up, popped the remainder of the granola bar in his mouth, and headed for the stairs.

Upstairs, he stopped at Colin's room and pounded a fist on the door.

"You up, Colin? You start your new job today!"

Aaron listened for sounds of life, and when he didn't hear any, he pounded on the door again, harder this time.

"Colin! Wake up!"

He still didn't hear anything, and he was about to pound the shit out of the door when there came the soft *snick* of a lock being disengaged. The door opened a few inches, just enough so that Aaron could see one of Colin's half-open eyes.

"You don't have to yell," the boy mumbled. "I heard you."

Aaron had to resist saying *I wasn't yelling*. Colin had hit that phase of adolescence where everything he said to his parents sounded like a challenge, and most of the time Colin wasn't even aware of it. Or so he claimed.

I never put up with that kind of shit from you, Martin's voice said.

"Big day, huh? Looking forward to it?"

Colin's eye stared at Aaron for several seconds. "I'm going. Isn't that enough?"

Aaron felt as if he should say something, pass on a tidbit or two of fatherly wisdom. Maybe "The first day's the hardest" or "The most important thing to remember is to try and maintain a good attitude." Or even something as simple as "I'm proud of you."

But before he could choose, Colin said, "Aren't you late for *your* job?" and closed the door. A second later the lock *snicked* into place one more.

Aaron stood looking at Colin's door for several moments before sighing and heading off for the shower.

He was standing at the sink mirror, naked and mostly dry, and running an electric razor across his face when Kristen walked into the bathroom.

"Hey there, sexy." She came over, patted his ass, and gave him a kiss on the back of the neck. Her hair was tied back in a ponytail, the way she always wore it when working in the yard, even when it wasn't hot out. She had on a sleeveless green blouse and a pair of white shorts. Her feet were bare, and Aaron knew that she'd been wearing her ratty old gardening shoes, and that she'd left them in the garage when she finished working.

Aaron didn't want to snap at her, but he couldn't help himself. "Why didn't you get me up?"

Kristen stepped up to the sink to wash her hands, and Aaron moved over to give her room.

"I tried. Three times, as a matter of fact, but you were dead to the world. Did you stay up late last night?" She finished washing her hands and dried them on the towel hanging next to the sink.

Aaron didn't take his gaze off his reflection in the

mirror. He was mostly finished shaving, had only his neck to do, but that was always the hardest part. He could never seem to shave there as close as he'd like. Not for the first time he wished he had the sort of job where you could go in grubby one day and no one would care. But people expected health-care workers— vets included—to have impeccable hygiene.

"I had trouble sleeping," he said, which was true enough. Now he would find out whether Kristen was aware of how long he'd stayed out last night.

"Poor baby. You work too hard." She hugged him from behind, circling her arms around his waist. "I know what might help you relax." She slowly lowered her right hand to his penis. "If you've got the time for a quickie, that is."

Aaron sighed. He moved away from Kristen before she could begin fondling him and turned off his razor.

"You always do this," he said.

"Do what?"

Aaron answered as he put his razor away and then applied aftershave to his face. "Always try to initiate sex when you know we can't do it. Like now, when I'm late for work. And then you say, 'Next time you complain that we never do it, remember that you turned me down.' If you really wanted to have sex, you'd pick a better time to make your move."

She scowled and Aaron thought that he'd done it now. She'd start yelling and they'd get into a major fight, and in the end nothing between them would change, and he'd be even later for work than he already was.

But Kristen's features relaxed and she managed a

smile. "Maybe this *isn't* the best time. How about I take a rain check, and we pick up where we left off tonight after the kids have gone to bed?"

Aaron had heard this line before, too. When he reminded her of her "rain check" later tonight, she'd say, *I'm sorry, honey, but I can barely keep my eyes open. Tomorrow night, I promise.* But tomorrow night it would be the same thing all over again.

Still, he was too late to get into it this morning, and really, what good would it do? None, that's what.

He smiled. "Sounds good," he said. Then he kissed her, gave her a quick hug, and went into the bedroom to get dressed.

Aaron backed his Lexus out of the driveway, thumbing the garage door remote attached to the visor. The garage door descended as he backed into the street and put the car in drive. Given his mood, he felt like tromping on the gas and peeling out, but he pressed his foot to the pedal gently, and the Lexus slid forward at a more leisurely rate of speed. He knew Kristen was looking out the picture window to wave good-bye to him—she did this every day, as long as she was home when he left for work. He didn't want to look, didn't want to smile and wave, but she'd know something was wrong if he didn't play his part in their morning ritual. So he looked, saw her, smiled, and waved, doing his best not to seem too perfunctory about it. Then he pressed the gas pedal down farther and accelerated away from the house.

They'd moved to this neighborhood not long after Aaron had opened his veterinary practice. Back then, this had been *the* part of town for young professionals to live in, and though it wasn't quite the hot location it used to be, if you told someone you lived on Kenyon Avenue, they were still impressed. The houses were much of a kind here, his included, two-story houses with large yards, three- and four-car garages, and immaculate landscaping. McMansions, his brother had called them the last time he'd visited, during Christmas five years ago. Aaron hated to admit it, but the term fit. Back when Kristen and he had moved here, it had seemed like they'd snagged the brass ring and would be living the good life from then on. But now the neighborhood felt foolish, pretentious, hollow . . . more like the facade of a Hollywood set than a place where real people lived and loved.

Aaron followed the curve of the road until he drew near the Langdons'. He eased off the accelerator and gazed at their house. Save for a few superficial differences, it looked almost exactly the same as his, although Caroline and Phillip didn't have any children. They did have two cats that Caroline brought in for him to check over once a year or so. He tried to remember the animals' names, but they wouldn't come. He liked animals well enough, but he didn't get all moony-eyed and sentimental over them like some vets did. That was a big part of why he had trouble remembering pet names—animals didn't really need names as far as he was concerned. When he saw a patient, in his mind it was Adult German Shepherd with Canine Hip Dysplasia, and that was all. An animal was a problem to be solved, a task to attend to, nothing more.

Aaron didn't really expect to see Caroline out, certainly not this early on a Monday, but he couldn't help slowing down even more and watching the front door of her house, glancing at the windows to see if she might be looking out. Once on his way to work, he'd driven past a house—not in this neighborhood, but close to his practice—where the front door had been open and a gorgeous, long-haired, and very naked blond woman had been bending over to retrieve the morning paper from the front stoop. She'd looked up in shocked surprised as Aaron had driven by, then fled into the house, her large firm breasts jiggling so much that Aaron had nearly run his car—he'd been driving a BMW in those days—into one of her neighbors' yards. Since then he'd passed the blonde's house hundreds of times, but he'd never again seen the door open, let alone caught her outside clothed or unclothed. It wasn't completely out of the realm of possibility that he might see Caroline in a similar compromising position one day. And so every day he checked out her house as he drove by. And he *really* wanted to catch a glimpse of her after what he'd witnessed last night at the Valley View Shopping Center. But as he drove past her house, the door didn't open and a naked Caroline Langdon didn't step outside to fetch the paper, nipples hardening in the morning air, pubic hair stirring in the breeze. And the curtains were drawn over all the windows.

Enough fantasizing, kid. Back to the real world.

Though Aaron had known he wouldn't see anything, he nevertheless experienced a wave of disappointment as he tore his gaze away from Caroline's house and faced forward.

And there, framed in his windshield, wearing a T-shirt and shorts, was Caroline. She was jogging toward him and his Lexus was heading straight for her.

Aaron had time to register the alarm on Caroline's face before he yanked the steering wheel to the left and slammed on the brakes. Though he hadn't been traveling all that fast, the car still swerved as it squealed to a stop.

Aaron sat there for several seconds, terrified that he'd hit Caroline, hurt her bad, maybe even killed her. He imagined her body crushed beneath the wheels of his Lexus. Blood bubbling up from her throat as if she were some sort of grisly fountain, her abdomen split open like a flesh sack that had been stretched too far and finally burst open to spill its wet, ropy contents all over the street.

You heard no scream, no thump.

Aaron turned his head, looked out the passenger-side window, saw Caroline standing there, not looking frightened in the least. In fact, she looked almost amused. Aaron turned off the engine, opened the door, and jumped out of the Lexus, already babbling apologies before his feet had touched the ground.

"Oh my God, are you all right? I'm *so* sorry, I didn't see you, was off in my own little world, I guess. But as long as you're okay . . . you *are* okay, aren't you?"

Aaron had walked around the front of his car as he talked, and now he stood next to Caroline.

"I'm fine," she said. "A burst of adrenaline is a great

pick-me-up in the morning. Maybe you should try to run me down every day." She smiled, and there was no anger in her tone.

"A little too much excitement for me," Aaron said. "But I'm glad you're not hurt, and I appreciate your being a good sport about my lousy driving. Guess I'm still not awake."

Now that Aaron knew Caroline was unharmed, he marveled at what had just happened. He'd been hoping to see her this morning, and now here he was—not merely looking at her from a distance as he drove by, but standing less than two feet away and talking with her. *Who says that dreams don't come true?*

While she might not have been naked, the fabric of her white T-shirt was thin, and he could tell that she wasn't wearing a bra underneath it. The legs of her black shorts were high enough to permit a glimpse of the rounded curve where leg became ass, and she wore no socks with her running shoes, displaying her slender ankles. No, she wasn't naked, but she was still sexy as hell.

"Understandable," Caroline said. "I'm not exactly a morning person myself."

Aaron took a quick glance up and down the street to make sure no other cars were coming. His Lexus sat more or less in the middle of Kenyon Avenue, but he didn't want to get back in and move it yet. Not if it meant cutting short his conversation with Caroline. But the street was empty at the moment, so no worries there.

"But you're out jogging," he said.

Her smile took on a secretive edge, and a look that he couldn't define came into her eyes.

"I'm unusually full of energy this morning, and I had to do something to burn it off. So I decided to go for a run."

Aaron nodded. "That explains why I've never seen you out alone when I leave for work."

Caroline's words echoed in his mind. *Unusually full of energy.* Was she still basking in the afterglow of last night's carnal adventures?

"I'd think you'd be tired after—" Aaron realized what he'd been about to say and snapped his mouth shut.

Caroline frowned. "After what?"

Asshole, asshole, asshole!

Aaron forced a smile. "You know . . . after a busy day at work yesterday." He couldn't remember what Caroline's job was, or even if she worked at all. He knew Phillip was in real estate somehow, though the details eluded him at the moment—if he'd ever known them in the first place. And real estate agents worked on weekends, right? Besides, Caroline didn't strike him as the sort of person to be content with living as a kept woman, but you never could tell. "Too tired to get up early and go running, I mean."

Caroline's frown deepened into a scowl. "Yesterday was Sunday."

Aaron's dream come true of getting a chance to talk with Caroline this morning was rapidly becoming a nightmare. "I'm sorry. I thought you and Phillip worked in real estate."

Caroline continued scowling for another moment before finally smiling and nodding. "I see. Yes, we do make our living from real estate, but we don't sell it. We *own* it."

"Oh." Aaron felt like an even bigger asshole than he had a minute ago.

"We own several properties. Apartment complexes, businesses, that sort of thing. Believe me, it's not as glamorous as it sounds, and it hasn't made us rich, though the bank's not going to foreclose on our home any time soon. We do work odd hours at times, inspecting properties, arranging for maintenance and repairs, sometimes even doing them ourselves, when we can. So it's not unusual for us to work on a Sunday, but it so happens we took the day off yesterday."

Aaron felt a bit less of an idiot now, and he decided to push his luck some more. "I hope you took advantage of your time off and had some fun."

Caroline's scowl didn't return, but Aaron sensed wariness in her voice as she replied. "We spent most of the day at home, resting." She paused and looked at him intently, as if she were trying to decide whether or not to continue, and if so, how much she should say. "We did go out last night, though." She kept her gaze locked on his as she said this, as if she wished to gauge his reaction to her words.

Aaron concentrated on keeping his expression neutral, but inside he felt a surge of excitement. He'd gotten her to talk about the club! Maybe not in any detail—he knew that would be expecting too much—but he was certain that it was the club behind the fuckle door that she spoke of.

"I hope you had a good time." Aaron purposely didn't include Phillip in this statement.

Her eyes narrowed as she continued looking at him,

but her voice sounded perfectly normal as she spoke. "As a matter of face, I did. I enjoyed myself quite thoroughly."

I'll bet Striped Shirt enjoyed you quite thoroughly as well. "Good. Glad to hear it."

Silence fell between them then, and though Aaron didn't want to leave her presence, he couldn't think of anything else he could say that would give him an excuse to talk to her any longer. Not unless he was willing to admit that he'd seen her with Striped Shirt at the shopping center last night. And he wasn't about to do that. A few (mostly) innocent double entendres were about all he could manage. Besides, if he stood here speaking to her any longer, he would start to notice flaws in her appearance. A tiny roll of fat around her belly, earlobes drooping because she often wore earrings that were too heavy, teeth that could stand to be a shade or two whiter. Given his personality, it was inevitable, and he didn't want to do that to her, didn't even want to think such things in her presence. Caroline Langdon was perfect for what he needed her for, a fantasy woman, and he didn't want to spoil that fantasy by injecting any irritating reality into it. It would be best if he just departed and left things as they were.

"I hate to leave, but I'm late enough for work as it is," Aaron said. "All the sick pets in Ptolemy won't survive if Dr. Rittinger isn't there to trim their toenails, clean their teeth, or empty their impacted anal sacs."

Caroline grinned. "Ah, the exciting life of a medical professional."

"You know it. See you later. Enjoy your day." He

gave her a small wave, more to stall for one last second than to say good-bye, then turned and walked back to his Lexus. He got in, started the car, put it in drive, and carefully pulled forward, giving Caroline a final wave as he passed her.

She waved back, but she wasn't smiling this time. And when he checked his rearview mirror, he saw that she was standing on the street in front of her house, watching him go. He pressed the gas pedal a little harder, and as his Lexus continued around the next curve, he lost sight of her. But though he could no longer see her, he knew she remained standing and staring in the direction he'd driven. He wasn't sure how he knew this; he just did. He couldn't decide if this knowledge excited or scared him. Perhaps both.

Caroline watched Aaron drive off, mulling over what, if anything, this unexpected—but not altogether unpleasant—encounter might mean.

I'd think you'd be tired after . . .

For some reason, Caroline had expected Aaron to finish his sentence with the words *last night*. And that bullshit about assuming she worked on Sundays that he'd tried to cover with had clearly been the product of desperation. She'd gone along with it, more to see how Aaron would react than anything else. He'd been so relieved that she'd accepted his lie at face value that it was almost comical, even cute, in a boyish kind of way. Obviously, he knew something, or at least suspected. The question was, how much?

It had been a while since she had taken either of the cats in for a check-up. They were long overdue, she was sure. Of course, suddenly taking one or the other of them in for an examination would seem far too convenient. But if one of them were injured . . .

She turned and started up the walkway toward her house, trying to remember where she and Phillip had stored the cat carriers. Since her back was turned, she didn't see the light blue VW Bug drive by, following the same direction Aaron had gone . . . didn't see the man behind the wheel turn to stare at her as he passed, rubbing his stubble-covered head with rapid, nervous motions of his fleshy hand.

CHAPTER FOUR

There were already seven patients—human ones, that is—in Aaron's office when he got there. Among them, they'd brought ten different animals. A Weimaraner, a chow, two tabby cats, an iguana, a pair of lovebirds, a ferret, a fat dachshund, and a descented skunk. One of the humans—a young boy—removed a guinea pig from his jacket pocket and held it up for Aaron to look at as he walked by.

Make that eleven animals.

Diane sat at the counter behind the reception window. She looked up as Aaron passed, gave him a disapproving frown, and glanced meaningfully at her watch. Diane Forrester was a pear-shaped matronly woman with white hair and a tendency to dress in loud, colorful blouses. She was hyperefficient, and if not for her, Aaron's practice wouldn't be nearly as successful as it was. This made it easier to tolerate her almost manic perfectionism—especially when she expected the same from her coworkers.

Aaron sighed, gave Diane a quick nod, and hurried though a doorway at the back of the waiting area that led to the examination rooms. Patti Morrilier, his chief vet tech, was standing in the hallway with an armload of charts, as if she'd been lying in wait for him. Patti was young, short, petite, with straight blond hair that fell just past her shoulders. She'd been out of college only a couple of years and still possessed an often annoying abundance of youthful energy.

"I've already got the examination rooms ready, and I was just about to finish putting the charts in the rooms. I've done the first one, though. Examination room three, the Weimaraner."

Patti's words tumbled out of her mouth in a breathless rush, and Aaron frowned slightly as he listened, hoping he didn't miss anything.

"Sounds good, Patti. Thanks."

She beamed. "You're welcome, Dr. Rittinger."

He almost told her to call him Aaron, but he remembered what Diane had said about the girl having a crush on him. She was attractive in a diminutive sexelf kind of way, but he didn't want to encourage her. Doing so might have been good for his ego, but it wouldn't be good for the office environment. Diane would pitch a fit if she found out.

So Aaron merely gave Patti a nod. "When you're finished putting out the remaining charts, start bringing the animals back, starting with the dog."

Then he headed off to examination room three, wishing he'd drunk the entire pot of coffee before leaving home.

* * *

By midafternoon, Aaron was ready for a nap. He'd been thinking on and off for the last few years about inviting another vet to join his practice in order to lighten his workload a little. After the day he'd had so far, he was seriously considering it again. He was also considering taking up smoking again, even though he'd quit twenty years ago. A cigarette break would do a lot to help him relax right now. But both Kristen and Diane would give him holy hell if he so much as looked at a pack of smokes, so that was out. Just one more unfulfilled fantasy to add to the list.

He was wondering if there was some way to skip out an hour or two early, maybe get Patti to cover for him, when he walked into examination room one and saw Caroline Langdon waiting for him.

She sat in the orange plastic chair in the corner, below a poster showing a cross-section of a dog infested with heart worms. She sat with her shapely, toned legs crossed, and a cat on her lap. The animal, an American short-haired calico, was shivering and mewing pitifully. She wore a short-sleeved white top, a short black skirt, and blue flip-flops with tiny plastic flowers on top where the straps crossed. He took his gaze off her legs, though it wasn't easy.

"We meet again," Aaron said. "A pleasant surprise, for me at least. It doesn't look so pleasant for your little friend there." He knelt next to Caroline and reached out to stroke the shivering cat on the top of its head. "What's the matter?"

"I think he's broken his leg, Aaron. Or at least

sprained it really bad. I found him around noon, limping across the backyard."

The way Aaron was kneeling, his face was level with Caroline's breasts. He took a quick glance at them, saw her top was unbuttoned to display a good amount of cleavage, and her nipples pressed against the thin white fabric. They didn't jut out stiffly, though, and Aaron figured she was wearing a bra, but a sheer one. Not black, because he'd be able to see it through her white top. Beige, maybe.

He reluctantly returned to his attention to the cat. He wished he could remember the animal's name, but he hadn't consulted the chart before he began talking to Caroline, and he didn't want to do so now, for it would mean moving away from her side, and he wanted to remain there as long as he could.

"Do you have any idea what happened to him? Did he get into a fight with another cat? Maybe fall off the roof or out of a tree?" While cats did often land on their feet when they fell, if they fell from high enough up, it didn't help them much.

Caroline shook her head, setting her gold hoop earrings to swinging, the motion also resulting in a slight quiver of her breasts. Though Aaron wasn't aware of it, he began stroking the cat's head even faster.

"Like I said, I just saw him walking in the backyard. The last time I saw him before that was when I let him out just after I got home from jogging. Our backyard is completely fenced in, and Mr. Jinks still has his claws. I figured he'd be all right. He always has been before."

Mr. Jinks! Now Aaron remembered, the cat had

been named after some old cartoon character. The Langdons' other cat was named Snagglepuss, after yet another toon feline.

Aaron took a deep breath through his nostrils, inhaling Caroline's scent. Her perfume was subtle, and applied in Goldilocks fashion. Not too much, not too little: just right. There was another scent, too, underlying the perfume and mingling with it. At first Aaron thought it was the smell of Mr. Jinks. Aaron had been a vet for so long that he normally didn't notice animal smells—not unless they did something nasty, like puke or shit on the examination table. It was a wild, feral smell, primitive and in a strange way arousing.

You dumb kid. What you're smelling is her pussy, and I don't mean the shivering ball of fur on her lap. The woman's not wearing any panties.

The realization hit Aaron like an electric jolt to his testicles, making his penis twitch inside his pants. He knew that, scientifically speaking, whenever you smelled something, you drew molecules of the thing into your nose where they adhered to scent receptors. So technically, in order to smell something, you had to take tiny bits of it into your body. He imagined Caroline's vagina slick with moisture, pictured molecules of cunt juice detaching and drifting into the air, only to be sucked into his nasal passages and absorbed into his body. He was eating her out with his sense of smell.

His penis began to harden, and he stood up so the bulge in his pants wouldn't be so noticeable. "Let's put Mr. Jinks up on the examining table and have a look," he said, sounding cool and professional, though inside his hormones were raging as if he were a horny teenager who got an erection every time the wind blew.

He walked over to the examining table in the center of the room. Caroline stood and carefully carried Mr. Jinks over and set him gently down on the tabletop. When the cat's left rear leg came in contact with the table, he yowled and drew it up against his body.

"He's sure acting like it's broken," Aaron said. "Pet him gently and say sweet things to keep him calm while I have a feel, okay?"

Caroline nodded. She stroked Mr. Jinks's head and back, though she was careful not to run her hand all the way down to the base of his spine, lest she cause his wounded leg any more pain than necessary.

"Good kitty, sweet kitty, Mama loves her kitty . . ." Her voice was practically a purr itself, and Aaron's cock got even harder. He was glad he stood on the other side of the examination table so Caroline couldn't see. But part of him did want her to see, wanted to witness her reaction. Would she be shocked or pleasurably surprised?

He reached out and with practiced fingers took hold of the cat's damaged leg and began probing it as gently as he could. Mr. Jinks meowed in protest and turned his head back several times, teeth bared as if to bite Aaron, though he never did. When Aaron was satisfied, he took his hand away and gently stroked the cat's side.

"God job, Mr. Jinks. You're one brave cat."

"How bad is it?" Caroline asked. "Is it broken?"

"I believe so. It feels like a clean break, though, and those are the easiest to set and fastest to mend. We won't know for sure until we have a few X-rays taken.

Is that all right?" Unlike human medicine, when it came to making decisions about animal health care, it was up to the pet owners to decide just how much money an animal's life and health were worth.

Caroline nodded. She was no longer smiling. Her face was drawn and haggard, as if she was having a terrible time accepting Mr. Jinks's injury. She didn't ask how much the X-ray would cost, which was a good sign of her love for and commitment to her pet.

"All right. You make sure Mr. Jinks stays where he's at, and I'll go get my vet tech." He gave Caroline what he hoped was a reassuring smile, then left the examining room. He found Patti in the reception area collecting a completed new patient form from a woman in her sixties who had an animal carrying case with a plump white rabbit inside it.

"Could you do me a favor and X-ray a cat for me? I think he might've broken his left rear leg, but I want to be sure before I do anything else."

Patti nodded and left the rabbit woman and accompanied Aaron back to the examination area. They went into examination room one, and Patti took Mr. Jinks off the table, holding him lightly so as not to upset the cat any more than he already was.

"Nice kitty," Patti soothed. "This'll all be over in a flash, and it won't hurt a bit." Some people spoke to animals as if they were thinking beings on an evolutionary par with humans, and Patti was one of them. Patti then looked at Caroline, her eyes narrowing slightly, as if she'd noticed how attractive the woman was and wasn't happy about it. "Don't worry. I'll take good care of him."

Caroline simply nodded and looked as if she might cry. Patti left with Mr. Jinks, closing the door behind. Aaron turned to tell Caroline that the X-rays would only take a few minutes, and that he'd return to look over them with her when they were finished. While things weren't as busy now as they had been this morning, there were still plenty of other pet owners waiting in other examination rooms or out in the reception area. He could go take care of some of them while Caroline waited. But just as he was about to say all this, Caroline reached across the table and took his hand.

"Would you mind staying with me?" she asked. "I'm just so worried."

Aaron hesitated. Vets had their own version of the Hippocratic oath. Would he be violating a portion of that oath—to work for the relief of animal suffering—by staying here instead of using the time to attend to other patients? But Caroline had hold of his hand, and he liked the feel of her flesh too much to break contact. He wasn't going anywhere.

Smart kid.

"Sure." His voice sounded dry and a little hoarse. "No problem."

Several moments passed like that, with the two of them holding hands across the examining table. Aaron was surprised by Caroline's sudden emotional fragility. She'd always struck him as a strong, confident woman. The kind who was always in control of her emotions. But he supposed he really shouldn't be surprised. People could get funny when it came to their pets. The sweetest little old lady might have her beloved doggie put to sleep without batting an eye, while a big strong macho he-man might weep like a little girl when faced with the same decision. After twenty years as a vet, Aaron still couldn't tell how people would react to a pet's illness or injury.

Caroline let go of his hand then, and Aaron felt a pang of disappointment. He'd known his role of comforter would be temporary—it always was—but he'd hoped it would last longer than–

She came around to his side of the examining table, her expression no longer one of worry. All traces of fear and anxiety had vanished, and she now moved with a confident grace that Aaron found at once enticing and intimidating. A small smile played about her lips as she closed to within a few inches of him and put her hands on his shoulders.

"I really enjoyed seeing you this morning." She pressed her body closer until they were just touching. Aaron was taller than her, and his crotch pressed against her abdomen just above her pubic mound. Aaron felt feverish, and his penis jumped as if an electric current surged through it. He wondered if she'd felt it, was certain she had, he *wanted* her to, though he knew he shouldn't.

"Me too." His reply came out as a whisper. It was lame, but it was the best he could manage at the moment. The cognitive functions of his brain had been placed on hold as blood was diverted southward, and really what use was intellect at times like these anyway?

"I've noticed you looking at me before." She leaned forward, stood on her tiptoes, and brushed her lips softly against his. "I mean *really* looking." She took her right hand from his shoulder and reached down to begin rubbing his hardening penis through his pants. "I liked it . . . Do you like this?"

She got a good grip on his organ and squeezed.

Aaron's breath caught in his throat and he couldn't respond.

This was like something out of a dream. No, better, for this was real.

Yeah, but that also makes it dangerous. What happens if Patti comes back and sees this? What if Diane finds out? Worse, what if Kristen does?

He knew what he *should* do. He should gently push Caroline away, then take a step back to put even more distance between them. He should remind her that they were both married, and as tempting as it might be to give in to their feelings, they had their spouses to think about. That's what he should do. What he *wanted* to do was bend Caroline over the examination table, lift up her skirt, and fuck her senseless.

She kissed him, the moist tip of her tongue sliding past his lips and into his mouth. At first he was hesitant to meet it, for doing so would mean that he was choosing to be part of this, that for the first time he was willingly cheating on his wife. But her hand continued kneading his cock, and his reluctance vanished like morning fog burned away by a blazing summer sun. He opened his mouth wider and probed her tongue with his. Circling, sliding, sucking . . .

Caroline removed her other hand from Aaron's shoulder, reached down, and began undoing his belt buckle. He reached beneath her blouse with his right hand, unhooked her bra, and began fondling one of her breasts. With his left hand he reached beneath the back of her skirt and found the smooth taut skin of her ass. He now knew for certain that she wore no underwear. Caroline finished unbuckling his belt, and his pants—which were made of light fabric—slid smoothly down his legs and around his ankles. Caroline's kisses became more intense as she hooked her fingers around the waistband of his underwear and began to tug it down. He felt the fabric move over his penis, and then the cool air hit the skin as his cock bobbed free. His organ throbbed in time with his pulse, almost as it were already experiencing mini orgasms. He moved his right hand to her other breast, pinching the stiff nipple between his thumb and forefinger and rolling it around. He moved his left hand from her ass around to her vagina, intending to slide his fingers into her, but he only managed to brush her pubic hair before she pulled away from him.

At first he feared that she had changed her mind, that she'd had second thoughts and unlike him had chosen to listen to them. But when she got down on her knees before him, gripped the shaft of his penis with one hand, and began tonguing the slit in his glans, he knew she hadn't changed her mind at all.

Aaron had only just managed to rebuckle his belt when Patti came back with Mr. Jinks and the X-rays. As he looked at the pictures of the cat's broken leg, Caroline petted the animal, who once again stood on the examination table. Aaron's penis ached and semen still oozed from the tip to dampen his underwear. Patti stood nearby, waiting for him to render his prognosis. He wondered if the odors of Caroline's and his ... lovemaking wasn't the proper term, not for what they'd done. And you couldn't call it fucking, since it had only gone so far. Messing around would do, he decided. He wondered if the smells of their messing around—the rich musk of Caroline's cunt, the ripe odor of his jism—lingered in the air, still strong enough for Patti to smell. If so, he doubted she'd recognize them for what they were, would most likely put it down to the everyday animal miasma that hung in the air here. At least, that's what he hoped.

Mr. Jinks' break was clean, the X-ray confirming what his probing fingers had already told him. He was about to ask Patti to help him get ready to put a cast on the cat's injured leg when he realized there was something odd about the X-rays. He looked at them again, paying closer attention this time. From the way the broken edges of the bone looked, it appeared that the break hadn't been caused by an impact but was rather the result of applied pressure. In other words, someone had broken the cat's leg on purpose.

Aaron looked up from the X-ray pictures to tell Caroline what he suspected, but then he remembered what she'd said. Mr. Jinks had been fine when she returned from jogging and let him out, and her backyard was completely enclosed. That would make it difficult for someone—like a bored neighbor kid who had grown tired of committing virtual mayhem on his X-Box and longed to try the real thing—to sneak in and break Mr. Jinks's leg. Difficult, but not impossible. Whoever had taken the cat's leg, gripped it with both hands, and snapped the bone in two would most likely have gotten clawed during the process. Unless it was someone the cat knew and trusted . . . someone ruthless enough to break the bone fast, in a single violent motion, and release the animal before it could strike back.

Caroline had no scratches on her hands. But then, she was Mr. Jinks's owner, the one who fed him, petted him, called him a good, sweet little kitty . . . While Mr. Jinks might wonder why his favorite human took his rear leg in her hands, he'd have let her do it. And though he also might've sensed something was wrong when her grip began to tighten, he still wouldn't have struggled, wouldn't have swiped at her with his claws. And when the first fissures began to appear in the bone . . .

Aaron thrust the thought away. It was ridiculous to even fantasize that Caroline might've broken the leg of her own cat and then bring it in to be seen by a vet. What possible reason could she have for committing such a horrible act?

To have an excuse to see you again, of course—and to get you alone so she could slurp down a little man milk.

Caroline was looking at him expectantly, but there was no hint of guilt in her eyes, no sign of concern that Aaron had realized what she'd done. In fact, there was nothing to indicate that only a few moments ago she'd practically swallowed his cock while he pumped his load down her throat. She looked like any other patient waiting for him to give her his prognosis.

He imagined the loud crack of Mr. Jinks's leg snapping, could almost hear the cat's shrill scream of agonized betrayal . . .

He forced himself to smile. "Like I said earlier, it's a clean break. Once we get a cast on it, Mr. Jinks should heal quickly." He turned to Patti before Caroline could say anything. "Would you mind assisting me?" He could set a bone and put a cast on it by himself when need be, but the procedure went faster when he had help. Besides, he didn't want to be alone with Caroline, not right now.

"Not at all, Doctor." Patti glanced at Caroline, as if to say, *Screw you, sister. You're not getting any more time alone with him.* Then she went over to the cabinet against the wall where medical supplies were kept and began gathering the materials necessary to take care of Mr. Jinks's leg.

Caroline smiled. "What a relief. Thank you so much, Aaron."

Patti scowled when Caroline called Aaron by his first name, though she didn't turn to look at the other woman this time.

Caroline took a step toward him, though she didn't come close enough to touch him. In a lowered voice, she said, "Some friends and I are getting together later this evening. Maybe you'd like to join us?" Her tone was innocent enough, but her eyes smoldered with lust and secrets, promises and mysteries.

Aaron couldn't believe what he was hearing. Was Caroline actually inviting him to visit the club—or whatever it was—that lay behind the gray door?

He glanced in Patti's direction, but she was still sorting through the supplies in the cabinet, searching for what she needed. But Aaron was certain she was still paying attention. He turned back to Caroline, and in a voice barely above a whisper said, "I'd like that. I'll drop by if I can make it." He didn't want to seem too eager, not with Patti in the room, undoubtedly listening to their every word.

Caroline grinned. "Great!"

He wanted to see if she would tell him where tonight's gathering was going to be held. Normally, that would be the next step in the conversation. *We're getting together at Tess's tonight. Tess and Bill McPhereson? Do you know them? Here, let me write down directions for you.* But there would be no need for directions—not if Aaron already knew which place she was talking about.

"Ready, Doctor," Patti said, her voice a touch too loud.

Aaron looked at Caroline. She looked back, still grinning, but she didn't say anything further.

"Okay, then," Aaron said. "Let's take care of Mr. Jinks, shall we?"

Caroline gave him a meaningful look, as if to say, *And later tonight we'll take care of you.*

CHAPTER FIVE

Aaron's last patient for the day was a toy poodle in desperate need of a flea dip. The little fucker nipped a couple of Aaron's fingers while he'd been examining her, so he let Patti do the dip. She had a more natural way with animals than he did and hardly ever got bit, clawed, or pissed or shit on.

Aaron took care of some paperwork while Patti finished with the poodle. She stopped by his office to say good night, gave him a funny look that he couldn't interpret, then left. A few minutes later, he powered down his computer and left as well. He walked into the waiting room and even though it was closing in on six o'clock, he saw that Diane still sat at her desk, fingers flying across the keyboard of her computer with the speed and grace of a concert pianist.

He walked up to the reception window and leaned on the counter. "Why don't you go on home, Diane? Whatever you're doing, it can wait until tomorrow."

Diane's husband had passed away a while back, so she was never in a hurry to go home. Even so, Aaron figured she had to have something better to do with her time than get a leg up on tomorrow's work. And if she didn't, then she needed to find something, and she sure as hell wouldn't be able to do so sitting at her desk.

"Just a few more minutes, Doctor, and then I'll knock off. Promise." Diane didn't take her gaze from her monitor as she spoke. The fact that she didn't make eye contact and that she'd called him *Doctor* instead of *Aaron*, as she always did when there were no patients around, told him something was wrong.

"Everything okay?" He wanted to get out of here, was planning to drive by the Valley View Shopping Center on his way home, maybe cruise through the parking lot and take a look at the fuckle door before heading home for dinner with his wife and kids. But he couldn't simply walk away from Diane. She'd worked for him too many years for him to blow her off, much as he might want to.

"Nothing," she said in a tone that made it perfectly clear she meant something.

It's obvious what's bugging her. She knows about your afternoon delight with Caroline.

How she knew, he had no idea, but as soon as the thought occurred to him, he knew it was true. Maybe Patti had suspected something, perhaps even come back to the examination room before Caroline and he were finished, had heard them and scurried off to return several minutes later, when they were finally done. Patti hadn't shown any sign of it at the time, but maybe she was a better actress than she seemed. And if Patti knew, it wouldn't have been long before she told Diane.

However it had happened, the damage had been done. The question was what to do about it.

"Uh, Diane . . ."

"No need to say anything, Doctor." She kept her gaze fixed on her monitor, her hand in constant motion on the keys. He couldn't tell for sure from this angle, but it looked like she had a word processing program open and was typing a string of nonsense syllables, as if she were only pretending to work. "Everyone is entitled to one mistake." She paused and gave him a quick glance. "But only one." Then she turned back to the screen.

Aaron nodded slowly. "Message received. Good night, Diane." Feeling like a naughty little boy who had just been scolded by his grandmother, he turned and started for the front door.

"Good night," Diane said, and then so softly he almost didn't hear it, she added, "Aaron."

Aaron's office, the Ptolemy Veterinary Clinic, was located on the western edge of downtown between Tiny Tots Day Care and Advanced Medical Imaging. The three businesses shared a single too-small parking lot in back of their buildings, and it tended to get a little crowded at times. But it was after business hours, and there were few cars in the lot. Aaron always parked in the back so his patients could park closer to the building. He usually didn't mind the walk. It wasn't very far, and he figured he could use every little bit of exercise he could get. But the heat and humidity were oppressive and sapped the life out of him. He felt beads of sweat begin to run down the back of his neck, along his spine, pooling at the small of his back. It didn't help that he felt like a complete bastard after Diane's warning. He was confident that she wouldn't say anything to Kristen—this time. But the fact that someone he worked with, someone he cared for and respected, knew what he'd done and strongly disapproved made him feel like a grade-A, first-class, number-one shitheel. Hot, depressed, and miserable, he kept his gaze downcast as he walked toward his car. Maybe he shouldn't go to Caroline's club tonight . . . hell, of *course* he shouldn't go. But even after Diane's scolding, he still wanted to, as much as ever. And in a perverse way, maybe even more. If Caroline was forbidden fruit before, then she was doubly so now.

As he drew near his Lexus, he heard a car door open. Aaron looked up and saw a man getting out of a light blue VW Bug—not one of the new ones, but an old sixties or seventies Bug, rust-eaten around the edges, tires so bald they had no visible tread—that was parked only a couple of spaces away from his Lexus. The man was medium height, stocky, with a pronounced gut. His shaven head was covered with patchy stubble, scabs, and white flakes of peeling skin. His facial features were soft and doughy, cheeks saggy, dewflap under his chin, puffy discolored bags beneath his bloodshot eyes. The man was in dire need of a shave. The lower half of his face was covered by dark blue, as if he had a large bruise there. His five o'clock shadow was so strong as to be almost comical, and it made Aaron think of Fred Flintstone's perpetual caveman stubble.

The man shut his car door, then vigorously rubbed

his scabbed and flaking scalp, causing pieces of dry skin and crumbly scalp to drift down onto the shoulders of his white T-shirt. At least, Aaron assumed it was white, or had been once. It was now a sour yellowish color, like germ-ridden pus, and splotched with numerous stains, many of which looked like dried blood. He wore his shirt untucked over a pair of old jeans, holes in the knees, cuffs frayed, bare toes with yellowed and cracked nails sticking out from underneath. The asphalt had to be burning hot given the temperature, but the man showed no sign of discomfort as he walked barefoot toward Aaron, still rubbing his scalp.

Aaron assumed the man was homeless, maybe one of those people who lived out of their cars. And from the look of him, he was also one of those individuals that liked to engage in deep philosophical conversations with brick walls on city street corners. Aaron had nothing against the homeless or mentally ill, and he knew better than to automatically equate the two. But this guy seemed to fit the worst stereotypes of both. He looked crazy, dangerous, and worse yet, like he wanted to hit up Aaron for a handout.

Got any spare change? I just need a couple of bucks to tide me over for the next day or two. Anything you can give, I'd sure appreciate it.

When Aaron had been younger, he'd almost always given people money when they asked for some "spare change." But he'd grown cynical in his middle age, or perhaps simply more realistic. He knew that any money he gave this guy would end up in a liquor store cash register within the hour. Aaron couldn't decide how best to deal with the scab-headed man. Should he continue walking to his Lexus, try to ignore the guy, get in, shut the door, lock it, and get the hell out of there as fast as he could?

He parked close to your car on purpose. He figured whoever owned a Lexus could afford to front him a few bucks.

What if Scab-Head was one of those persistent, belligerent beggars? The kind that won't take fuck-off for an answer. What if he tried to make Aaron fork over his money? What if he wasn't a beggar but a mugger instead?

Aaron wanted to turn around and head back toward the building, but he was already halfway across the parking lot, and Scab-Head had closed to within twenty feet of him. If Aaron turned and ran, would the guy pursue him? Aaron was no athlete, but he was thinner and in way better shape than Scab-Head and could most likely outrun him.

Don't be such a pussy. You're a grown man, not a little boy who runs away whenever someone says boo. Show a little backbone, kid.

The Dad Voice was right. He'd let his imagination get the better of him. He'd just continue to his car and try to avoid making eye contact with Scab-Head. And if the man started talking to Aaron, maybe following him to his car, then he'd deal with it—one way or another.

Aaron became aware of the smell when he and Scab-Head had closed to within ten feet of each other. Greasy and rank, like the inside of a garbage can that hadn't been washed out in years. It clung to the insides of Aaron's nasal passages, coated the back of his throat. His eyes began to water and his stomach roiled.

Jesus Christ, did the son of a bitch bathe in raw sewage?

Aaron quickened his pace, more determined than ever to avoid Scab-Head now. But the man angled toward him, obviously intending to intercept Aaron before he could reach his car. Aaron decided to go with the old offense-is-the-best-defense routine. Without slowing, he turned to face the man and said, "I don't know what you want, but I'm in a hurry, and I really don't have the—"

Before Aaron could say anything more, Scab-Head began running toward him, moving with a burst of speed that Aaron hadn't thought the fat man capable of. So surprised was Aaron by Scab-Head's sudden attack that he could only stand and watch as the man came at him, gut joggling seismically. Scab-Head grabbed hold of Aaron's shoulders and pushed him toward the ground. Aaron's right knee hit the asphalt, sending a jolt of pain through his leg. Scab-Head's weight and momentum forced Aaron onto his side, his right hip and shoulder struck the ground, the impact knocking the wind out of him. Scab-Head half crouched, half lay on Aaron, holding him down. The fat man's chest heaved as he took in gulps of air, breath wheezing in and out as if he were in danger of cardiac arrest. This close, the man's stink was truly horrendous, and Aaron thought the man needn't have bothered to use his weight to render him immobile; his body odor could've done the job by itself. Scab-Head's breath was just as lethal. His teeth were yellow, gums sore and bleeding, and his tongue was coated snail-belly gray. When he exhaled, it smelled like he had eaten a shit sandwich with picante sauce, sour milk, and extra onion.

"Get off . . . me . . . damn you!" Aaron had trouble drawing enough breath to speak, and he gritted out his words through clenched teeth.

"Stay still, don't struggle." The man's voice was calm, his tone detached, as if he attacked people in parking lots every day and it was no big thing. "I just want to talk to you for a couple of minutes. I'm not going to hurt you."

Aaron tried to throw Scab-Head off him, but the man weighed too much, and Aaron couldn't get his arms or legs beneath him to give him any leverage. At the moment, it was all he could do to continue drawing air into his lungs.

"You're already . . . hurting me!"

"Sorry about that," Scab-Head said, though he made no move to shift his bulk off Aaron. "But I had to make sure you'd stay put and listen. What I have to tell you is too important."

"I'll listen, I . . . promise. Just get . . . off me!"

Scab-Head chuckled. "The way I look and smell? The minute I get off you, you'll jump to your feet and run like hell. You probably think I'm some kind of lunatic, don't you?"

"The thought had . . . occurred to me."

"Well, I'm not. I look this way on purpose." He lowered his voice, as if imparting a secret. "It's camouflage."

Despite the man's protestations to the contrary, Aaron was certain that he was completely bug-fuck. But the fat, smelly son of a bitch had made no move to hurt him since he'd brought him down. Maybe if

Aaron listened to whatever crazy horseshit the bloat had to say, he'd let him go. If nothing else, maybe it would give Aaron a chance to get into a better position to free himself.

"So . . . talk."

Scab-Head looked around as if to make sure that no one was watching or listening. Other than the two of them, the parking lot was deserted, which was too damn bad for Aaron. He could've used a witness or two right now—preferably one with a cell phone that had 911 on speed dial. The fat man then leaned his mouth close to Aaron's ear, the movement causing more of Scab-Head's weight to press down on Aaron. The pressure was incredible, and Aaron thought he could feel his ribs grind against each other.

"She was here today. Don't bother denying it. I saw her pull into the lot and get out of her car. She had an animal with her in a carrier. A cat, maybe, though I wasn't close enough to get a good look."

Aaron thought he might be mishearing due to lack of oxygen and impeded blood flow, but it sounded as if Scab-Head was talking about Caroline.

"I saw you, too. Last night, in the parking lot. The *other* parking lot, I mean. Saw you watching her. Saw you talking to her this morning, too."

Aaron felt a stab of cold fear in his gut. Scab-Head *was* talking about Caroline, and worse, he had evidently been spying on her. Or maybe it was Aaron he'd been spying on. Either way, Scab-Head had just moved up a notch from crazy to dangerously crazy.

"Did she invite you yet? If she hasn't, she will. It's . . . what they do. When she does ask, say yes.

Once you're in, keep your eyes and ears open. Participate, of course. You'll have to so they don't get suspicious." Scab-Head grinned. "Besides, it'll be fun." His grin fell away then. "They probably won't take you in back. Not your first night, but if for some reason they do . . ." He trailed off. A faraway look came into his rheumy, bloodshot eyes, his jaw went slack, and he began to tremble, the vibrations making his flab quiver as if he were a thin sack of flesh filled with gelatin.

He gave a quick shake of his head, and his eyes snapped back into focus. He rubbed his scalp vigorously. "We'll talk again."

Scab-Head ponderously lifted his bulk off Aaron, rose to his bare feet with a grunt, and started walking toward his Beetle. Aaron lay on the ground, gasping for breath, so relieved to be free of the man's oppressive weight that for the moment he gave no thought to getting up. Right now, it was enough to be able to take in lungfuls of air once more.

Scab-Head got into his Bug and started the engine. The car gave a shrill whine as if a belt was bad, and there was a rapid clanging sound, as if the fan blade was striking something as it rotated. Scab-Head put the car in gear and backed out of his space. He ground the gears putting the transmission into first, and Aaron—who was still drawing in deep gulps of air—realized that the lunatic might run him over, whether on purpose or by accident. The Bug lurched forward, and Aaron jumped to his feet, ready to throw himself to the side if the car came at him. But Scab-Head drove by, missing Aaron by a good yard or more. The fat man glanced at Aaron as he sped past, gave him a nod, and then pulled onto the street and raced off, leaving behind a gray-blue cloud of acrid exhaust.

Aaron rose to his feet and brushed dirt and small pebbles off his clothes. He turned in the direction Scab-Head had taken, but the Bug was no longer visible, and the whiny-rattling sound of its engine was quickly fading in the distance.

"What in the hell was *that* all about?"

When Aaron got home, he made no mention of his encounter with Scab-Head. He'd driven home with the windows open and air conditioner blasting to help cut the stink that had rubbed off on him, and while his clothes had dirt and oil ground in at several spots, he often came home from work with mysterious stains on his clothing. Kristen was used to him being a little messy and—thanks to the animals he worked with— somewhat aromatic. She and Colin were already eating dinner, so after a quick hello he went upstairs to the bedroom, changed into a blue polo shirt and white shorts, then tossed his soiled clothes into the hamper. As he changed, he gave his body a quick once-over. He was scraped and bruised in numerous places, but he hadn't bled—much, anyway—and while his ribs were sore, he didn't think they were broken. Cracked, maybe. He'd have to go easy on them for a few days.

He went back downstairs only to find his wife and son had vacated the dining table. Kristen had fixed him a plate of grilled teriyaki chicken breasts, brown rice, and peas, but everyone else had cleared their places. It looked like he was going to be dining alone . . . again.

He walked into the kitchen. Kristen was rinsing the dinner plates and stacking them in the dishwasher.

"What's up?" Aaron said. "I know I'm home a little late, but I'm not *that* late, am I?"

Kristen answered without turning away from the sink. "Lindsay's over at Rosemary's house, and Colin has a date with a girl he met at the pool today."

"He does? I'm impressed. First day on the job, too."

Looked like Aaron hadn't been the only one getting lucky at work today. He thought of Caroline sucking him off in the examination room, the moist tight seal of her lips, the way she wiggled the tip of her tongue against his foreskin . . . He expected to feel a wave of guilt thinking about these things in the presence of his wife. He *wanted* to feel guilty, because that would mean he was still a decent man despite what he'd done. But he felt no guilt whatsoever. What he did feel was horny. He wanted to fuck Kristen, right here, right now. If Colin still hadn't been in the house, he would've, too. He imagined grabbing Kristen, pulling her clothes off, saying, *Caroline Langdon gave me the best head I've ever had today. Let's see if you can top her.*

Good Christ, what the hell was the matter with him? It was bad enough he'd cheated on his wife. Even if she did have a low sex drive, he'd promised to be faithful to her when they married, and today he'd broken that promise. But to be standing here thinking such nasty things . . .

You're a man, and you're thinking with your dick, that's all. Doesn't mean you have to let it control you— not unless you want to.

He walked over to Kristen until he was standing directly behind her and encircled his arms around her waist. He then gave her a gentle kiss on the cheek. "How was your day, sweetheart?"

The words rang hollow in his own ears, as if he were an actor pretending to be Aaron Rittinger, loving husband. And a poor actor at that.

But Kristen leaned back against him, giving no indication that she sensed the awkwardness he felt. He'd almost thought she would, that she had some sort of wifely sixth sense that would instantly detect his infidelity the moment they touched.

"Not bad," she said. She put the dish she was in the process of rinsing back in the sink, dried her hands on a towel, then turned around, put her hands on Aaron's shoulders, and kissed him. She tasted of teriyaki sauce.

"Sorry I can't stay and keep you company while you eat," she said. "But I have to go pick up Lindsay."

"What about Colin?"

"He's going to ride his bike downtown and meet his date at the Tastee-Freeze. He's probably already left."

"He has?" Aaron hadn't seen Colin since his brief stop in the dining room before going upstairs. Had Colin left while Aaron was changing? He couldn't keep track of that boy. It was like he'd sired Casper the Surly Adolescent Ghost.

"That's okay," Aaron said. "I don't suppose you can leave Lindsay at her friend's a while longer—"

"Wish I could, sweetie, but I promised Kate that I'd get Lindsay on time."

Aaron had no idea who Kate was. The mother of Lindsay's friend, he guessed.

"Maybe later tonight, once the kids are asleep?" he said.

If she says yes, I won't go tonight. I'll stay home, be a good husband, and never stray again.

Kristen gave him a quick kiss on the nose and then withdrew from his arms. "Maybe. I'm pretty tired already, but who knows? I may rally and find some extra energy for later."

Aaron forced a smile. He'd heard this before. Translated, it meant *Not tonight.* "Sure. Sounds good."

CHAPTER SIX

Kristen was asleep by 10:45. So was Lindsay, and Colin . . . well, his door was closed and, asleep or awake, he'd keep it closed all night. Aaron considered leaving a note for Kristen. She normally slept through the night, but in case she *did* wake up and find herself alone in bed and start wondering where her husband was, it would help to have some sort of alibi in place. The trouble was, he couldn't think of a good one.

I couldn't sleep so I went for a walk sounded lame, as did *An old college buddy called after you went to bed and asked if I wanted to have a few drinks with him.* So in the end, he decided against writing a note. If Kristen woke while he was gone, he'd just have to deal with it.

He put on his shoes, grabbed his keys and wallet, then headed for the garage.

He pulled into the parking lot of the Valley View Shopping Center at 11:04. He drove slowly through the lot, on the lookout for a light blue Volkswagen Beetle.

He'd been watching out for Scab-Head ever since leaving his house. But Aaron had seen no sign of the man on his way here, and he saw no Beetles in the parking lot, light blue or otherwise. Aaron looked for Caroline's Infiniti, but he didn't see it either. Maybe she'd gotten cold feet—though that was hard to imagine given the . . . enthusiasm she'd demonstrated earlier. Maybe she'd changed her mind, or met someone else.

You were all right for a onetime quickie, Aaron, but I found someone longer-*lasting, if you know what I mean.*

What was he doing here? This was ridiculous. He was acting like a stereotypical middle-aged man in the throes of a midlife crisis. And a pathetic, tawdry one at that. He should swing his car around, head for the parking lot's entrance, and go back home where he belonged.

Headlights flashed in his rearview mirror. He couldn't tell what make of car that they belonged to, but when the driver hit the brights a couple of times to get his attention, he knew it was Caroline.

Time to put up or shut up, kid.

Aaron pulled his Lexus into an empty spot in front of I'd Buy That For a Dollar and parked. A moment later, Caroline pulled her Infiniti into the space next to him. Aaron turned off his lights and cut the engine. As he removed the key from the ignition, he glanced out the driver's-side window. Caroline smiled and waved at him. He smiled and waved back, feeling like a teenager who'd sneaked out of the house to meet a girl his parents disapproved of. It was foolish, but at the same time exhilarating. His heart was pounding and he felt a little sick to his stomach. He was nervous, he was excited, but most of all, he was *alive.*

He got out of his Lexus, locked it, and pocketed the keys. Caroline was already out of her car and walking toward him. She wore a black minidress with stiletto heels that clacked on the asphalt as she walked. Without a word she put her arms around his neck and kissed him. It was a long, passionate kiss, and when it was over, Caroline leaned close to his ear and whispered, "I've had the taste of your cum in my mouth all day."

Her voice was low and throaty, and her breath was warm in his ear. His penis, already partially erect from their kiss, became hard as rock. Above them, moths and smaller flying insects dipped and dove as they circled the parking lot's fluorescent lights.

"Ready?" she asked. There was a hint of a challenge in her voice, as if she thought he might back out. But he'd come too far to turn away now. Or perhaps not far enough.

"You bet."

She nodded, grinned, then took his hand and started leading him toward the door. The night air seemed suddenly cold to Aaron, and he had to fight the urge to shiver. *Just nerves,* he told himself. *Just try to enjoy the sensation; it's all part of the experience.*

"Considering what you're wearing—and by the way, you look fantastic—I think I'm a little underdressed," Aaron said.

"Don't worry about it. We're not much on dress codes in Penumbra."

"Is that the name of the place? Penumbra?"

Caroline nodded.

The word was familiar to Aaron, though at the moment he couldn't recall the definition. He could've asked Caroline, but he didn't want to appear stupid in front of her. He considered telling her about his encounter with Scab-Head after work. It was clear the lunatic had some connection to Penumbra . . . and, it seemed, to Caroline as well. *Did she invite you yet? If she hasn't, she will. It's . . . what they do.* But Aaron didn't want to spoil the mood by bringing up the incident now. There would be plenty of time to tell her about Scab-Head later.

Aaron and Caroline reached the sidewalk that stretched the length of the strip mall and stepped up onto it, still holding hands.

"Is there anything I should know before we go in?" he asked.

"Not really. Just relax, be yourself, go with the flow. You'll be fine."

Easy for her to say. She was an old pro at this kind of thing, but Aaron was as green as green could be. He'd come this far, though, and he wasn't about to back out now.

Caroline led him up to the fuckle door, then released his hand. She carried a tiny purse in her other hand, and she opened it and took out a single key. Just as she had last night, she inserted the key into the lock and turned it. Only now Aaron was standing next to her instead of secretly observing from behind the wheel of his Lexus. The lock clicked open, and Caroline removed the key, dropped it back in her tiny purse, then closed it with a soft snap.

She gestured toward the doorknob. "Go ahead and open it. Visitors always are the first to enter."

Aaron forced a smile. "Come into my parlor, eh?" Caroline smiled back but otherwise didn't reply.

C'mon, dumb-ass. Don't just stand there with your dick in your hand. Open the fucking door!

Aaron reached for the knob. He remembered how it had felt last night when he'd tried it. Warm, soft, yielding, almost as if it were made of flesh instead of metal. But this time as his fingers closed around it, he found the metal cold and hard. He turned the knob and gently pushed the door open. The first thing that he was aware of was the smell. A musty odor that was a combination of dust, mold, cigarette smoke, and dried semen. He heard the rattle-hum of an ancient air conditioner at work, but though it cooled the place, it did little to cut down the smell. Faint yellow light spilled through the doorway, and as Aaron stepped inside, he saw that the illumination, such as it was, came from two old floor lamps with rust nibbling at their metal stands and shades that were torn and stained. There were two additional lamps, one apiece atop the end tables flanking a Naugahyde couch with cracks in the surface, many of which had been crudely repaired with silvery metallic strips of duct tape. The walls were covered with tacky butterfly-patterned wallpaper that was faded and peeling. The cheap tile covering the floor was warped, yellowed, and cracked in numerous places. The couch sat between two easy chairs that were old and threadbare, with stuffing and springs sticking out and more patches of duct-tape repair jobs. On the other side of the room opposite the couch was a crude bar made of a wooden plank set atop a pair of sawhorses. There were three stools in front of the bar, and several cardboard boxes filled with booze and a mini fridge sitting on the floor behind it. At one end of the bar, a portable CD player had been set up, wired to small speakers instead of earphones. Music played softly, some sort of smooth jazz, Aaron thought, though he knew little about jazz of any flavor. He was more of a classic rock man.

Aaron didn't know what he'd expected from Penumbra, but this wasn't it. He might've thought he was in the wrong place—or that Caroline was playing some sort of elaborate practical joke on him. But toward the back of the room, set on either side of a door that had been painted black, was a pair of mattresses. They lay on the floor without boxsprings, sheets and blankets clumped together in sloppy piles. Each mattress had a number of pillows, most of which didn't have cases.

Maybe it's supposed to look like a cheap backroom whorehouse, Aaron thought. *A sort of sexual kitsch to add to the fun.*

Maybe, but he wasn't sure he could buy that idea, not even for a dollar.

Caroline and Aaron weren't the only ones in Penumbra that evening. The place was already full, and the others all turned to look as Caroline closed and locked the fuckle door. There were six—two women and four men. One of those men was Phillip, Caroline's husband. Of Striped Shirt, there was no sign.

Most of Penumbra's patrons looked at Aaron with a

neutral expression, but Phillip grinned, rose from the chair where he'd been sitting, and started toward him, hand outstretched to shake.

"Aaron, glad you could make it!"

Phillip reached Aaron, clasped his hand warmly, and gave it a couple of vigorous pumps. To say the least, Aaron felt odd to be shaking hands with the husband of a woman he'd come here to hopefully screw—especially when said woman was standing right next to them both.

Don't sweat it, kid. Different strokes and all that. 'Sides, that's what you came here for, wasn't it? A little kink-a-kink-a-doo?

Unable to think of anything else to say—*Appreciate the opportunity to boff your wife* didn't seem appropriate—Aaron took his hand away from Phillip and simply said, "Thanks."

Caroline walked over to Phillip and kissed him with lips that had engulfed Aaron's dick only a few hours earlier, lips that had tasted his cum and found it sweet.

Phillip was a tall man—taller than Aaron by a good five inches. He was thin, with a runner's build, and he had the same fragile and bony look that serious runners possessed, as if their limbs might snap like twigs in a strong wind. His black hair was silver gray at the temples, giving him a distinguished, scholarly aspect. Aaron supposed he was handsome in an effete, sterile sort of way, and not for the first time he wondered what a firebrand like Caroline saw in him. Phillip was dressed more simply than his wife, in a white shirt with the sleeves rolled down but the cuffs unbuttoned.

The shirt was tucked neatly into jeans that looked so new Aaron wouldn't have been surprised if Phillip had purchased them earlier in the day.

Caroline took Aaron's hand. "C'mon, I'll introduce you to everyone while Phillip makes you a drink." She looked at her husband. "Right, hon?"

"Sure thing. What'll you have, Aaron?" He continued to speak as he headed for the makeshift bar. "We've got beer, wine, some harder stuff . . ."

Aaron didn't really feel like anything, but he didn't want to appear unsociable, so he said, "A shot of vodka will be fine, thanks." Actually, he could probably have used a double, but he didn't want to get drunk. He didn't want to lose control, not so early, anyway.

As Phillip stepped behind the bar and went to work, Caroline led Aaron around the room and made her introductions. Everyone was sitting—in chairs, on the couch—and though all of them seemed happy to meet Aaron, none of them stood or offered to shake his hand. They seemed normal enough at first glance, but a closer look revealed that each was odd in his or her own way.

Wyatt McGlothin was a sturdy broad-shouldered man with a thick bushy mustache. He wore a short-sleeved blue shirt, navy blue pants, and black shoes. There was something about the clothing that put Aaron in mind of a uniform, and he understood why when Caroline said Wyatt was a deputy sheriff. Though handsome enough, Wyatt possessed a facial tic that made his left eye wink erratically, and he had yellowish crusts at the corner of his mouth.

Gillian Russell was a petite bird-thin woman in her early thirties with short strawberry-blond hair and delicate ivory-skinned features. She was barefoot and wore a sheer yellow dress with spaghetti straps that looked more like a nightie. She wore no bra and her stiff nipples—which were so large they seemed to account for half her breast size—pressed against the thin green fabric. There was a shadowy triangle between her legs, and Aaron realized she wasn't wearing any panties either. Caroline said Gillian was an opthalmologist who had a practice in Ash Creek, which Aaron thought was ironic since half of her right eye was bloodred, as if the capillaries there had burst.

Sitting on the couch were Trevor and Shari St. Pierre, a married couple who also worked together as a dentist and dental hygienist. They were both almost naked, wearing only black thong underwear. Aaron judged them to be in their early fifties, but they were in such good shape that, if you just looked at their bodies, you'd guess they were ten years younger. Trevor had brown hair and wore glasses, and when he smiled, he displayed a mouthful of silver-capped teeth. Shari was a curly-haired blonde whose tresses spilled onto her shoulders. Her full naked breasts defied gravity in a way that told Aaron that they were probably implants, but the nipples were little more than tiny pink nubs of scar tissue. Had the surgeon who'd done her tits botched the job? And if so, why hadn't Shari sought reconstructive surgery on her nipples?

The last member of Penumbra Aaron was introduced to was a man named Spencer Fielding, an insurance agent whose office was at the far end of the shopping center. Spencer sat on the couch with Trevor and Shari. He was dressed in a gray suit and tie, as if he'd been working late and hadn't had a chance to go home and change. He was short, with a round face, balding head, salt-and-pepper beard, and a belly that protruded over his waistline, hiding his belt from view. Spencer's oddity was a slow trickle of blood that flowed from his left nostril, causing him to constantly lick his upper lip like a toddler lapping up snot from a runny nose.

Of everyone assembled, Caroline and Phillip were the only ones completely normal—or who at least appeared to be.

"Hail, hail, the gang's all here," Phillip said as he brought Aaron his drink. His tone was pleasant enough, but there was a calculating coldness in his gaze that bothered Aaron. Maybe Phillip knew about Aaron's afternoon suck-fest with Caroline, or perhaps he simply suspected something and was jealous. After all, she *had* brought Aaron as her "date" tonight. He'd assumed that everyone here, Phillip and Caroline included, were swingers. But if that was true—and so far he'd seen nothing to indicate otherwise—why would Phillip be jealous?

Maybe that's part of the kink. Maybe Phillip likes feeling jealous of the other men his wife screws.

Maybe, but Aaron sensed it was something different than that, though he had no idea what it might be.

He detected movement out of the corner of his eye, accompanied by a skittering-rustling sound. He turned toward it and saw a small cage sitting on the floor next to the couch, pushed back behind one of the end tables. Inside, huddled in a ball atop a pile of bedding, was a plump brown rabbit.

"I see you've spied our friend Peter over there," Trevor said.

"What do you mean over there?" Shari said, reaching into the front of Trevor's underwear and grabbing her husband's cock. "Peter's right here!"

Wyatt and Spencer laughed, but Gillian rolled her eyes at the terrible joke.

Aaron kept his gaze on the rabbit as he took a sip of his vodka. It stung his mouth and burned pleasantly as it slid down his throat.

"I've always considered myself pretty open-minded," Aaron said. "But I have to warn you all: Even though I'm a vet, I draw the line at fucking rabbits."

For a moment no one said anything, and then Caroline burst out laughing. The others joined in, and Aaron grinned as he took another sip of vodka.

Across the street from the Valley View Shopping Center was a Speedy Lube, and sitting in the parking lot— far enough from the fluorescent lights so that it was hidden in shadow—was a Volkswagen Beetle. Gerald had parked facing the street so he had a good view of Penumbra, and the binoculars he held to his eyes provided him with an even better one. He watched the vet pull into the shopping center's lot, followed almost immediately by Caroline. He watched them park and get out of their cars, and when Caroline touched Aaron, Gerald felt a sharp pang of jealousy. Once, that had been him meeting Caroline in the middle of the night, being touched by her, kissed by her, having her hold his hand as she led him to the gray metal door that opened onto the heaven and hell that was Penumbra.

As he watched Caroline unlock the door and usher Aaron in, Gerald wondered for perhaps the thousandth time how different his life would be now if he'd been able to resist Caroline's charms. And if he had, knowing the dark ecstasy he had experienced behind that door, would he have regretted resisting her, even after everything that had happened? It was a foolish question. To know the touch of the Overshadow was to know pleasure beyond pleasure, pain beyond pain, sensation so intense that it was beyond the limited capabilities of language to describe. He'd do anything to know that touch again. *Anything.*

A muffled sound like someone trying to speak through a mouthful of cotton came from the VW's cramped backseat. Gerald put his binoculars down on the passenger seat and turned around. Lying scrunched up in the back, wrists and ankles bound by duct tape, was a young blond woman wearing a white T-shirt, blue shorts, white socks, and running shoes. Her mouth was covered with tape as well, and her eyes were wide open and filled with terror.

"You're awake," Gerald said and rubbed his scabby scalp. "That's good. I'm never sure just how hard to hit. The last girl I took . . . or was it the next to last?" He let out an apologetic chuckle. "The memory's the second thing to go."

The girl's eyes widened farther, making her look almost comical, as if she were a cartoon character that had stepped out of the TV and into the real world.

"Anyway, one of the last girls I took ended up dying

because I hit her way too hard. I used a hammer to knock her out, and though it didn't look like I hurt her too bad, I must've messed up something in her brain because she died less than three hours later. And once she was dead, she wasn't any fun." He paused. "Well, not as *much* fun, anyway."

The girl—who Gerald had found jogging in the park at dusk—shook her head back and forth in denial, but then she grimaced and stopped moving.

"You're gonna have a headache for a while. Sorry about that. I've been doing this long enough that you'd think I'd be good at it by now, but no matter what I use—hammer, rock, baseball bat—I either hit too hard or not hard enough. But what matters most is that you're still alive, so I guess I shouldn't be too hard on myself, right?"

The girl's eyes darted right, then left, as if she were a terrified animal desperately seeking some avenue of escape. She began making high-pitched whines in her throat, making her seem even more animalistic. From the way she was acting, Gerald wondered if his blow— he'd used the handle from an old croquet mallet this time—had damaged her brain. He mentally shrugged. So what if he had? She was young, in her midtwenties at the most, and full of life and vitality. In the end, that was all that mattered.

"You just be still and try to get some sleep. It'll make the time go faster for you. If you make too much noise . . ." He faced forward, bent down, and picked up the croquet mallet handle from the passenger-side floor. He held it up so the girl could see it.

"If you aren't quiet, I'll just have to hit you again."

He slammed the mallet handle down hard on the back of the passenger seat, and the girl jumped at the sound. She also stopped whining.

Gerald smiled and turned back around to face the front, dropped the handle on the floor, picked up the binoculars, and resumed his surveillance. He focused his gaze on the gray metal door, was able to read the word *fucl* scratched on its surface, so powerful were his binoculars. He could well imagine what was going on behind that door right now, and doing so gave him an erection.

He continued staring through the binoculars at the door, ignoring the soft, snuffling sobs of the girl who was bound and gagged in the backseat of his car.

"Feeling good, lover?"

Aaron wasn't sure who asked this question. It was a woman's voice, but he couldn't tell if it belonged to Caroline, Gillian, or Shari. Considering that he'd screwed all of them in one orifice or another over the last few hours, he supposed it didn't really matter who spoke.

"You know it."

Aaron lay naked on one of the mattresses and stared up at the ceiling. From the way it appeared to be rippling like water, he assumed that he was drunk. He had a vague memory of someone—one of the men, he thought—handing him some pills and a bottle of rum to wash them down. Aaron didn't remember taking the pills or drinking any of the rum, but he figured he must have. So he was drunk *and* wasted. Shaked and baked.

The woman to his right got to her feet, and Aaron

saw it was Caroline. He made a grab for her leg, intending to pull her back down, but she avoided his grasp easily.

"I'm just going to get some water," Caroline said. "You two thoroughly dehydrated me. I'll be back in a minute." She gave Aaron a wink and walked off, putting a little extra sway into her hips for his benefit.

Aaron let his hand flop back down on the mattress. He hadn't really hoped to stop Caroline. As many times as he'd come tonight, there was no way he could get it up again. Hell, he wasn't sure he even *had* a dick anymore. He could've worn it down to a nub, like a pencil that had been sharpened one too many times. He imagined the tiny remnant of a number-two pencil sticking out from between his legs, the point rounded and blunt. The image amused him and he chuckled, causing the woman still lying next to him to giggle, as if she'd somehow read his mind and also found the image funny. The woman sat up and Aaron realized it was Gillian, the ophthalmologist with the single blood-red eye.

"You are absolutely *yummy*, Aaron." Gillian circled his nipples with her index finger, her voice almost a purr. "Too bad Morgan's not here. He was AC/DC, you know. He'd have loved to play with a stud like you." Gillian sighed and her tone became wistful. "He had the most amazing tongue, and he howled like a fucking banshee during orgasm." She sighed again and shook her head. "It's a goddamned shame."

Aaron was tired and drowsy, and though he wasn't bisexual, he felt too good at the moment for Gillian's talk about Morgan to bother him. "Where is he?"

Phillip—naked, sweaty, and covered with fresh bruises and scratches—came over and stood next to their mattress.

"Morgan couldn't make it tonight," Phillip said. He was smiling but there was no warmth in his eyes. "He has a very demanding schedule and can't come as often as he'd like."

Gillian let out a snort that sounded like a cross between a laugh and a sob. "He used to come plenty when he—"

"That's enough, Gillian."

Phillip glared at Gillian, and she glared right back. The crimson part of her bad eye seemed to glow with an angry flame, and her lips pursed in determination. For a moment Aaron thought she might defy Phillip, but then she looked away, ending the staring contest.

Phillip turned to Aaron, his gaze softening. "Sorry to come across like such a hard-ass, but Morgan's frequent absences are something of a sore point with some of us. We don't think that he displays the proper commitment to the group."

"I understand," Aaron said, though he didn't.

Caroline returned then, carrying a half-empty bottle of water. She took another swig, then spoke to Phillip. "It's getting late, sweetheart. If we're going to go in back, we ought to get to it."

"What about Aaron?" Phillip asked.

"I say he joins us. Provided he's capable of standing and walking on his own."

Aaron had no idea what they did "in back," but considering what they did in front, he was determined not to miss out.

"You know we don't take first-timers in back," Phillip said. There was a slight edge to his voice, as if he was beginning to get angry.

"Usually. But Aaron's different. There's a real . . . *hunger* inside him. I've got the bruises to prove it."

"And just where would those bruises be, my love?" Instead of sounding jealous, Phillip sounded aroused.

"Wouldn't you like to know? Seriously, I think Aaron can handle it."

Aaron wanted to say something in his own defense, but as he opened his mouth, Caroline caught his eye and shook her head. The message was clear: Let Phillip decide on his own.

"All right," he said at last, nodding. "Let's do it."

Caroline stood on her tiptoes and gave Phillip a quick peck on the lips. "Thanks, lover."

Not so long ago those lips had explored every nook and cranny of Aaron's body. He thought he'd experience a wave of jealousy at seeing Caroline kiss her husband with them, but he didn't. He felt turned on, and his exhausted cock actually gave a twitch, as if it might rally for another go-round.

Aaron sat up and Caroline knelt next to him.

"How are you doing?" she asked.

Before Aaron could answer, Gillian rose to her feet. "I hope you'll both excuse me, but I need a drink." She nodded toward the bottled water Caroline held. "Something stronger than that." She walked off toward the bar, shoulders hunched as if she were trying to keep herself from crying. Whatever the deal was with Morgan, Gillian was clearly upset by the situation. Aaron decided it wasn't any of his business, though, so he put the matter out of his thoughts and answered Caroline's question.

"I'm sore, but happy. What's up?"

"There's something special we do here in Penumbra. Not all the time, but we're going to do it tonight. We'd like you to join us."

Aaron looked around. Phillip was moving through the club, speaking to each member in a low voice. When he finished, they nodded, eager grins on their faces, and started to get dressed.

Gillian returned with a glass of Jack Daniel's in her hand. "So our new playmate's going to get the full experience tonight? Wonderful!" She sat back down on the mattress next to Aaron and started nuzzling his neck.

A sudden feeling of revulsion overwhelmed Aaron. A naked woman who he hadn't known existed a few hours ago was nibbling his neck, while another knelt next to him. Both of them had his cum on and in them in various places, and he was slathered in their saliva and vaginal juices. A sour musk clung to the three of them, the smell rank and nauseating. Aaron's stomach roiled, and he felt hot bile splash against the back of his throat. He feared he was going to vomit forth the whiskey and whatever drugs Phillip had given him. With an effort, he fought his nausea down, and the urge to throw up subsided, though it didn't entirely go away.

"What . . . what time is it?" Aaron asked. He looked at his wrist, but though he'd been wearing a watch when he came in here, he didn't have it on now. He had no idea where it was. "I probably should be getting home. You know, before my wife wakes up and discovers I'm not there."

Gillian nipped Aaron's shoulder hard enough to hurt. "You're not going to bail out on us now, are you? Not when things are just about to get *really* good!" Gillian no longer seemed to be upset about Morgan's absence. It was as if she'd completely forgotten about him. Or wanted it to seem like she had.

Caroline reached out and put a hand on Aaron's shoulder, her eyes full of concern. "It's only natural that you should feel a little . . . awkward. Phillip and I went through the same thing the first time we came to Penumbra."

"And came *inside* Penumbra," Gillian added with a giggle.

Caroline ignored her and continued. "It's only natural to feel overwhelmed after experiencing so much pleasure, to feel guilty for indulging your own desires far more deeply than you ever have before. But doesn't a part of you—an important part that's been neglected for far too long—feel satisfied? Fully and completely, perhaps for the first time in your entire life?"

Aaron wanted to deny it, but Caroline's words rang too true, and he said, "Yes."

She smiled. "Then trust me when I say that if you stay, if you join us in the back, you'll know fulfillment beyond anything you've experienced here tonight. Beyond anything you've ever imagined."

"She's not shitting you, sweetheart," Gillian whispered in Aaron's ear. She took hold of his earlobe in her teeth and shook her head back and forth several times, almost as if she were a dog playing with a chew toy. She released his earlobe and said, "It's fan-fucking-tastic."

She stuck her tongue in his ear then, and a chill

shivered down his spine. His cock, despite everything it had been through tonight, began to swell.

"All right, I'll do it," he said.

Caroline's smile broadened. "Excellent! Let's get dressed." She rose to her feet, and Gillian released her hold on Aaron and stood as well. As the two women moved off to find their clothes, Aaron saw that the others were already dressed. Phillip had hold of the pet carrier containing the rabbit. The animal was awake and seemed to be content enough in its captivity. It sat looking out through the bars, eyes wide and moist, nose twitching as it scented the air.

"Why are we getting dressed?" Aaron asked no one in particular.

"Because it's respectful," Phillip answered.

Aaron looked at Phillip for a moment, trying to determine just what in hell he meant by that. Finally Aaron nodded. "Okay," he said, and started looking for his clothes.

CHAPTER SEVEN

The mood in Penumbra had turned almost somber, but with an underlying current of anticipation. No one spoke as Aaron finished dressing, and his hands were trembling so much that he had trouble buckling his belt.

He felt odd putting his clothes on, reassuming a veneer of modesty after everything he'd done—and that had been done *to* him. Though they were only a polo shirt and shorts, his clothes felt restrictive and scratchy, like the suit his father had used to make him wear to church when he was a boy.

This place is about as far away from church as you can get, he thought.

"Everyone ready?" Phillip asked.

They all nodded. Still no one spoke, but their eyes shone with eagerness. Whatever lay within the back room, they couldn't wait to get to it.

This is your last chance, he thought. *You can still back out. All you have to do is turn around, walk to the front door, open it, and step outside.*

Yeah, said the thought-voice that sounded too much

like his father. *And what if they try to stop you? That fat guy wouldn't give you much trouble, but those other three—Wyatt, Travis, and Phillip—they're all in pretty good shape. Better than you, anyway, especially Phillip. You won't get out of here unless they let you go.*

Aaron told himself that he was just being paranoid, probably an aftereffect of the booze and drugs. And yet, from the way the others kept sneaking glances at him, Caroline most of all, he couldn't help feeling that he was committed to following them into the back room—whether he wanted to or not.

Though the other men had put on their pants, Aaron could see the bulges made by their stiff cocks. Jesus Christ, what did these guys do, swallow a couple of bottles of Viagra apiece before coming here tonight? And what the hell was in the back room that would give them all hard-ons, especially after everything they'd already done in the front room? Maybe the *real* kink was waiting in the back room. Maybe they kept a sex slave imprisoned back there, maybe even several. But then why would they put their clothes back on, and what was the deal with the rabbit?

Given the current atmosphere in the place, Aaron thought there might be some sort of ceremony to the opening of the door that led to the back. But Caroline simply removed a single key from her purse—he couldn't tell if it was the same one she'd used to open the fuckle door or not—and inserted it into the lock. A turn, a click, and then she removed the key, put it back in her purse, took hold of the knob, and, after a second's hesitation, opened the door.

It was dark inside, and Aaron had the impression that there was nothing beyond the doorway, that it was only a frame for empty blackness. But then Caroline stepped aside, and one by one the others proceeded into the darkness, Phillip and the rabbit going last.

Caroline turned to Aaron and gestured toward the door. "After you."

"Said the spider to the fly."

Caroline grinned. "We're all spiders here, Aaron. You included."

Unsure what to make of this remark, Aaron stepped through the doorway.

Aaron couldn't see anything inside. The light from the front room didn't penetrate into this one, almost as if the darkness were somehow holding it back. Caroline stepped through after him and closed the door. He waited to hear the sound of her locking the door, but she didn't. This came as a comfort to him; if he had to escape, he could.

Though the front room was air-conditioned, after the group's sexual escapades it had become warm and somewhat stuffy. But this room was cooler, so much so that the temperature change gave Aaron a jolt. Breathing in the cool air made his throat and sinuses ache, and a wave of dizziness came over him. He thought he might faint, but then Caroline took hold of his hand, almost as if she sensed his vertigo, and her touch steadied him.

"Let me guide you, Aaron," Caroline said in a near whisper. "The rest of us don't need to see to get around in here, but since this is your first time . . ."

Aaron was suddenly put in mind of going through a

Halloween haunted house, the kind where drunks in rubber masks reach out to grab women's asses as they pass by. He reached out into the darkness, half expecting the hand that found his to be cold and skeletal. But if was soft, warm, and feminine, and he gripped it gratefully.

Caroline pulled him farther into the room, and he found himself counting the steps. *One, two, three, four, five . . .*

"Stop here," Caroline said, and he did so. "Now, I don't want to frighten you, but it's very important that you don't take another step forward, not even an inch. Do you understand?"

Not really, but he said yes anyway. His head was beginning to throb and his mouth felt like it was filled with steel wool. Whatever it was that they were going to do in here, he wished they'd get started.

"Keep looking straight ahead," Caroline instructed. "You probably won't be able to see much tonight, but you should be able to see more clearly next time."

"*Much* more," Spencer said, causing a couple of the others to chuckle. From the sound of their voices, Aaron had the impression that the eight of them were standing close but—with the exception of Caroline and him—not shoulder to shoulder. *We're in a circle,* he thought, though he wasn't sure how he knew this. Instinct, perhaps, or maybe his eyes were adjusting to the darkness, at least a little.

The room was filled with a strange sort of coolness. Aaron heard no hum of an air conditioner, no soft hiss from a central air vent. The cold seemed to emanate from directly in front of him, as if he were facing a pillar of black ice. What's more, the air felt clammy, like the atmosphere in an old basement with crumbling stone walls and greenish black mold growing everywhere.

"Since you can't see, Aaron, I'll tell you what I'm doing." It was Phillip, and it sounded as if he were standing on the opposite side of the circle from Aaron and Caroline. "I'm kneeling at the edge of the circle. You can't see it, but the floor's made of concrete. The circle was drawn when it was freshly poured and had yet to dry."

Aaron stared through the darkness in the direction he judged Phillip was kneeling. He thought he saw a black shape move, a shape that was darker than the darkness around it. But this shape wasn't kneeling; instead it seemed to be undulating from side to side, almost serpentlike. The motion became faster, more intense, and Aaron thought that whatever the shape was, it was getting excited.

Not whatever—whoever. It has to be one of the eight of us. Probably Gillian. She's a complete horn dog. Aaron could picture her shimmying and swaying, most likely fondling her breasts and fingering her cunt as she did so, so turned on was she by what was about to happen. But the rippling dark shape seemed taller than Gillian, broader too. Probably just a trick of the light, he decided. Or rather a trick of the dark. But he couldn't bring himself to fully believe it.

"I'm putting our good friend Peter's carrier on the floor now," Phillip said.

Aaron heard the soft sound of plastic gently coming into contact with concrete, accompanied by the rattle-ping of the metal bars of the carrier's doors. The rabbit scuttled in its cage, the claws scratching against the carrier's plastic bottom.

"Now, this is important, Aaron, so listen close. I've just put the carrier down *outside* the circle. We never go inside the circle, no matter what. Got that?"

Aaron wanted to ask why, but he also wanted to get whatever they were about to do over and done with, so he just said, "Yes."

"Good. Now I'm going to open Peter's cage door. I've set the carrier's front end so close to the circle that when Peter bolts for his freedom, he'll have no choice but to go into the circle."

"What if he doesn't come out?" Aaron asked. He knew from years of vet experience that frightened animals would often huddle in a corner of their carrier and refuse to leave, even when the door was opened.

Aaron heard the cold smile in Phillip's voice as he answered. "Then we grab hold of the little fucker and toss him in."

Before Aaron could ask any more questions, he heard Phillip open the carrier door. The room fell completely silent then, and Aaron realized that everyone, himself included, was holding his or her breath in anticipation of what would happen next. More scuttling came from the cage, louder and more frantic, and Aaron knew that Peter was gearing up to make a break for it. He heard the rabbit shoot out of the carrier, heard its nails scrabble on the concrete floor—was it inside the circle or outside? And why the hell did that matter anyway?

Almost as soon as Aaron thought this, the scrabbling sound stopped. At the same moment the black shape in the middle of the circle stopped undulating and went completely still. What looked like an arm—though thinner and longer than Aaron would've thought possible—snatched out toward the floor. And then the rabbit screamed.

Though he was a vet and well aware that rabbits could indeed scream when they needed to, the sound still startled him, making him jump. Caroline squeezed his hand in reassurance, but he could feel that she was trembling, as if she too was upset by what was going to happen. But perhaps her tremors had little to do with fear . . . at least, not fear for the rabbit.

The hand—no, the *tentacle*—pulled the rabbit up to the main mass of darkness. The rabbit screamed once more, this time far more loudly and higher-pitched, but its screams ended abruptly, almost as if they were a recording that someone switched off. The eight men and women standing around the circle, Aaron included, exhaled in unison, the collected sound reminding him of the satisfied sigh of someone who'd just experienced a particularly good orgasm.

What happened to the rabbit? Aaron wondered. Was it injured? He was tempted to step forward and feel around for it to see if it needed medical attention. But then he remembered what Phillip had said about not crossing into the circle.

He was probably just shitting me, playing up the drama of the moment, Aaron thought. *What could possibly happen if I walked into the circle?*

His father-voice replied: *The same damn thing that happened to the rabbit.*

Aaron remained standing where he was.

When Phillip spoke again, his voice, soft as it was, ripped through the silence like a shotgun blast. "I'm standing up again now, Aaron. It's going to be hard to describe what happens next. I think it's probably best to let you experience it for yourself. Just stand still and no matter what happens, don't move. And for Christ's sake, don't take so much as a half step forward. Understand?"

"Yeah, sure." Aaron couldn't keep the irritation he felt out of his voice. He was beginning to suspect that this was all bullshit, a practical joke to play on the new guy. Normally, he might've gone along with it good-naturedly enough, but right now he didn't feel so damn hot, and he wasn't in the mood. He turned toward Caroline to tell her that he was going to go, but before he could speak, he felt something cold brush against the sweat-slick skin of his forehead. Instead of startling him, the touch felt good. Soothing, relaxing, like the feel of a cool damp cloth pressed against the forehead when one is overheated or ill. Without thinking, Aaron turned to face the circle again, and he saw a tendril of darkness come toward him, felt its cool tip touch his forehead once more. It pressed against his skin, not painfully, but with slow determination, as if it weren't going to let something so inconsequential as skin and bone prevent it from going where it wished. The pressure intensified, though it still wasn't painful, and Aaron wondered if whatever was pressing against his head had somehow anesthetized the area so it wouldn't hurt. The pressure increased even more, and just as

Aaron thought he might be shoved off his feet, he felt a silent *pop!* like the sensation during anal sex when the anus finally accepts the penis and allows it inside. The dark tendril had penetrated Aaron's forehead and now burrowed into the tender sweet meat inside.

Aaron understood what was happening. The dark thing that inhabited the circle etched into the concrete floor—whatever it was—was digging into his brain. He should've been in agony, should've been terrified, should've been screaming until his throat was raw and bloody. But it didn't hurt and he wasn't scared. In fact, he felt fantastic, as if whatever was rooting around inside his skull was directly stimulating the pleasure center of his brain. Sensations coursed through his body, raced along his nerve-endings, filled every cell of his being. He felt warm and safe, loved and teased, fucked and fed, praised and admired . . . every positive emotion he'd ever known he now experienced all at once, and far more intensely than ever before. The physical sensations were equally incredible. He felt as if his body had been dipped in warm honey while his cock exploded with one orgasm after another, sperm shooting out of the tip as if he were a come fountain. He heard music more beautiful than the finest orchestral arrangements ever penned, tasted food that would've put the gods' ambrosia to shame. His veins were alight with golden fire beyond any drug ever discovered or manufactured, and his optic nerves were overwhelmed by a riot of swirling, dancing colors, many of which he'd never seen and had no names for.

Aaron felt a presence inside his mind, then. Not an

intelligence, exactly, at least not as he understood the word. But whatever the nature of the presence, Aaron knew he was no longer alone inside his own skull. He could sense the Other reaching out to him, striving to connect on a deep level, almost as if it were trying to communicate with him . . .

And then, just like that, it was over.

The dark tendril pulled free from Aaron and withdrew back into the circle. The sudden emptiness that he felt was so overwhelming, so crushing, that his legs buckled beneath him and he started to fall. Hands grabbed him beneath his arms and kept him from collapsing.

"A little help here," Caroline said, her voice strained. Aaron heard rapid footsteps, and then several other pairs of hands took hold of him.

"C'mon, let's get him back into the other room," Phillip said.

Aaron's head lolled on his chest as he was carried away from the circle. He was perfectly conscious, but he felt as if the connection between his mind and body had been severed. Fear slammed into him as he remembered how the dark tendril had burrowed into his brain. Jesus, what if the goddamned thing had fucked him up inside, caused him to be paralyzed? He could be a basket case for the rest of his life!

He heard the door open, saw faint light splash into the room. He was carried through the doorway and over to the couch. They laid him down and gathered around, some looking concerned, others amused.

"Get back," Caroline said. "Give him some air."

The others did as she said, moving off to the bar and

speaking in low tones. Aaron couldn't make out what they were saying, but they kept glancing back toward him and smiling in amusement.

Caroline knelt next to the couch and patted the back of his hand. "Don't mind them. They're just remembering their first time. It can really knock you on your ass, even when you know what to expect."

Aaron felt his strength slowly beginning to return. He tried sitting up and with Caroline's help, managed to do so.

"What . . ." His throat seized up, and he had to swallow several times before he could speak again. "What the hell *was* that?"

Caroline's smile fell away, and there was a soft, almost reverent tone in her voice as she answered, "The Overshadow."

The word was unfamiliar to Aaron. He was about to ask Caroline to explain further, but then he remembered the dark tendril stretching toward his forehead, burrowing through his skin and into his skull. Panicked, he reached up to feel his forehead, expecting to find torn flesh, sticky blood, jagged bone, and soft brain tissue. But his forehead was uninjured, the skin smooth and unbroken.

"What happened in there?"

Caroline looked at him for a moment, as if she were considering how much to say right now. "It's getting late. How about I fill you in on the ride home?"

Aaron frowned, not understanding. "But I drove myself."

"I know, but you're in no shape to drive yourself home. I'll drive you there in your car, then just walk back to my house." She smiled. "One of the advantages of our being neighbors."

Aaron wanted to protest. What if Kristen woke up and discovered Caroline bringing him home? No way would he be able to explain it. But Caroline was right; the way he felt right now, he doubted he'd be able to pull out of the parking lot without hitting another car, let alone make it home without getting into an accident.

"Yeah, all right." He held out his hand and Caroline took it and helped him off the couch. His legs still felt wobbly, but he could stand on his own.

Phillip came over, carrying a shot glass filled with vodka. "Glad to see you on your feet, Aaron. The first time always hits like a punch to the gut. Knocks the wind out of you for a bit. But you'll be back to normal before morning." He grinned. "Hell, you'll be *better* than normal." He held out the shot glass for Aaron to take.

Aaron thought about declining. The last thing he needed was more booze or drugs polluting his system. But on the other hand, a strong bracing shot of alcohol might be just what he needed to get going again. He smiled gratefully to Phillip and nodded as he took the drink. He held the small glass up to his nose and inhaled the acrid smell of vodka. He put the rim of the glass to his lips and downed the alcohol in one gulp. It burned going down, but pleasantly so, as if it were clearing away the residue Aaron had accumulated from breathing in the back room. He handed the empty glass back to Phillip.

"Better?" Phillip asked.

Aaron was surprised to discover that he indeed felt a

little better. Ah, the wonders of distillation! "I think so. Thanks."

Phillip smiled. "And thank you for fucking the shit out of my wife. I can't wait to take an inventory of her bruises and scrapes—both external *and* internal—when we get home." He gave Caroline a lascivious leer, and she laughed and swatted him on the arm.

"You're just an overgrown teenager!" she said, though not without affection.

Aaron thought the vodka he'd just swallowed was going to come back up. It was one thing to participate in an orgy, if that was the right term for what had taken place here tonight. But to have Caroline's husband thanking him for having sex with her . . . that was too damn strange.

"Don't forget Gillian!" Trevor said. "Aaron drilled her so hard, her pussy has openings in both the front and back now!"

"Fuck you," Gillian said, though she didn't sound upset by the comment.

Everyone laughed. Everyone except Aaron, that is.

"I really need to go," he told Caroline.

She nodded, linked arms with him for support, and led him toward the outer door.

"Good night, all," she said. "Screw you later."

More laughter, punctuated with farewells and Phillip saying, "See you at home, darling!"

As Caroline opened the fuckle door and helped Aaron step out into the night air, he realized something. He had no idea what had happened to the rabbit.

* * *

Gerald was wide awake when Aaron and Caroline stepped into the parking lot. He hadn't needed to work very hard to stay alert, for he didn't need to sleep anymore—at all.

From the way the vet was staggering—and from the way Caroline was helping him—Gerald knew that they'd taken him to see the Overshadow . . . and on his first night in Penumbra! He clenched his teeth as a toxic mix of envy and jealousy twisted his gut. *He'd* had to wait until his third visit to Penumbra to see the Overshadow, and even then he'd had to work to convince the others that he was ready. What was so bloody fucking special about Aaron Rittinger that he'd been invited back on his first visit?

Maybe Caroline took him back on purpose tonight . . . maybe she knows that I'm watching, and she did it to taunt me.

The thought both pleased and alarmed him. If Caroline wanted to tease him, that meant she was thinking about him, that he was still important to her. But if she knew he was watching Penumbra and she told the others . . . then he was a dead man. He experienced an urge to start his VW, throw it in gear, and get the hell out of there as fast as he could. Forget Aaron Rittinger, forget the plan—just save himself.

He got as far as reaching for the key in the ignition, actually grasping it between his thumb and forefinger. But instead of turning it, he removed his hand from the key and reached up to vigorously massage his scalp. He felt the wetness beneath his hand as scabs tore off and blood welled forth, but he didn't care. The pain was minor and it helped calm him.

He continued rubbing his scalp, smearing blood over the top of his bald head as he watched Caroline help Aaron to the passenger seat of his car. She buckled him in, closed the door, then went around to the driver's side and got behind the wheel.

"Had a little too much of the good life tonight, huh, Aaron?" Gerald muttered.

A rustling sound came from the backseat. Gerald thought the girl had fallen asleep, but she was awake now.

"Settle down back there," he said in a toneless voice. "I don't want to have to mess you up any more than I already have." He kept his gaze trained on Aaron's Lexus while he said this. The girl whimpered softly and then fell still, so Gerald figured that she'd gotten the message.

The Lexus's headlights came on and the car pulled out of its parking space. Gerald started his VW but he didn't hit the headlights; he didn't want to give his presence away. When the proper time came—when Aaron was ready—then Gerald would have no problem making a scene.

Caroline drove Aaron's Lexus onto the street. Headlights still off, Gerald backed out of his space, then moved forward, hoping he'd be able to keep up with Caroline. But as he pulled his VW Bug out of the lot and onto the road, there was more rustling in the back, louder this time, frantic.

"Goddamnit, I warned you!" Gerald tromped on the brake, causing the Volkswagen to fishtail. When the car came to a stop, he slid the gearshift into neutral and set the parking brake. He wasn't wearing a seat belt, so he had no problem turning around, leaning over the backseat, and pounding the bound and gagged girl as hard as he could. Once, twice, three times . . . When he was finished, his hand was sore and swollen, and he wondered idly if he'd broken a couple of knuckles. The girl hadn't made a sound after the first strike, and she appeared to be unconscious. Cheeks and jaw red and swollen, nose mashed and broken, bleeding as if her nostrils were twin faucets gushing crimson. Gerald had no idea if she were still alive, and at this point he didn't care.

He turned back toward the windshield and looked for the taillights of Aaron's Lexus, but he saw nothing. Not that it mattered; he knew where the man lived. Caroline, too, since she and Aaron were neighbors. He caught movement out of the corner of his eye, and he turned to look out the side window. The other members of Penumbra were leaving the club and heading for their cars.

He had to get moving again before the others saw him parked in the middle of the street. But where should he go? Should he follow Aaron and Caroline? If he did, he risked Phillip being behind him since they'd be driving to the same place, and of all the current members of Penumbra, Phillip Langdon was the hardest to fool. He'd be bound to notice that Gerald's rattletrap VW didn't belong in his neighborhood, especially at this hour. And if Phillip decided to check out the ancient junker, who would he find behind the wheel but his old friend and orgy partner Gerald Messer? Gerald doubted he'd live very long once Phillip caught him. Gerald would've liked to talk with Aaron some more, get his reaction to his first visit to

Penumbra, maybe bask in the smell that was sure to still be clinging to him. Body wash, aftershave, perfume, mold, and most of all, the more odiferous remnants of sex.

To hell with it. He could always catch up to Aaron tomorrow. Despite the lateness of the hour, right now the other Forsaken were back at the Homestead waiting for him—and for the plaything he'd procured for them this evening.

He released the emergency brake, put the car in gear, then pressed down gently on the gas pedal. When he was half a mile away from the Valley View Shopping Center, he turned on his lights and started heading out of town toward the country. He really hoped he hadn't killed the girl, but if he had, it wouldn't be a complete waste. There were other things they could do with her then. *Lots* of things.

Whistling, Gerald continued driving down the road.

CHAPTER EIGHT

Aaron sat in the passenger seat of his Lexus, the side of his face resting against the window. The cool of the glass felt good on his skin, but the vibrations of the car moving down the road were giving him the beginnings of a fierce headache. He supposed he should sit up straight, but he was too tired to bother.

Caroline had turned the radio to an eighties station, and the sterile sound of new wave synth-pop drifted out of the speakers. She sang along with the song, and though Aaron felt he recognized the tune, he couldn't remember the name of it or the band. He decided it didn't matter; so much of the music of that decade was interchangeable.

He looked out the window as they drove through the night streets of Ptolemy. He was rarely out and about at this hour, and he was surprised by how dark it was. The neon signs of businesses and fast-food restaurants were off, and aside from his Lexus, there were no other cars on the road. The houses they passed were dark as well, no lights glowing in the windows, no porch lights shining like lonely beacons in the darkness. It seemed like the entire world was asleep. No, more than that—like it was dead, deserted, and empty, and Caroline and he were the only two people left on the planet.

The commercial district gave way to residential. The trees growing forth from the lawns here seemed like large black masses of concentrated shadow, and Aaron imagined they were kin to that thing in the back room of Penumbra—the Overshadow, Caroline had called it. He envisioned dark tendrils unfurling from the black shapes on either side of the street, pictured the shadowy strands snaking toward the Lexus, wrapping around the car, covering it in darkness as they yanked the vehicle to a stop and searched for a way to get inside . . . to get at *him*. For a moment the image seemed so real that Aaron thought he wasn't just imagining it, and he jerked his face away from the window with a terrified gasp.

"What's wrong?" Caroline asked, voice filled with concern.

"The trees . . ." Aaron trailed off. The trees outside were just trees once again, nothing more. He let out a shaky breath. "Never mind. I guess I was just seeing things."

"I wouldn't be surprised. The first time you experience the touch of the Overshadow it can really mess with your head." Her smile was visible in the glow of the dashboard lights. "After my first time, I refused to eat or drink for two days. I was convinced the Overshadow would never touch me again if I soiled my body by taking any nourishment. Luckily, I got over it. As diet plans go, that one was a little extreme for me."

Aaron smiled at her joke, but the smile didn't last long. "These . . . aftereffects. Are they permanent? I mean, did it"—he couldn't bring himself to say the word *Overshadow* yet—"damage my brain somehow?"

"Of course not, Aaron. You're perfectly fine." She didn't turn to look at him as she answered, though, and her tone seemed too deliberately casual. Still, Aaron wanted to believe her, so he didn't press the issue.

"What is it? That . . . thing in the back room in Penumbra. What did it *do* to me?"

"Not just to you—to *all* of us. Everything else we do in Penumbra—the sex, the booze, the drugs—is only a prelude, an appetizer for when we go in back and . . . *experience* the Overshadow, when we receive the pleasure it offers. Be honest with me, Aaron. You've never felt better than you did when the Overshadow touched you, when it *entered* you." Caroline shivered as if she were experiencing the Overshadow's cold touch anew.

Aaron couldn't deny it. Whatever the Overshadow had done to him, the sensations had been so intense that for a time it was as if he'd ceased to exist, as if the being that was Aaron Rittinger—his personality, thoughts, memories, emotions—had been obliterated, leaving behind in its place nothing but absolute raw pleasure.

"It was beyond anything I've ever imagined," he said.

"And that was after just a rabbit," Caroline said. "If you thought tonight was something, wait until—" She broke off and closed her mouth, lips pressed tightly together.

"Wait until what?" Aaron asked.

Caroline didn't respond. Instead she slowed and hit the turn signal. Aaron glanced out the window and saw that they'd reached their subdivision. They'd be at his house in another minute or so. Caroline turned onto their street and pressed the gas pedal, driving faster than she had a moment ago.

Anxious to get home or hoping to get me there before she has to answer my question? He decided to try a different angle during the short time he had left.

"What was the rabbit for? What happened to it?"

Caroline didn't say anything, and Aaron thought she wasn't going to answer any more questions tonight. But as they drove past her house, she said, "Before the Overshadow will touch us, it must be . . . fed."

"You mean it *ate* the rabbit?" He couldn't believe he was sitting here in the passenger seat of his Lexus, still weak and shook-up from the aftereffects of the most wild experience he'd ever had, and discussing the feeding habits of some kind of monster or demon or whatever the hell it was.

Caroline slowed as she approached Aaron's house. She pulled into the driveway and turned off the lights. She put the car in park, but she didn't turn off the engine. She then turned to regard Aaron for a long moment before speaking once more.

"The rabbit wasn't a meal, exactly. More like a . . . a sacrifice."

Aaron felt his balls shrivel and draw in close to his body as the implications of Caroline's words hit him. The Overshadow wasn't a monster, at least not to Caroline and the other members of Penumbra. It was a god.

* * *

"What's wrong with him, Doctor?"

Aaron looked down at the animal sitting on the examination table. *What isn't?* he thought. The creature was the size of a smallish dog or medium-sized cat, but it had features of both. It possessed feline eyes and ears, but its elongated snout was definitely canine. Its upper gum was bereft of teeth, and yellowed nubs that resembled human teeth protruded from the lower jaw. Instead of fur, its body was covered by a feathery white down, like a recently hatched chick of some sort. Its tail was serpentine and covered with mottled scales, ending in a snake head that glared at Aaron, mouth stretched wide, venom dripping from wickedly curved fangs. Worst of all was the thing's smell, like a cancer-ridden skunk had sprayed its diseased stink on a piece of rotting meat that someone had then taken and marinated in a septic tank for a month. Aaron kept trying to breathe through his mouth so the smell wouldn't make him vomit, but it didn't help much. The stench was so thick that he could've bitten a hunk of it out of the air and chewed.

Aaron struggled to maintain his professional composure as he responded to the creature's owner. "It's difficult to say. We don't see too many animals like this around here, and while I do treat exotic pets, I have to admit that it's, ah, not a specialty of mine." He gave the owner an apologetic smile.

The man frowned and vigorously rubbed his scabrous bald head. "Well, aren't you going to run some tests on him? Take some blood, stick a thermometer up his butt, *something?*"

Aaron looked at the creature's hindquarters. The snake head at the tip of the tail hissed at him, as if to say, *Don't even think about ramming one of your cold glass sticks up* my *ass, pal!*

"Maybe if we rolled the animal over, Doctor?"

The voice was female, and it came from Aaron's right. He turned to see Caroline standing next to him, wearing a white examination coat encrusted with what Aaron thought might be cum stains.

"Roll it . . . I mean *him* over? What for?"

In answer, Caroline reached out, placed her hands on the creature's sides, and gently urged it over onto its back. Its belly was smooth and pink, like the skin of a newborn rodent, but there was a seam running down the middle, something like an operation scar, though this was more pronounced, almost as if the skin hadn't rejoined completely.

The bald man pointed at the creature with an index finger tacky with blood. "*That's* what I've been talking about, Doctor! You need to do something about it—the seam keeps opening up and spilling Fluffy's entrails all over the floor. It makes a hell of a mess, and the stains are a real bitch to get out of the carpet!"

Aaron was about to ask Caroline what she thought he should do next, but then he noticed that the examining room had disappeared. The four of them—Aaron, Caroline, the bald guy, and Fluffy—were now inside Penumbra's front room. Instead of lying on an examination table, Fluffy now reclined on the black Naugahyde couch. The bald guy and Caroline were dressed the same as they had been a second ago, but Aaron was naked. He felt a slow draining sensation in his penis, and he looked down to see globs of yellow-white semen drip from his opening and fall to the floor in a steady rain of ejaculate. *Plap-plap-plap-plap-plap* . . . He willed himself to stop dripping, tried to tighten his groin muscles to squeeze his penis shut, but his efforts only made the sperm come out faster.

He looked up to see if either Caroline or the bald guy had noticed, but both of them were gazing at Fluffy with concern. The fleshy seam in the creature's hairless pink abdomen was starting to split open. Slowly, bloodlessly, like a zipper it pulled apart, moving downward until its body cavity yawned open. The creature yowled in pain, its cry sounding uncomfortably close to that of an infant, and it began to thrash. Caroline grabbed the thing's back legs to steady it, and Aaron pressed the fingers of his left hand on the creature's chest to hold it down. The tail whirled around and the snake head shot toward Caroline's wrist and buried its venomous fangs in her flesh. She shrieked and yanked her hand away from the creature, tearing open a wide gash in her wrist. Blood gushed out onto the creature, spilled onto the table, and Caroline cradled her hand to her chest and sobbed as she tried to stanch the flow of blood. Aaron saw the skin around Caroline's wound was already beginning to blacken and swell. The snake's poison was going to work.

Cum ran out of Aaron's cock in a steady stream now, and the widening puddle of jism on the floor mixed with Caroline's blood. Aaron pulled his hand away from the howling creature and took a step toward Caroline, intending to help her, but then the bald man screamed, "What did you fuckers do to my Fluffy?"

Aaron turned back in time to see the bald man pick up the creature and then hurl the yowling, thrashing thing straight at his face. Dark tendrils emerged from the gaping cavity in Fluffy's stomach and wrapped around Aaron's head. The bloodless slit in the creature's gut—which now resembled a shaven vagina—slipped over Aaron's head, cutting off his oxygen and plunging him into absolute darkness.

"Fuck!"

Aaron sat up. He reached for his face, intending to claw the goddamned conglomerate thing off him, but he stopped when he realized he could see his hands. He looked around and saw that he was sitting on the couch in his family room. Bookshelves, fireplace, entertainment center, flat-screen TV on the wall, the expensive abstract painting over the mantel, the one Kristen had insisted they buy, though it looked to Aaron like what was left after a bug collided with a car windshield at a hundred miles an hour . . . He was home.

Jesus Christ, what a shitty dream! He supposed he shouldn't be surprised that he'd have nightmares, though, after what he'd experienced tonight. He glanced at the cable box on the entertainment center to check the time, but his eyes took a couple of seconds to focus on the glowing blue numbers. *Middle age sucks,* he thought.

When his vision sharpened he saw that it was 4:48. He wasn't sure what time it had been when Caroline brought him home, but he doubted he'd been asleep for more than two hours, if that. He was tempted to lie back down on the couch and sleep some more, but he resisted. In another hour or so his family would begin rising, and he had some things to take care of before then. Besides, now that he was awake he didn't feel all that tired. In fact, he felt pretty damn good. Rested, full of energy, like he could go outside right now and jog a few miles around the neighborhood without breaking a sweat. He remembered what Phillip had said just before Aaron had left Penumbra with Caroline.

You'll be back to normal by morning. Hell, you'll be better than normal.

It seemed Phillip hadn't been exaggerating. Grinning, Aaron stood and left the family room, walking with an honest-to-God spring in his step. He headed down a short hallway to the downstairs bathroom, went in, flipped on the light, then closed and locked the door. When he got home, he hadn't gone upstairs and crawled into bed with Kristen for several reasons. One, he felt guilty as hell after what he'd done tonight. It had felt great, but there was no point in deluding himself: He'd betrayed his wife. And not only her, but his kids as well. He was their father, and it was his responsibility—along with their mother—to provide a stable home environment for them. Participating in orgies and bizarre rituals wasn't exactly conducive to familial stability. Two, he didn't want to wake Kristen. If he did, she might realize just how late he was coming home. This way, she'd (hopefully) have no idea how long he'd been gone—if she even realized he'd gone at all. Third, and this was the most practical reason, he smelled rank as hell. Sweat, semen, and the vaginal juices of two different women. If Kristen woke up and he was in bed with her, she'd be sure to smell the sin on him. So he'd decided to catch a few z's on the couch—actually, he hadn't had much choice as he'd practically passed out on it—and then shower in the downstairs bathroom.

Just like a criminal trying to cover his tracks, he thought. But he didn't feel as much guilt and regret as he had a moment ago. He couldn't help it; he just felt too goddamned *great* to feel bad. He shucked off his clothes, which smelled about as fragrant as pig shit, turned on the water nice and hot, just the way he liked it, then stepped into the shower.

As he began to soap up, he started humming the eighties song that Caroline had been singing along to on the car radio. He burst out laughing when he remembered the title: "Tainted Love."

Caroline lay spread-eagled on a cold metal table, feet up in stirrups as if she were about to undergo a gynecological exam, wrists and ankles bound by leather straps so tight they threatened to cut off her circulation. She was naked and her flesh was covered with goose pimples. Phillip insisted on keeping the temperature low down here so that her nipples would always be hard, just as they were now. Stiff and jutting, the flesh so dark purple that they almost looked black. Her discomfort was delicious.

They were in the basement, or as they referred to it, the "workshop." The walls were padded with black leather, chains ending in fur-lined handcuffs dangled from the mirrored ceiling, and the white-tiled floor contained drains set in strategic locations. The lights set into the ceiling could project different colors of illumination, and tonight Phillip had chosen red—Caroline's favorite. Stretching the length of one wall rested a large worktable covered with dildos of varying shapes and sizes, along with parts cannibalized from leaf blowers, hedge trimmers, and lawn mowers. From these odds and ends Phillip constructed their homemade toys, and a dozen of the finished products sat on the table, nightmarish combinations of marital aids and mechanical equipment that might have been designed by the Marquis De Sade.

Phillip, also naked, stood next to her and gently stroked her inner thigh with his fingertips.

"How do you think it went tonight?" he asked.

Caroline closed her eyes and shivered as Phillip's fingers brushed her matted pubic hair. She'd wanted to take a bath once she got home, but Phillip had wanted her to stay *soiled*, as he put it. "You mean, how did Aaron do?"

"Yes." Phillip pinched the tender skin at the juncture of her leg and crotch between his fingers and gave it a hard twist. Caroline bit her lip and took in a hissing gasp of air.

"I think he did fine," she said. "We might have found ourselves a new member."

She kept her eyes closed, and now she felt Phillip's breath hot on her sex. She wondered what he was going to do to her, and the anticipation drove her crazy. She was so wet she could feel her juices running down her thighs.

"I'm not so sure," Phillip said, his mouth so close to her cunt that she could feel the vibrations of his voice shudder through the engorged flesh of her clitoris. "He enjoyed himself, sure. Who wouldn't? But he seemed . . . I don't know . . . hesitant, somehow. As if he were holding part of himself back. Besides, I'm leery about taking on a new member so soon after losing Morgan."

She felt the tip of Phillip's tongue lightly graze her clit, and she was so hypersensitive after everything her body had experienced tonight that she almost came right then. But she managed to hold her orgasm at bay.

She practically purred as she spoke. "You know we have to keep our numbers up unless you want to increase our risk of dementing."

"You're right, of course," Phillip said. "I'm just afraid that Aaron won't be able to handle the next step."

Caroline shrugged. "If that happens, then we'll give him to the Overshadow and look for someone else. But he'll be okay. You'll see."

She felt Phillip's breath recede. "For his sake I hope you're right."

She heard her husband walk away, and she opened her eyes to watch as Phillip headed over to the worktable and looked over the variety of machines he'd created over the years. She knew them as well as she did her own body: the Violator, the Intruder, King Dong, the Tingler . . . She wondered if Phillip was going to treat her to something new or if he would select one of their old standbys. In the end, he hefted the bulky Devastator off the table, and Caroline felt her vagina clench with a combination of anticipation and fear. The business end of the Devastator terminated in a two-foot-long clear dildo covered with prominent metal studs with openings at the tips. Phillip returned to the table and flicked a switch on the Devastator's side. The machine came to life, its motor making soft *chuf-chuf-chuf* sounds as the dildo began spinning around at the same time as it thrust forward and back.

Phillip gazed down at her, his naked body bathed in crimson light and a wild glimmer dancing in his eyes.

"It looked like you and Gillian gave Aaron the fucking of his life tonight."

Caroline stretched languidly, causing the leather restraints around her wrists and ankles to creak. "He gave as good as he got, darling, believe me."

Phillip thumbed another switch on the Devastator. The internal tubing began feeding lubricant to the studs and clear liquid sprayed out of the nozzles as if the plastic shaft were some manner of bizarre pornographic sprinkler.

"As good as I'm about to give you, my love?"

Caroline grinned at her husband. "We'll just have to see about that, won't we?"

Phillip positioned the spinning-thrusting tip of the Devastator between his wife's legs, and with a single violent motion shoved the studded dildo inside her.

Ricia woke to pain and darkness. She thought at first she was in a boat—the sound of a motor, the rocking motion—but then she realized she was lying on the backseat of a car and memory returned to her. She tried to open her mouth to scream, but her lips refused to part. She remembered then that they were sealed with duct tape, the same tape that bound her hands and wrists. She was going to scream anyway, as muffled and useless as the sound would be, if only to release the terror building inside her. But the pain throbbing through her body warned her not to make a sound, for if she did, he would beat her again and this time she might not survive. The fear had to come out somehow, though, and tears began to stream down her face, soaking into the upholstery she lay on. She forced herself to cry quietly and took a dispassionate mental inventory of her injuries.

Each breath felt like a knife sliding into her lungs, so she probably had some cracked or broken ribs. Her jaw throbbed and her skull pounded with every bounce and jostle of the car, which meant there was a chance she had a concussion. She remembered something she'd heard once somewhere, about how it was dangerous to fall asleep if you had a concussion. The thought almost made her laugh—right now falling asleep was the least of her worries. Her eyes—make that *eye*, for it seemed one of them had swollen shut—had adjusted to the darkness. She turned her head, making damn sure to do so quietly, and looked out the back window to get a sense of where she was. All she saw was black sky, ice-bright stars, and looming shadows that she hoped were trees. She didn't think she was in town anymore, for the lights of Ptolemy kept the stars from coming through so clearly. But otherwise, she had no idea where she was.

Ricia Lockhart, twenty, worked at the Burrito Bungalow, a fast-food joint that was open twenty-four hours and located just off the exit from State Route 75. It wasn't the greatest job in the world, but it allowed her to set her own hours, which meant she could work around her college schedule. She was a sophomore at the University of Cincinnati, majoring in nursing, although lately she'd been toying with the idea of changing to respiratory therapy. Her uncle had died of lung cancer last year, and going into respiratory therapy seemed like a good way to honor his memory.

She got off work at ten, and she clocked out and left the restaurant by the back door. The employees were required to park behind the building so that prime spaces would be open for customers. She was anxious to get back to her cramped apartment, take a quick shower, and study for a physio exam she had tomorrow. She wished she could take off college in the summer, like so many of her friends did, but she already had too many student loans to repay. The faster she graduated and went to work, the better. Plus, she'd be able to quit working fast food all the sooner.

When she saw the blue VW Bug parked next to her gold Saturn, she didn't think anything of it. She'd never seen the car before, but that didn't mean anything. There were always new workers starting at the Bungalow—the turnover rate in fast food was high—and she figured the Beetle probably belonged to an employee she didn't know yet. But as she got closer to her car, she saw the silhouette of someone sitting behind the wheel of the Volkswagen, and a warning chill rippled along her spine. Ricia was a petite woman of Asian descent, with long black hair bound in a ponytail and a model's slim build. She wasn't a particularly fearful person, but she was a realistic one. Small as she was, there wasn't a lot she could do to defend herself physically. For an instant she considered going back inside the bungalow and asking one of the guys, maybe Artie Schaeffer, who was sweet and mild as a lamb but built like a linebacker, to walk her to her car. But then she thought about how much studying she needed to do, and she decided to just hurry to her car and get in. After all, it was only ten o'clock and the parking lot was lit well enough. Even if the guy in the VW wanted to try something, he'd be crazy to do so. Unfortunately, the one thing Ricia hadn't counted on was the possibility that the man in the Volkswagen was, in fact, insane.

·   She was less than five yards from her car when the man got out of his. She knew at once that he wasn't a fellow employee. He was too old for one thing, and the way he was dressed would've gotten him a write-up from management for sure. He looked like a homeless person, and even from this distance, she could tell that he smelled like a backed-up sewer. As he came toward her, she saw the cold dead look in his eyes, and she opened her mouth to scream. But before any sound came out, the man with the dead eyes rushed forward and shoved his hands toward her face. She saw that he held a length of silver duct tape, and then he pressed it to her open mouth, sealing the lips together.

Now that she couldn't scream or call for help, she knew she had two options: run or fight. Though she was small, she'd learned enough about human anatomy in the last couple of years to know the vulnerable areas to strike at: the eyes, the throat, the genitals . . . But knowing the best places to attack and actually bringing herself to lash out at another human being— even one who was in the process of assaulting her—

were two entirely different things. Ricia had only a split second to make her choice, and as she was introverted by nature, she chose to run. It was a mistake. She did manage to turn away from her attacker, but before she could take a single step, she felt something hard strike the base of her skull—the man's fist?—and bright light flashed along her optic nerves. Her knees folded beneath her and she lost consciousness before she hit the ground.

Ricia had regained consciousness a couple of times since then, but each time she'd made too much noise and managed to upset her captor, and he'd hit her until she passed out again. He struck her enough times tonight that she feared she might have permanent brain damage, might even be bleeding inside her head. What was that called again? A subdural something-or-other. Whatever its name, it was nasty and could kill her if she didn't get medical attention soon. But to do that, she had to escape her captor, and she had no idea how she was going to accomplish that miracle. She decided she would just have to remain conscious, keep alert, and hope a chance presented itself, and when it did, that she'd be in a condition to take advantage of it.

She did her best to relax on the backseat and ignore the pain throbbing through her body as the Volkswagen continued going wherever it was going. She had no idea how long she lay like that—time meant nothing to her right now—but eventually the car slowed and turned. The ride became bumpier now, and the Bug moved more slowly. Ricia could hear the crunch of gravel beneath the car's tires, and she decided they'd left the main road and were now traveling down an unpaid side road, or maybe a country driveway. And then, far sooner than she expected, the car came to a stop. Faint fluorescent light filtered in through the Volkswagen's windows, though from what source, Ricia couldn't tell. The man turned off the engine. A moment passed as she listened to the engine tick as it cooled, and then the driver turned around and looked at her with those dead eyes of his.

"Still alive?"

She made no sound, no movement, lest she anger him again. But she kept her eyes wide open, so he could see that she was awake and still among the living.

"Guess so," he said.

From his tone, she couldn't tell whether this knowledge pleased him or not. For that matter, she wasn't sure whether it pleased her. Maybe it would have been better if she'd died during the drive. She suspected she was soon going to find out.

"We're going to get out of the car now, you and me. You're small enough that I can carry you if I have to, but I'd rather you walk under your own power. It's more respectful. Do you understand?"

Ricia didn't, but if he wanted her to walk that meant he would have to unbind her legs. And once he did that, she'd be able to run.

She nodded.

His eyes narrowed and he nervously rubbed his scab-encrusted bald head. "I know what you're thinking, but you can't get away. We're way out in the country, and there's nowhere for you to go. If you try to escape, you'll just make things harder for yourself. Get me?"

She got him, all right. But that didn't mean she still wouldn't try to get away from him the first chance she got.

She nodded again.

The man looked at her one last time, as if trying to gauge whether she was lying to him or not. Finally, he turned back around to face the front, opened the driver's door, and got out of the car.

This is it, she told herself. *Stay calm . . . wait for your chance . . .*

He reached into the car and flipped the switch that made the front seat fold down. Then he reached in with his other hand, this one holding a large hunting knife. The sight of the blade almost made Ricia lose it, but she forced herself to look way from the weapon and concentrated on breathing evenly. *Relax. He's just going to cut the duct tape around your ankles, that all.* She hoped.

The bald man carefully slid the steel blade between her feet and worked it under the tape. Then, with a series of swift, steady sawing motions, he cut her free.

Instinct screamed *Now!* and adrenaline surged through her. When he'd confronted her in the parking lot behind the Burrito Bungalow, she'd chosen to run instead of fight. Now she chose both. She was still wearing her work uniform, which meant she had on comfortable black walking shoes. She would've preferred steel-toed boots, but one had to work with the resources at one's disposal.

She lashed out with her right foot and slammed the heel into the bald man's chin. His head snapped back and he made a gurgling-choking sound as he fell backward. Ricia didn't hesitate. Ignoring the pain from the beatings she'd taken, she sat up and scooted toward the open door. Moving with her wrists still bound by tape was more difficult than she'd thought it would be, but she had a hell of a lot of motivation and she managed. She was off balance and nearly fell as she got out of the car, but she remained on her feet. The bald man was lying on the ground, blood tricking from his mouth, hand still holding tight to his hunting knife. She felt a thrill of triumph at seeing the blood. The kick had made him bite his lip, the inside of his cheek, or maybe even his tongue. It wasn't much in the way of payback, but it would do for a start.

He groaned and started to sit up, and Ricia was faced with another choice. Go for his knife—though how she'd get it with her hands bound the way they were she didn't know—or get the hell out of there as fast as she could. In the end, there really wasn't any choice at all. Her instincts screamed for her to run, and she couldn't have disobeyed them if she wanted to. She did, however, pause long enough to stomp on the fucker's throat three times. If she was lucky, she'd crushed his larynx. If nothing else, she hoped she'd slow him down enough to give her the edge she'd need to get away. One more throat stomp for good measure, and then she took off running into the night.

Her senses were on high alert, and as she ran she took in her surroundings in a single glance. Old two-story wooden house with peeling white paint, ancient barn so weathered it was impossible to tell what color it had once been. Between them a telephone pole upon which a fluorescent light was attached, flying insects swarming around it, its sterile white wash illuminating the immediate area but doing little to hold back the vast sea of darkness beyond. Fields of waist-high grass swayed in the night breeze, and Ricia instantly added all these details up to form a single judgment: abandoned farmhouse.

We're way out in the country, and there's nowhere for you to go.

But the bald man was wrong. There was one place she could go: *away.*

She ran like hell toward the waving grass.

Gerald struggled to breathe as he sat up. His throat hurt like a son of a bitch, and it felt like his Adam's apple had swollen to the size of a grapefruit. He turned to look in the direction the girl had taken off in, but she was already beyond the circle of illumination created by the fluorescent light pole. She was only a retreating shadow blending with the surrounding darkness, soon to be lost to view altogether.

Gerald tried to yell for help, but all that came out of his injured throat was a soft, raspy croak, nowhere near loud enough to be heard by the others. He was furious with himself. If he hadn't been distracted by Caroline and Aaron, he could've focused all his attention on the girl, and she never would've had the opportunity to escape.

I should've killed her when I had the chance, he thought.

He pushed himself into a standing position and staggered toward his car. He opened the driver's door, leaned inside, and pressed his palm hard against the center of the steering wheel. The VW's horn blared, and a moment later the barn door slid open and the other Forsaken came running to help.

Gerald grinned and pointed in the direction the girl had run. Without question or hesitation, the Forsaken ran past the Bug and raced off in pursuit.

Ricia was grateful for the long pants that were part of the standard Burrito Bungalow uniform. Tall grass, weeds, and thin thorn-covered branches whipped at her legs as she ran. If it hadn't been for her pants, her legs would've gotten cut up something fierce. She ran at a steadied, measured pace, afraid to go any faster. Her bound wrists threw her off balance, and if she wasn't careful, she'd trip and fall. And if that happened, then the bald man would have an opportunity to catch up to her. Whatever else he did, she was certain the man would never give up and let her go. Not after the way he'd abducted her and then brought her out to this place, wherever it was. He'd gone to too much effort, broken too many laws to allow her to escape.

She started when she heard the blare of a car horn cut through the night, and without thinking she looked back over her shoulder toward the noise. The motion caused her to wobble and her right foot shot out from under her. She spun as she fell and landed hard on her right side, the impact forcing the air from her lungs in a sudden gust. She lay on the flattened grass for a moment, stunned and gasping for oxygen. Her breath slowly returned, and she managed to sit up, wincing in pain as she did so. Her side felt as if it were on fire; if her ribs hadn't been broken before, they surely were now. She brought her bound wrists up to her face and inspected the tape, hoping that by some miracle it had torn when she'd fallen. But this was duct tape—the chosen tool of do-it-yourselfers and amateur repairmen everywhere. Nothing so minor as a simple fall was going to damage it. Frustrated, Ricia maneuvered her hands closer to her face, grasped the edge of the tape covering her mouth, and yanked it off. It stung and she felt sharp pinpricks of pain on her lips. She guessed the tape had taken some skin with it, but she didn't care. Both of her lips could've been torn off right then, and it wouldn't have mattered to her. Just so long as the tape was off so she could breathe easier as she ran, scream for help, and release the terror seething inside her like steam in a pressure cooker. She looked at the tape still binding her wrists. Now that her mouth was uncovered, she wondered if she could try tearing the tape off with her teeth. Sure, the stuff was strong, but if she could get it off she could—

The sound of bodies thrashing through the tall grass and weeds, ragged breathing as lungs unused to physical activity struggled to take in and process oxygen fast enough. Someone was coming after her, and from the sounds, not just the bald man. Many someones.

Ricia forgot about trying to bite off the tape. She pushed herself awkwardly to her feet, letting out a bleat of pain as her broken ribs once more made their presence known. She stumbled forward, nearly tripping again, but then she found her balance and resumed running.

"You might as well stop, sweetie! There's nowhere to go!"

A man's voice, from behind her. Not close, but not far away, either. It wasn't the bald man, but someone else. One of the others. How many of them were there? she wondered frantically. But of course the answer was obvious: too many.

"Come on back! You don't want to miss out on the fun!" A woman's voice.

"Maybe *she* does, but *I* sure don't!" Another man, not the bald-headed one. That meant there were three others beside her abductor—at least.

Though it was a cool night, the air was humid and Ricia's body was slick with sweat. A detached part of her mind—one that would serve her in good stead if she survived to become a respiratory therapist—realized that this was her chance. If her wrists were sweaty enough, the moisture might loosen the tape's hold and make it possible for her to grip the tape with her teeth and pull her hands free. But she couldn't afford to stop even for the few seconds that such a maneuver would take. Could she do it while she ran? What if she lost her balance again and fell?

Before she could decide what to do, the matter was rendered academic. A dark shape loomed before her, seemingly having appeared from nowhere, and before she could turn to avoid it, a fist lashed out and struck her hard on the jaw, instantly breaking it. Ricia moaned as she collapsed to the ground, then whimpered as her broken ribs ground together. She gazed upward and through blurry tear-filled vision saw the dark outline of the bald-headed man standing over her.

"Dumb bitch," he muttered in a hoarse whisper. "You got turned around in the dark and started heading back toward the Homestead. Don't know why we were even bothering to chase you—you were already coming back to us." He leaned down and she could see a slash of white cut through the darkness as he grinned. "Almost like it was meant to be, huh?"

He scooped her up then as if she weighed no more than a small child and tossed her over his shoulder. As he started carrying her back toward the barn, she didn't resist. She was too tired, too hurt, too mentally and emotionally exhausted to fight anymore. Others joined them as they neared the barn, three of them—two men and a woman—just as Ricia had guessed. They looked just as dirty, haggard, and crazy as the bald-headed man, and their eyes gleamed with the same burning intensity.

"What are we going to do with her, Gerald?" one of the men asked. He looked to be in his sixties, though it was difficult to judge his age, unkempt and unhealthy as he was. It also didn't help that his face was a jigsaw puzzle of scar tissue.

"Something special, I hope," the woman said. She looked to be in her forties, maybe older. Her gray hair hung in long braids with bits of jagged bone tied in. "It's been *ages* since we've had a new playtoy."

"It's been three days, Meredith," a cadaverously thin man in his early thirties pointed out. Though he had thick black hair, he had no eyebrows and no teeth.

"I know!" The woman—Meredith—cackled. "That's practically an eternity!"

The others, including the bald man, laughed softly, an edge of hysteria in their voices.

From her current vantage point, Ricia couldn't see

where they were going, but then she didn't need to. She knew they were heading for the barn. She could see the fluorescent light glowing on the ground, see the liquid black shadows of her captors sliding along behind them.

"Don't worry," the bald man said. "After all the trouble she's put me through tonight, I think she's more than proven herself to have a strong spirit. I believe she's worthy of being added to the Tapestry."

"Aw, man . . . I was hoping we could have some fun with her first," the toothless man said.

Ricia didn't want to know what these people—whoever and whatever they were—considered *fun*. She heard shoes crunch on gravel and knew they were back on the driveway . . . almost at the barn.

"Don't forget what we're trying to do out here, Ned," the bald man said, a tone of admonishment in his voice. "We're here to do more than merely sate our lusts."

"Not that there's anything wrong with that," Meredith said, then cackled again.

Still riding over the bald man's shoulder and looking downward, Ricia saw gravel give way to bare earthen floor. The light changed too, from blue-white fluorescence to a glaring bright yellow, as if work lights had been strung up in the barn. She took a breath and nearly gagged. Once, when she still lived with her parents, she'd been mowing the backyard and accidentally run across a dead rabbit that some neighborhood dog had killed, chewed on for a while, then left behind. The rabbit had been out in the sun for too long, and what remained of its carcass was bloated and rotten.

As the mower's blades tore the animal's corpse apart, it released a rank, greasy smell of death and decay into the air that lingered for hours. The stench inside the barn was like that, only a thousand times worse.

"Well, we finally made it," the bald man said. He removed his hand from Ricia's back and leaned forward. Ricia slid off his shoulder and flopped onto the ground. Her broken ribs screamed in agony, but no sound came out of her mouth. Why bother? She was already as good as dead.

The bald man squatted down on his haunches so he could look her in the face. He gestured, then spoke in a hushed, reverent voice. "Behold the Tapestry."

She didn't want to look, knew that she'd regret it more than anything else she'd ever done in her life, but she couldn't help herself. She slowly turned her head and gazed in the direction the bald man indicted.

She saw the Tapestry, and she realized then that there were worse things than death. Infinitely worse. She screamed then, and she was still screaming several hours later when she became the Tapestry's latest addition.

CHAPTER NINE

Aaron had breakfast on the dining table before anyone else was up. Pancakes, sausage, scrambled eggs, and hash browns. Not the most healthy of breakfasts, perhaps, but a mouthwatering one, if he did say so himself.

He waited for several minutes, sipping coffee, to give his family a chance to wake up on their own. Finally, he couldn't stand it anymore and he went upstairs. He woke Lindsay first, whispering, "Time to get up—breakfast," in her ear. Then he went into Colin's room and stood by his son's bed as he tried to decide the best way to wake up the boy without irritating him. He decided Colin would most likely be pissed no matter what he did, so Aaron gently shook his shoulder and said, "Wake up," in as neutral a voice as he could manage.

Colin opened one eye partway. "What time is it?" he growled and rolled over to squint at the clock radio on his nightstand. "Shit! C'mon, Dad, it's *summer!*"

Normally Aaron would've called his son on the use of profanity, but he felt too good to bother.

"I made breakfast. Get up if you want some. Go back to sleep if you don't."

Colin fixed his one open eye on Aaron and scowled in a mixture of confusion and suspicion. Aaron didn't want to stick around and get into an argument with the boy. He'd either come down to breakfast or not. Aaron turned and left Colin's room—the groggy teen muttering what were most likely more obscenities at Aaron's retreating back.

Aaron ignored Colin and continued down the hall to the master bedroom. He opened the door just as the alarm switched on, playing an oldies radio station that Kristen liked. In the darkened room, he heard the rustle of blankets as his wife began to stir. He crossed to his side of the bed and pulled back the covers, so Kristen wouldn't realize that he hadn't slept beside her all night. He then sat down on the edge of the bed and put his hand on Kristen's shoulder.

She rolled toward him and smiled sleepily. "Hey there." She reached out to turn off the alarm and glanced at the time. "What are you doing up so bright and early? Usually you're still dead to the world when I wake up."

Aaron shrugged. "I just got up early today."

She sat up and rubbed her eyes. "Is something wrong? Don't you feel well?"

"I'm fine." Light-years better than fine, but he couldn't tell her that. "Since I was awake I decided to surprise everyone and make breakfast. Better come on down and eat before it gets cold."

She frowned. "You . . . *made* breakfast?"

146

He laughed. "I know I don't cook much, but it's not *that* unheard of for me to make a meal, is it?"

"If it doesn't involve a gas grill and raw meat, yes." She was wide awake now. Eyes open and clear, voice smooth and strong.

"Then we'll make this an annual Rittenger family holiday. Henceforth, this day shall be forever known as Dad Made Breakfast Day."

He hoped she'd laugh even though it wasn't that great a joke. But instead her eyes narrowed and she gave him an appraising look. Aaron knew that he had just tripped her wifely radar. He'd deviated from the well-known script of their morning routine, and she was suspicious. At first he felt unjustly accused by her look and almost said so, but then he remembered she had plenty of reasons to be suspicious after what he'd done last night.

It'll be a onetime thing, he told himself. *I won't go to Penumbra again, won't talk to Caroline anymore. I'll do my best to put the whole bizarre experience behind me and rededicate myself to being the best husband and father I can be.*

But even as he thought this, he knew he was lying to himself. He *would* talk with Caroline again, and despite the oddity of the Overshadow, he'd return to Penumbra in an instant to feel its touch again.

Regret and guilt blossomed like twin poisonous flowers in his heart. *Tell her now, tell her everything—before things go too far.*

Aaron wanted to, and to his credit he was just about to start when a wave of well-being washed through him, draining his guilt, wiping away his regret, until once again he felt *great*.

He grinned, took Kristen's hand, and began to pull her off the bed. "C'mon, slugabed! Your breakfast awaits!"

Kristen laughed as she struggled to pull free of his grip. "Okay, okay! Let go!"

Aaron did so and Kristen collapsed onto the bed, still laughing. Aaron smiled, pleased to see his wife so happy. It had been a while since he'd heard her laugh like this. So long that he couldn't remember the last time he'd heard her laugh with such joy.

See? Going to Penumbra wasn't a bad thing. You're happy, and your happiness has spilled over onto Kristen. What's that old cliché about an affair being good for a marriage? Looks like it's true.

He wasn't surprised when his Dad Voice spoke up after that.

Rationalize it any way you like, kid. But the truth is you fucked around on your wife last night, and if she knew, she'd be devastated. You're a shit heel, and you know it.

Maybe so, Aaron thought. *But for the first time in a hell of a long time, I'm a* happy *shit heel. What do you have to say to that?*

Evidently nothing, for the Dad Voice was silent.

Aaron pulled Kristen off the bed and onto her feet, then put his arms around her and kissed her. His body pressed against hers, her flesh soft and yielding beneath her flimsy nightgown. He thought of the things he'd done last night with the lips that he now pressed against hers, but it didn't bother him, even though a distant corner of his mind whispered that it should've.

When they parted, Aaron said, "Let's go eat."

She looked at him for a long moment before finally nodding. "All right, just let me go get my robe."

Breakfast went well, even better than Aaron had hoped. Everyone ate—including Colin, who surprised Aaron by actually coming down. There was hardly any grumbling or bickering from the kids, and a general atmosphere of something that could almost be called family togetherness filled the house for a change.

This is what we need, Aaron thought. And it wouldn't have happened if he hadn't gone to Penumbra last night. Maybe he *was* rationalizing his actions, but that didn't make the results of them any less real, did it?

When Aaron was ready to leave for work, Kristen gave him a long lingering kiss in the kitchen instead of her usual perfunctory peck. When she drew back, Aaron said, "What was that for?"

"Just a little thank-you for being so sweet this morning." She smiled and a mischievous glint came into her eyes. "And a promise of things to come later."

He arched an eyebrow. "Such as?"

She leaned forward and whispered in his ear, "Such as you and me."

Aaron laughed, gave her another kiss, then headed for the garage. As he backed his Lexus down the driveway, he breathed in the scent of sweat, perfume, and sex—Caroline's smell. His penis started to harden, and he realized that during the entire time Kristen had been kissing him so passionately, his dick hadn't so much as twitched. This realization disturbed him, but he was determined not to let it spoil his mood, so he pushed the thought from his mind.

As he started to pull away from the house, he saw Kristen standing at the front door. As he looked, she opened the front of her robe and gave him a quick flash of her left breast. Laughing, Aaron honked the horn in appreciation and continued down the street.

The events of last night seemed like a dream to him in the bright light of day, but he had no doubt they'd happened. He had no clue what the Overshadow was or what exactly it had done to him, but he didn't care. It was almost as if the shadowy creature *was* a god of some sort, one that had granted its blessing to Aaron. The incredible pleasure he'd experienced at its cold touch last night, the domestic harmony that he'd enjoyed this morning . . . they were gifts, and Aaron was grateful for them.

And yet . . .

He approached Caroline and Phillip's house, and he slowed and looked for any sign of them. No, not *them:* Caroline. The curtains were drawn, and he saw nothing, though.

Well, what did you expect? That Caroline would be standing naked in her front yard waving hello as you drove by on your way to work?

Even so, he was disappointed not to see her. He remembered what Phillip had said just before Caroline and Aaron had left last night.

I can't wait to take an inventory of her bruises and scrapes—both external and internal—when we get home.

He wondered if Phillip had been joking, or whether even after everything that he and his wife had done in Penumbra—though not to each other—they'd had more sex after Caroline had dropped him off and walked home. He wouldn't have been surprised, didn't think he was capable of surprise anymore after his visit to Penumbra. He tried to imagine what Caroline and Phillip might've done to each other in the privacy of their own home, but while the images that passed through his mind made his dick grow even harder, they unsettled him as well. It wasn't jealousy that he felt— at least, he didn't think so. Whatever it was, it made him feel sad and a bit depressed.

"No biggie," he told himself. "You're just coming down from your high."

He'd meant it as a joke, but as soon as the words left his mouth, he wondered if they were true.

He drove on past Caroline and Phillip's house, determined to hold on to whatever positive feelings he could for as long as possible. But by the time he reached work, he felt like shit, both physically and emotionally.

You had your fun last light, and now it's time to pay the piper, kid. The Dad Voice sounded smug and amused.

Maybe so. But it was worth it. The thought lacked conviction, however.

As Aaron pulled his Lexus into the parking lot behind his practice, he looked for Caroline's car, and he was both relieved and disappointed not to see it. He also looked for the blue VW Bug that had belonged to the bald lunatic that had confronted him yesterday, and he was glad to note its absence as well. A sudden memory flashed through his mind.

Did she invite you yet? If she hasn't, she will. It's . . . what they do. When she does ask, say yes. Once you're in, keep your eyes and ears open. Participate, of course. You'll have to so they don't get suspicious. Besides, it'll be fun. They probably won't take you in back. Not your first night, but if for some reason they do . . .

These were the words that Scab-Head had spoken to him last night. At the time, Aaron had dismissed them as the simple ravings of a madman, but now he realized that the man had been talking about Caroline and about Penumbra. Whoever the crazy son of a bitch was, he *knew*. The things the man had said yesterday hadn't made sense at the time, and so much else had happened to Aaron at Penumbra that he really hadn't given the man and his lunatic ramblings much thought. Only now they didn't seem so crazy, did they? But as for who Scab-Head was, what his connection with Penumbra might be, and what he wanted from Aaron, Aaron couldn't guess. But that the man wanted *something* was pretty damn clear. The first chance he'd get, he had to give Caroline a call, tell her about his encounter with Scab-Head yesterday and find out if she had any idea what he was going on with him.

Depressed, tired, nauseated, and now worried, Aaron headed across the parking lot to his office.

The morning was busy, filled with sick pets and anxiety-ridden owners, and it was close to noon by the time Aaron had a spare moment to himself. He walked into the reception area to tell Diane that he was going back to his office for a few minutes to make some calls. But as he approached her, Diane held out the phone receiver for him to take.

"Call for you, Aaron. It's Caroline Langdon." Disapproval was clear in Diane's voice, and Aaron wouldn't have been surprised to see her curl her upper lip in a sneer as she spoke Caroline's name.

Aaron had been feeling increasingly normal as the day wore on, though he was still far from a hundred percent. He'd managed to forget his guilt, or at least suppress it, but Diane's disapproval was enough to bring all the guilt and remorse flooding back, stronger than ever. Aaron struggled to keep his response as neutral as possible. Diane was suspicious enough as it was; he didn't want to make things worse by appearing too eager to take Caroline's call.

He made no move to take the receiver from Diane's hand. "Could you transfer the call back to my office?"

Diane looked at him for a moment. He'd heard the phrase *steely gaze* before, but this was the first time he'd actually seen one. It felt as if Diane was looking past his flesh and into his soul, the sins that he'd committed last night plain for her to see.

At length, Diane smiled. "Of course, Aaron." She brought the receiver to her face, asked Caroline to please hold, then pushed the button to forward the call. She then put the receiver down—a bit too hard than was strictly necessary, Aaron thought.

"She'll be waiting for you in your office," Diane said.

Aaron tried to determine if Diane was purposefully engaging in innuendo or if he was just being paranoid. He forced a smile, said, "Thanks," then turned to go.

"Aaron?"

He turned back to face her. "Yes."

Her gaze was far from steely now. It contained only sadness and concern.

"Never mind," she said. "It can wait."

Not knowing what to say to that, Aaron just nodded and headed for his office. Vets didn't starve, but Aaron was by no means wealthy, and his office reflected this. His desk was made of gray metal and purchased at the close-out sale for an office supply warehouse. Several filing cabinets—also gray metal, also bought at the sale—rested against one wall. A wooden bookshelf sat against the opposite wall, shelves filled with tomes on veterinary science that Aaron hadn't looked at since college. There were a couple of paintings on the walls, both landscapes, both brought in by Diane. He'd ignored them for so many years that he had no clear notion exactly what the paintings depicted. There were no pictures of his family in sight, though he had a couple of his daughter in one of the desk drawers. Looking at photos of his family usually depressed him, so he'd never brought many in.

Once inside, Aaron shut the door, sat behind his desk, picked up the phone receiver, and pressed a button to switch over to the line where Caroline was waiting.

"Hello?"

"Hey, lover. How are you doing?"

Caroline's voice sounded like honey and smoke in his ears.

"I was doing fantastic early this morning. Now I feel kind of blah."

"That's normal. The first time is kind of rough on you, but the aftereffects won't be so bad in the future."

"I . . . well, about that . . ."

"Don't tell me you're having *regrets?*" The way she stressed the last word made it sound as if she thought the entire concept of *regret* was both childish and ridiculous.

"Not exactly," he lied. "Just feeling . . . *unsettled* is the word. I think."

Caroline's voice was full of overdone sympathy as she replied, "Aw . . . would Aaron like Mama to come pay him a visit and make it all better?"

Talk about childish, he thought, but his cock gave a twitch anyway.

"Thanks," he said, "but it's pretty busy around here today. Besides, I think my office manager suspects there's something going on between us. If you come down here again today, she'd know something was up for sure."

"Is that the woman who answered the phone when I called?"

"Yeah, her name's Diane. She's a great employee and a good friend, but she can be something of a meddler sometimes. Always with the best of intentions, but if she knew I was having an affair, she might tell Kristen. For my own good: At least, that's how Diane would look at it."

"Does she suspect anything about Penumbra? Did you tell her anything about it, anything at all?" Caroline's playfulness was gone, replaced by a sharp intensity that made Aaron uncomfortable. He almost felt as if he were being interrogated.

"I haven't told her anything. Not about us, and certainly not about the club."

"Good. Keep it that way. Penumbra is a carefully guarded secret, and if word were to get out . . ." Caroline trailed off.

Aaron understood. The club members' reputations would be ruined if their activities at Penumbra were exposed. But more than that, the existence of the Overshadow—whatever the thing was—would be revealed. And if that happened, there was a chance it would be taken away from them. And if they couldn't have access to the Overshadow anymore, couldn't experience its touch . . . A sudden sick feeling swept through Aaron and he had to fight to keep from throwing up all over his desk. They couldn't lose the Overshadow—it was unthinkable!

"I understand," Aaron said, his voice thick. "Diane doesn't know a thing, trust me."

There was a soft click on the line then, as if a third party had gently put down a receiver.

"You still there, Caroline?"

"Still here, Aaron. But I think Diane just hung up."

Near the end of the day, after the last scheduled patient had been seen, Aaron suggested that Patti go home early. The vet tech was a bit puzzled by Aaron's generosity, but that didn't stop her from taking advantage of it and getting out of there. She had a date later on and could use the extra time to get ready.

Once she was gone, it was just Aaron and Diane. He

found her at her desk, going over a stack of delinquent accounts. It seemed like vets got stiffed more often than other health-care professionals, maybe because people weren't paying for themselves but for their animals. Whatever the cause, collecting on unpaid debts was a perennial hassle for Aaron.

"Can I talk with you for a minute, Diane?" Actually, Aaron would've preferred not to say anything and hope they could ignore the matter, but Caroline had insisted he check to make sure whether Diane had eavesdropped on their phone conversation. Aaron had promised he would, but while he recognized the necessity of doing so, he wasn't happy about it.

"Can it wait? I don't mean to be rude, but I really want to get these accounts done before I leave." Diane didn't look up from her paperwork as she spoke, and her voice was strained.

Aaron experienced a burst of anger then, so strong that it alarmed him. What business was it of Diane's where he put his dick? They were coworkers—no, employer and employ*ee*—and that was all.

"I know you were listening in when I spoke with Caroline before lunch."

Diane didn't respond; she just kept shuffling papers and typing on her computer keyboard.

"I don't appreciate being spied on. Don't do it again." Aaron's words came out harsher than he'd intended, but he was so angry that he couldn't help it.

Diane sat up straight, her shoulders stiffened, and she removed her hands from the keyboard. She spoke without turning to face him.

"What I did was wrong, Aaron, but I was just so

concerned. I know you haven't been happy in your marriage for some time. You never said anything, but you didn't have to. I could just tell. And I know it's not my place to judge, but you really need to think hard about what you're doing. I don't know what Penumbra is or what goes on there, but I do know that you're taking a terrible risk." She took a deep breath and continued, still not turning to look at him.

"Years ago, back when my husband was alive, I . . . made a mistake similar to yours, Aaron. It almost cost me my marriage, and what's worse, it broke the heart of the only man I've ever truly loved. I was lucky, though. He forgave me and we were able to put my mistake behind us and move on. But things never were really the same between us after that." Her voice began to quaver, and Aaron knew she was fighting back tears. "I guess I just want you to know that you're gambling with some mighty high stakes. And no matter how the game turns out, you're liable to lose in the end."

Listening to Diane's story had drained away his anger, leaving in its place only a hollow sadness.

Finally, Diane turned to face him, tears sliding slowly down her cheeks. "Promise me you'll think about what I've said."

Aaron understood then why Diane had interfered so strongly this time. He supposed he couldn't blame her, not after what she'd told him. "I promise."

She smiled, wiped away tears with her fingers, then turned back to her computer screen. "Why don't you go home now and leave me to finish this up?"

Aaron wanted to tell her that the delinquent accounts could wait until tomorrow, but he understood she wanted to be alone for a bit. "Okay, but don't stay too late."

"I won't."

He nodded, forced a smile, and left.

Out in the parking lot, Aaron looked around for Scab-Head's blue Beetle. He was relieved to see no sign of it. After his conversation with Caroline had turned to Diane and how much she knew, Aaron hadn't gotten the chance to tell Caroline about his encounter with Scab-Head yesterday. He'd have to remember to tell her tonight, at Penumbra. He didn't bother to pretend to himself that he wasn't going. Despite what Diane had told him, he knew he would go. He *had* to.

As he climbed behind the driver's seat of his Lexus, his cell phone rang. He answered it and heard Caroline's voice.

"So?"

"She *was* listening, and she did hear you mention Penumbra," Aaron confirmed. "I doubt she'll do anything with the knowledge, though. We talked before I left, and she urged me to think hard about what I'm doing. I think that'll be the end of it." *I hope.*

"She's still there?"

"Yeah. She often stays late to finish up some work. Why?"

"No reason." Caroline was silent for several seconds, and Aaron had the impression that she was mulling her response carefully. "I suppose we'll just have to wait and see. Hopefully you're right and nothing will come of it. So . . . see you at the club tonight? Twelve midnight, sharp?"

This is it; your last chance to say no.
"Sure. See you then."

Caroline sat in her Infiniti in the parking lot of a chiro-practor's a block away from Aaron's veterinary clinic. She turned off her cell phone, laid it on the passenger seat beside her, then looked out the windshield and waited. A moment later, she saw Aaron drive by in his Lexus. After he was gone, she waited a full minute before turning on her car's engine and pulling out of the lot. She drove onto the street and headed south—toward Aaron's practice.

CHAPTER TEN

Diane pretended to work for a full ten minutes after Aaron left. Finally—having accomplished next to nothing for her efforts—she stuffed the delinquent accounts paperwork back into its folder, returned it to her desk drawer, then shut down her computer. Aaron should be gone by now, which meant it was safe for her to leave. Telling him about her affair had been difficult, and she didn't think she could face him so soon afterward. She knew she shouldn't have been ashamed to tell Aaron the truth. He was in the same situation, and he *was* the closest thing to a best friend she had since Walter had passed on. But she was ashamed, deeply so, and she wanted some time to pass before she had to look Aaron in the eye again, so she *could* look him in the eye.

She gave the office a quick once-over. The cleaning people were due in tonight, and she liked to take inventory of the place before leaving, so that if anything turned up missing the next day, they'd know when it had disappeared and who'd taken it. A lot of the drugs a vet kept on hand were similar to a physician's—though the names and dosages often differed. After all, PCP's intended use was as an animal tranquilizer. Some of the substances could be used to make street drugs and reasonable facsimiles, if someone knew their way around a basic chemistry set.

When Diane completed her rounds, she was tempted to do it all one more time, just to be thorough. But she knew there was no real need, that she was just looking for excuses to postpone going home. She lived for her work because she honestly didn't have anything else to live for. She and Walter had produced no children, and though they'd discussed adopting or even fostering some, nothing had ever come of it. She often thought that was the reason she felt so close to Aaron. Though he was a bit too old to be her biological child, he was like the son—or perhaps the younger brother—she never had.

Diane straightened the magazines in the reception area, then turned off the lights. She stepped outside into the humid evening air, which actually felt rather good after being cooped up inside in the air-conditioning all day. She locked the front door, turned the knob to check it, then headed for her car.

She wondered if she'd done the right thing by listening in on Aaron's phone conversation with Caroline Langdon. Technically, it was a sneaky thing to do, but she'd only done it out of concern for Aaron. She'd had to know whether her suspicions about him and Caroline were correct before she said anything more to him about the situation. But even if she could justify her actions to herself, that didn't mean Aaron would view them the same way. He had every right to feel betrayed by her, and she wondered if he'd ever trust her again. Who knows? She supposed it might even be possible that he'd fire her, though she had a hard time imagining Aaron doing anything that extreme.

Like Aaron, she parked her Accord near the rear of the lot. She was only halfway to her car, her shoes *clack-clack-clacking* on the hot black asphalt, when sweat began to bead on her forehead. She decided she'd been an idiot to even think the hot summer air had been refreshing, and she was already looking forward to getting into her car and turning on the air conditioner full blast.

If she'd lost Aaron's trust today, even if she lost her job, it would all be worth it if she'd helped save his marriage. She didn't know Kristen all that well, but she knew she was a good woman. Diane didn't want to see her get hurt. Even more, she didn't want to see Aaron ruin his marriage and end up alone. She knew what it was like to be alone, night after night, with nothing but your memories to keep you warm in bed. It was a fate she hoped to help Aaron avoid.

As she drew near her Accord, she noticed a white Infiniti parked several spaces from it. She didn't recognize the car, but that didn't bother her. What *did* bother her was when the driver's-side door opened and Caroline Langdon got out. The woman wore a simple black blouse, old jeans, and worn, grass-stained shoes—the kind of outfit a person would wear for working in the yard. It was quite a contrast to how she'd been dressed yesterday.

Caroline started walking toward Diane, but before

the other woman could get too close, Diane said, "I'm sorry, but if you've come to see Dr. Rittinger, I'm afraid the office is closed and he's left for the night." She knew Aaron's home phone number of course, but she wasn't about to give it out to a client—especially *this* one.

"I didn't come to see Aaron. I've come for you." Caroline smiled, but her eyes were cold as ice chips.

Diane noted the woman's choice of words. Not *I've come to talk to you,* but rather *I've come for you.* The same instincts that had told her that Aaron and this woman were having an affair now warned her that Caroline intended her harm. Diane had a vial of pepper spray attached to her key ring, but her keys were in her purse. Could she open it and retrieve the pepper spray before Caroline intercepted her? The other woman had already closed to within twenty feet of Diane, more than near enough to make a dash for her the moment Diane reached into her purse. Still, she had no other weapon, and she was too old and out of shape to outrun the younger woman. Maybe if she casually reached into her purse as if she simply intended to take out her keys so she could unlock her car . . .

Diane started to open her purse, but then Caroline stopped, and reached behind her back. When she brought her hand forward again, she was holding a handgun. One that she'd presumably carried tucked inside her pants against the small of her back, just like in the movies.

"Don't move and don't say anything. I borrowed this from a friend of mine, and while I'm not a crack shot with it, I doubt I'd miss at this range." Caroline spoke in a calm voice, as if she pulled guns on people every day. That tone, more than anything else, convinced Diane that Caroline meant business. The barrel of the weapon was pointed at Diane's chest, and Caroline's hand was rock steady. Diane knew that Caroline would indeed shoot her if she didn't do exactly as the other woman said. Diane stopped walking, and though she didn't try to raise her hands—for Caroline hadn't asked her to—she made sure to keep them in plain sight.

"Good girl. Now I want you to keep walking toward me and go around to the passenger side of my car. Get inside, sit, put the seat belt on, and buckle it."

Diane nodded to show she understood Caroline's instructions and then started walking slowly toward the white Infiniti. Caroline kept the gun trained on Diane the entire time she walked, and Diane knew that if she took so much as a single step to one side or another, Caroline would fire.

As she walked toward the Infiniti, Diane struggled to understand what was happening. She felt certain it had to do with her eavesdropping on Aaron's and Caroline's phone conversation, though she had difficulty understanding why and how it could drive Caroline to take such drastic action. It wasn't as if Diane intended to expose the affair, so why should Caroline feel so threatened?

Caroline followed Diane back to the Infiniti and kept the gun pointed at her while she got in and buckled her seat belt as instructed. Caroline then closed the passenger door and hurried around to the driver's side. She got in, closed the door, and locked it, though she didn't put her own seat belt on.

Doesn't want to restrict her range of motion in case she needs to use the gun, Diane thought. *Smart.*

Diane supposed she ought to be scared, but right now she didn't feel much of anything beyond bewilderment. Perhaps she was in shock from having a gun pulled on her and, evidently, being abducted. Or—and this was a far more disturbing thought—perhaps on some level she actually welcomed what was happening. If nothing else, at least it was a change in the dull, predictable routine of her empty existence.

Caroline turned to her and in a cold, no-nonsense voice said, "Sit on your hands."

"Pardon me?"

"Sit on your hands," Caroline repeated, louder this time.

"Oh, I see. So I won't be able to make a grab for your gun."

"Just do it," Caroline said, nearly growling.

Diane did so, feeling as if she'd somehow walked into the middle of a bad television crime drama. Caroline reached up with her free hand and removed her keys from behind the visor. Another smart move, Diane thought. This way she didn't have to struggle to pull them from her pants pocket, but she hadn't needed to risk leaving them in the ignition where Diane might have gotten hold of them.

"You've done this before," Diane said. "Abducting someone."

Caroline inserted the proper key into the ignition and started the car.

"Once or twice." She switched the gun to her left hand, then put the car into reverse. She backed out of the spot, put the Infiniti in drive, and pulled out of the lot and onto the street. Caroline turned the air conditioner on, and Diane was grateful. Bad enough to be kidnapped in summertime; all the worse to have to ride in a stuffy, sweltering car.

"Why no rope?" Diane asked.

Caroline flashed her an angry irritated look. "What?"

"To tie my hands. And shouldn't you have gagged me? Don't get me wrong: I'm grateful you didn't, but it seems like you're taking an awful risk by not doing either."

Caroline glared at her and then smirked. "Aaron had you pegged. You really *are* a meddler. You can't even resist interfering with your own kidnapping."

The comment hurt, all the more so because she knew it was true. She'd always been a butt-insky, as her mother put it. She just couldn't help herself, even when she knew better. Like now.

"I'm just nervous, I guess. Yesterday you brought your cat in for a checkup, and today you're abducting me at gunpoint. Why?"

They drove in silence for a few minutes after that. Diane wanted to glance out the passenger-side window and get a sense of where they were, in hope that the knowledge might give her an idea where Caroline was taking her. But she couldn't tear her gaze away from the gun. The blackness inside the barrel seemed to swell in size until it encompassed her entire field of vision, as if there was nothing else in the universe except her and it.

"Because if I didn't have a gun pointed at you, you'd never have come with me," Caroline said at last.

Diane couldn't argue with that. "Where are we going?"

Another pause, but not so long as the last. "There's something I want to show you. Something that I think will help you understand about Aaron and me. Maybe you won't be so quick to judge us after you see it."

Diane had no idea what Caroline was talking about, but she didn't like the sound of it. She wanted to tell Caroline that she hadn't judged them. How could she after what had happened between her and her own husband? But she said nothing because she knew that she was lying to herself, if only partially. Maybe she hadn't judged Aaron, but fairly or not, she'd judged Caroline as a conniving, manipulative slut. She supposed she could now add *criminal* to the list of the woman's shortcomings, and probably *psychotic* as well.

"If you just want to show me something to help me understand, then the gun's not necessary. I *want* to understand, so I can help Aaron, if for no other reason. Why don't you put the gun away before either of us gets hurt?"

Caroline didn't take her gaze off the road, and the gun appeared steady in her grip. "I say what's necessary. Now shut up until we get where we're going." Caroline's voice was loud, though she didn't quite shout, and her tone was one of angry irritation.

Diane nodded and said no more. She sensed she'd

pushed Caroline as far as she could, though she'd learned precious little in the process. Still, she couldn't take her eyes off that gun, and she continued staring at the darkness hidden within its barrel until the Infiniti slowed and turned into a parking lot.

Diane finally risked a glance out the window and saw Caroline had brought her to the Valley View Shopping Center. Diane was confused; she'd expected to be taken somewhere isolated and disposed of, like a sick old dog whose owner takes behind the barn and puts a bullet through its brain. She had *not* expected to be taken shopping. Diane rarely came here. She lived on the other side of town and besides, this shopping center was a little too run-down for her tastes.

Instead of continuing into the lot and finding a place to park, Caroline swung her Infiniti past the bar on the building's corner and drove around behind the shopping center. Back here there was nothing to distinguish one business from another. Just featureless back doors, rain gutters, pipes, Dumpsters, and scattered bits of trash and cigarette butts. Though the sun was still up and would linger in the sky for a couple more hours yet, it rode close to the horizon, its light thick and orange. Because the front of the shopping center faced west, the back alley was draped in shadow, making everything seem fuzzy, soft-edged, and unreal.

Caroline stopped and parked the Infiniti next to a Dumpster. She removed the keys from the ignition and closed her hand into a fist around them.

"I'm going to get out of the car now. You're going to sit where you are and not move a muscle. I'll come around to your side of the car—keeping the gun pointed at you all the way—and then you're going to open your door and get out. If you look like you're even *thinking* about making any sudden moves, I'll shoot you. Do you understand?"

There was a hell of a lot about this situation that Diane didn't understand, but Caroline's instructions were perfectly clear. She nodded.

"Good." Caroline then got out and walked around the car until she stood on the passenger side of the Infiniti—far enough back so that Diane couldn't hit her leg opening the door too fast, but still close enough that she could get off a good shot at Diane if she had to. Caroline gestured with the gun, and Diane knew it was time for her to get out of the car. But for the first time since Caroline had confronted her outside Aaron's practice, terror gripped Diane and she began trembling. Maybe it was a delayed reaction, or maybe it was because the reality of what was happening had finally hit her. Caroline had brought her to an isolated place where all she'd have to do was put a couple of bullets in Diane's head, toss her body into a Dumpster, and get the hell out of here. It might not be the perfect murder, but it would be close enough.

Diane started when Caroline tapped the gun barrel against the window.

"Get out." Caroline's voice was muffled by the window glass, but otherwise intelligible. "*Now.*"

Diane was trembling so much that she didn't think she could make her body obey her commands. She would end up being shot through the window for the simple reason that she was too scared to move.

There's something I want to show you. Something that'll help you understand about Aaron and me.

Caroline's words came back to her, and with them came a tiny spark of hope. Maybe, just maybe, if she did what Caroline wanted, let the woman show her whatever it was, then Caroline would let her go. The rational part of Diane's mind knew that she was succumbing to the same foolish hope that endless victims before her had clung to in vain throughout human history. *If I please my tormentor, I will live.* But like all the others who had come and gone before her, she had nothing else left but a foolish hope. And so she opened the door and got out of the car. The hot, humid air hit her like a physical blow, and she felt suddenly weak and nauseated. She thought she might faint, but she managed to stay conscious.

"Hold out your hand," Caroline ordered.

Diane did so, ashamed to see how much it shook, angry at displaying weakness before her captor. Caroline had pocketed her car keys, but now she held out a single key and placed it in Diane's palm.

"See that door?" Caroline nodded and Diane turned to look in the direction she indicated. She saw a featureless gray metal door, just like all the others on this side of the building.

"Yes," she answered.

"The key I gave you opens that door. Use it."

Diane tried to swallow but it felt as if her throat was filled with concrete. She had never considered herself a very imaginative person, but now her mind went wild, conjuring one horrible image after another of what might be behind the metal door. Maybe it would be better if she refused to open it and let Caroline shoot her right here. Maybe a swift, clean death was preferable to what waited for her inside. But there was that spark of hope, however infinitesimal, and she stepped forward, inserted the key into the lock, and turned it. As badly as her hand shook, Diane feared she might not be able to unlock the door. But the lock turned easily, as if well maintained, and opened with a clear, crisp *snick!*

"Good. Now turn around slowly and hand the key back to me."

Diane did so and Caroline tucked it into her jeans pocket.

"Open it."

Up to this point, Caroline's voice had been firm and dispassionate. But now a note of eagerness crept into her tone, and that frightened Diane more than anything that Caroline had done since first pointing the gun at her. The spark of hope grew even fainter, but it was still there, so Diane reached out, took hold of the cold metal knob—how could it be so cold if it was so damn hot out?—and turned it.

The door swung open smoothly, hinges silent. Diane felt a wave of cool air roll over her, and she understood why the doorknob had felt so cold. Whatever was inside, the air-conditioning was turned up all the way. She peered through the open doorway, but no lights were on and all she could see was darkness.

"Go inside." Caroline sounded more than eager now. Her voice was husky, and if Diane hadn't known better, she would've thought the other woman was becoming aroused.

Maybe she is, Diane thought. *Maybe she didn't bring you here to kill you. Maybe she brought you here because she wants to do something else with you.*

The prospect of being used like that, being forced, whether by a woman or a man, sickened Diane, but it allowed her spark of hope to grow just a little larger. *If I give her what she wants, maybe she'll let me live. Especially if I'm good.*

Diane stepped through the doorway and into darkness.

The black enveloped her like a cold velvet blanket, the sensation at once disturbing yet somehow comforting. The cool air felt clammy, as if she had entered a cavern deep in the earth's bowels. When she turned around, she saw Caroline framed in the open doorway for an instant before the other woman pulled the door shut and sealed out the light.

"A word of advice." Caroline's voice seemed to come from all around her, and though Diane knew the effect was caused by the disorientation of being in complete darkness, she was unsettled nonetheless. "Just because *you* can't see anything in here doesn't mean that *I* can't. I have exceptional night vision. I can see you just fine, and I'm pointing my gun right at you. And if you think I'm bullshitting you, consider this: Even if I can't see you, I've got a full clip of ammo. If I shoot wildly, there's still a damn good chance I'll hit you."

Diane nodded, but then she said, "I understand," just in case Caroline *was* lying about being able to see so well in the dark.

"Great." Caroline took a deep breath. "We're almost finished, Diane. What I want to show you is about eight feet straight ahead of you. All you have to do is start walking toward it."

"It?" There was something about the way Caroline had said the word that bothered Diane, as if the *it* was some sort of *thing* instead of an object.

"Just start walking. I'll tell you when to stop."

As if of its own volition, Diane's right foot slid forward, then her left. She took small steps, feeling her way with her toes and outstretched hands. The air grew cooler and more clammy the farther she went into the dark room, and though she couldn't see, she thought her breath might well be misting in the cold air. How far had she gone? Three feet? Five? If Caroline was impatient with Diane's tiny steps and slow progress, she said nothing about it. A couple more steps, and Diane began to feel a tingly-crawly sensation at the base of her skull, and she sensed that she and Caroline weren't alone in the darkness, that there was something else here with them, and that something was directly in front of her.

A fist of ice gripped her insides, and she felt a strong, primitive urge to turn and run back toward Caroline, back where the door must be, and to hell with Caroline's gun, to hell with the possibility of getting shot. Diane would gladly take a couple of bullets if it meant she wouldn't have to confront whatever presence waited for her swaddled in the room's darkness.

But Diane wasn't by nature an irrational or impulsive person, and she hesitated a moment—and in that moment her left foot stepped across a thin curved line embedded in the cold concrete floor. She couldn't see the line, had no idea that it even existed, but she knew at once that she'd entered a Bad Place. The air was far more frigid here, and she could feel tiny particles of ice form on her nose hairs as she inhaled. The tingling feeling on the back of her neck got worse, and she had the sensation that she stood mere inches away from something . . . something that lay at the heart of this cold space, something that perhaps was even the *source* of it.

Without realizing it, she'd continued to walk with her hands held out before her, and now her flesh came in contact with something smooth and firm, though it yielded slightly beneath her fingers. When Diane had been younger—back before she'd met Walter and begun dating him—she and a girlfriend had driven down to Florida one summer vacation. Among the various sights and attractions they'd visited was Seascape Aqua-Park. Diane had never been much for either museums or zoos, and to her mind Seascape was simply a combination of the two. But one spot in the park changed her view. It was a large outside tank where people could reach in and pet dolphins while they swam. Diane hadn't wanted to touch any of the animals at first. Despite the dolphin's cheerful, friendly image on such TV programs as *Flipper*, Diane had read somewhere that the creatures could get *too* playful with humans at times and try to . . . mate with them, regardless of gender. The thought deeply disturbed Diane. Weren't dolphins supposed to be pretty smart? And if so, did that mean they chose to try to screw humans on purpose? Or rather, on *porpoise*? And they had those creepy little beaky mouths with tiny white teeth, and that weird, mocking laugh, like some kind of demented aquatic version of Woody Woodpecker. And their bodies looked like giant gray penises anyway, with a few extra barbs where their fins protruded from the shiny-slick flesh.

But Diane hadn't wanted to looked like a 'fraidy-cat in front of her friend, and there was no way that she was going to admit the truth about why she was hesitant to touch the dolphins. So she gritted her teeth, stuck her hand into the surprisingly warm water, and hoped the dolphins would sense her reluctance and avoid her.

Of course, the dolphins, perverse creatures that they are, swam straight for her. She closed her eyes as the first animal brushed its flank against her hand. The dolphin's skin felt exactly the way she'd always imagined it would: hard, slightly spongy, slick, and a trifle oily. But instead of being revolted by these sensations, Diane experienced a deep and profound sense of well-being, as if the dolphin was somehow using their contact to telepathically communicate reassurance to her, to let her know that it meant her no harm. So unexpected and exhilarating was this feeling that Diane's eyes snapped open and she laughed out loud. After that, she'd spent the rest of the day at the dolphin pool, touching the animals, experiencing the same feeling of well-being over and over, much to the frustration of her friend, who wanted to move on and see the rest of what Seascape had to offer.

The thing in the silent dark cold felt the same— except for the water, of course. And touching it gave Diane the same sense of contentment and joy that touching the dolphins had.

A happy smile spread across her face, and she was about to turn around and thank Caroline for bringing her here, when the smooth flesh turned burning cold. She yanked her hands away with a hiss of pain and backed away, but before she could get far, a tendril of solid darkness shot forward, inserted itself between her lips and began slithering down her throat. Diane wanted to scream, but the best she could manage was a soft, wet gagging sound. She grabbed hold of the tendril and tried to yank it free, but it was too strong, too cold to the touch, and she had to let go. She sensed something then, almost like a faint voice whispering. But this voice came from inside her mind, as if she were experiencing someone else's thoughts. She couldn't understand what it was saying: It seemed so far away, and she was too terrified to listen closely. And then the voice stopped, and Diane tumbled into a darkness far deeper than that of the thing that had taken her life.

As soon as Caroline saw the Overshadow reach for Diane, she tucked the 9mm between the waistband of her pants and the small of her back. She had no further need for the weapon. She watched as the Overshadow fed, having to resist the urge to reach inside the front of her pants and finger her vagina. If she allowed herself to get too turned on, she might lose control entirely, and that would be a very bad thing. The Overshadow was feeding on something far more substantial than a mere rabbit, and the pleasure it would grant in thanks would be more intense. Far more so than any one person could hope to absorb on her own. If she allowed herself to give in to temptation and accepted the Overshadow's thanks—all of it—alone, there was an excellent chance she'd sustain permanent brain damage or even die. She wouldn't be the first to fail to resist and suffer the consequences, but she couldn't imagine a better way to go. Still, she remained standing where she was and managed to keep her hand out of her pants as the Overshadow finished up.

When it was done, what remained of Diane's body was no longer capable of standing on its own. Two more tentacles of black emerged from the dark center of the Overshadow's being and gripped the woman beneath the armpits. Diane's body was lifted easily, as if it weighed no more than a bit of down. The Overshadow set the corpse down on the floor near the edge of the circle that served as both its home and its prison. The Overshadow couldn't reach much beyond the area defined by the concrete circle, but that was enough to allow it to shove Diane's body until it was almost all the way out of the circle.

Caroline approached the corpse cautiously, however. The Overshadow, while usually not greedy, definitely enjoyed a little dessert after a meal. Especially if said dessert was alone and unprotected. She slowly edged closer to Diane's body and then, without taking her gaze off the Overshadow, she took hold of the front of Diane's blouse and tugged. The woman was far lighter in death than in life, and Caroline had no trouble sliding her body away from the Overshadow, which continued standing in the middle of the room, constrained by the circle etched into the concrete around it. The Overshadow had not reabsorbed its three tentacles yet, and now it waved them lazily in the air, seeking the forehead of one of its worshippers so that it might properly give the thanks that such a fine, full meal deserved.

"Sorry," Caroline whispered as she backed toward Penumbra's rear entrance, pulling Diane's corpse along with her. "But I've got to go. You've done your work, and now I have to do mine." Now that the Overshadow had been fed—and a snooping outsider had been eliminated—there was only one thing left for Caroline to do.

Take out the trash.

CHAPTER ELEVEN

Aaron sat on the couch, pretending to watch an old Humphrey Bogart film on television. But what he was really doing was trying not to scream. He normally didn't drink much at home. A little beer now and again, maybe some red wine. Tonight he held a glass of vodka in his hand, gripping it tight as if it were a lifeline. It was his second in the last half hour, and it was already two-thirds gone.

He'd felt all right when he got home from work, but as the evening progressed, he began to feel increasingly agitated, nervous, and irritable. He'd barely spoken to his family at dinner for fear that he'd begin snapping at them—especially Colin. The boy seemed to effortlessly push all of Aaron's buttons these days, whether purposefully or not. Perhaps Colin reminded him too much of when he'd been a teenager, one who'd never been able to do anything well enough to please his father. Or maybe Aaron simply resented the boy's youth with the bitter envy of a middle-aged man who's seen his best days gone by.

"Fuck," he muttered, and took a sip of vodka. It was warm—the bottle had been leftover from last New Year's and tucked away in the back of a kitchen cupboard—instead of being refrigerated, the way he usually liked it. The warmth made the vodka seem to burn all the more as it trickled down his throat like liquid fire. It hurt, but that was okay. It was a small price to pay for taking the edge off his nervousness, even if only a little.

Intellectually, he understood what was happening. Caroline had said that the aftereffects of one's first touch of the Overshadow could be rough. Since last night he'd gone from exhilarated ecstasy to nausea and depression, and now to extreme agitation. Caroline had promised that the aftereffects would lessen over time, and maybe that was true, but right now he felt like putting his fist through the TV screen—right through Bogie's smug hound-dog face—and then going outside and running down the street. Faster and faster, until his lungs were on fire and his overtired heart threatened to explode.

What he did was take another sip of vodka.

Kristen had taken Lindsay over to a friend's house to go swimming. Kristen knew the girl's mother well, and they were no doubt chatting happily while the kids played in the pool. Colin had retreated to his lair after dinner—surprise, surprise—and hadn't emerged since, which suited Aaron just fine. The way he felt right now, the last thing he needed was—

"I'm going over to Steve's. I'll be back later."

Colin's voice echoed from the foyer, followed by the sound of his opening the front door. Aaron slammed his glass down on the coffee table, splashing vodka over the rim. He then leaped off the couch and ran out of the living room and toward the foyer. Colin—wearing a Mudvayne T-shirt and baggy jeans that rode too low on his hips—was already halfway out the door.

"Hold up! Where did you say you were going?"

Colin stopped but he didn't turn around to face Aaron. "Steve's."

Aaron stopped a foot away from Colin and stared at the back of the boy's head. His hair was greasy and tangled, and Aaron wondered when he'd last combed it, let alone washed it. He almost said something about the hair, but instead he said, "Steve who?"

"Jesus, Dad! Steven *Carsner?*"

The last name meant nothing to Aaron, but then he'd never been able to keep straight the names of his children's friends. Rather than admit this to Colin, he asked, "What are you going to do over there?"

Colin still didn't turn around, and Aaron experienced a violent urge to grab the boy by the shoulders and spin him around so he would be forced to look Aaron in the eye. With an effort, he kept his hands to himself as Colin answered with a sneering tone.

"We're going to smoke crack, watch porn DVDs, and jerk each other off. Christ, what do you *think* we're going to do? We're going to play video games."

Without waiting for his father's reply, Colin stepped outside, leaving the door open behind him.

Fury overwhelmed Aaron and he dashed outside. Colin was already off the porch and heading catty-corner across the lawn. It wasn't much past eight thirty, and the sky was a pinkish blue above, a rich fiery orange near the horizon. Aaron ran to catch up to Colin, grabbed the back of the boy's shirt, and spun him around. Colin cried out, "Hey!" and then he lost his balance. Aaron released his hold on the T-shirt, and Colin fell to the grass, landing hard.

Aaron squatted down next to his son, arms resting on his knees. He leaned forward and looked Colin in the eye. He was pleased to see glimmers of fear mixed in with building resentment. Fear wasn't exactly the same as respect, but it was close enough.

"Don't you fucking walk away from me when I'm talking to you, boy." The voice was Aaron's, but the words belonged to his father. Aaron had heard them himself during a similar incident long ago, though it had been winter and Aaron had refused to restack a pile of wood because his father wasn't pleased with the job he'd done. Aaron had gotten less than three yards before his father had him down in the snow, yelling at him so loud spit sprayed Aaron's face, feeling hot enough to burn his cold skin.

But instead of bleeding away Aaron's anger, this realization only served to intensify it for reasons he didn't understand.

Do it, Colin. Say one more smart-ass thing, and I'll—

The resentment in Colin's eyes faded then, leaving behind only fear and hurt. He suddenly looked like a frightened little boy instead of a teenager trying to seem tough and cool.

"I'm sorry, Dad, I didn't . . . I mean, I wasn't . . ." He lowered his eyes, now brimming with tears. "Sorry," he finished.

Aaron knelt next to his son for several more seconds,

feeling the cool of the evening air, hearing crickets call to one another. And then, just as if a switch had been thrown somewhere deep inside him, the anger and tension were gone, so suddenly and completely, it was as if they'd never existed in the first place. Shame rushed in to fill the emptiness the anger had left behind.

"Okay. Just . . . remember to look someone in the eye when they talk to you, and don't walk away until the conversation is over." The remark sounded ridiculous, as if he were a communications professor giving advice to a student.

"Yeah, sure. You bet." Despite his words, Colin didn't meet his father's gaze, and Aaron didn't blame him.

Aaron stood up and took several steps back to give Colin some room. The boy rose to a sitting position, sniffled, wiped his nose with his hand, then brushed it in the grass. He stood and then started walking across the yard once more. When he reached the edge of the property, he looked over his shoulder as if fearful that Aaron might come after him. When he saw that Aaron hadn't moved, he faced forward and started running down the street as fast as he could.

"That wasn't exactly one of my finer moments as a father," he muttered.

"From what I could see, the little son of a bitch had it coming."

Aaron turned toward the speaker. Despite the summer heat, the man still wore his gray sweater. His mouth was pinched in disapproval as he glared in the direction in which Colin had run.

"Do you really think so?" Aaron asked his father.

GET UP TO 4 FREE BOOKS!

You can have the best fiction delivered to your door for less than what you'd pay in a bookstore or online—only $4.25 a book! Sign up for our book clubs today, and we'll send you **FREE* BOOKS** just for trying it out...**with no obligation to buy, ever!**

LEISURE HORROR BOOK CLUB

With more award-winning horror authors than any other publisher, it's easy to see why CNN.com says "Leisure Books has been leading the way in paperback horror novels." Your shipments will include authors such as RICHARD LAYMON, DOUGLAS CLEGG, JACK KETCHUM, MARY ANN MITCHELL, and many more.

LEISURE THRILLER BOOK CLUB

If you love fast-paced page-turners, you won't want to miss any of the books in Leisure's thriller line. Filled with gripping tension and edge-of-your-seat excitement, these titles feature everything from psychological suspense to legal thrillers to police procedurals and more!

As a book club member you also receive the following special benefits:

- **30% OFF** all orders through our website & telecenter!
- **Exclusive access** to special discounts!
- **Convenient** home delivery and **10 days** to return any books you don't want to keep.

There is no minimum number of books to buy, and you may cancel membership at any time. See back to sign up!

*Please include $2.00 for shipping and handling.

YES! ☐

Sign me up for the Leisure Horror Book Club and send my TWO FREE BOOKS! If I choose to stay in the club, I will pay only $8.50* each month, a savings of $5.48!

YES! ☐

Sign me up for the Leisure Thriller Book Club and send my TWO FREE BOOKS! If I choose to stay in the club, I will pay only $8.50* each month, a savings of $5.48!

NAME: _____

ADDRESS: _____

_____

TELEPHONE: _____

E-MAIL: _____

☐ **I WANT TO PAY BY CREDIT CARD.**

☐ VISA   ☐ MasterCard.   ☐ DISCOVER

ACCOUNT #: _____

EXPIRATION DATE: _____

SIGNATURE: _____

Send this card along with $2.00 shipping & handling for each club you wish to join, to:

Horror/Thriller Book Clubs
20 Academy Street
Norwalk, CT 06850-4032

Or fax (must include credit card information!) to: 610.995.9274. You can also sign up online at www.dorchesterpub.com.

*Plus $2.00 for shipping. Offer open to residents of the U.S. and Canada only. Canadian residents please call 1.800.481.9191 for pricing information. If under 18, a parent or guardian must sign. Terms, prices and conditions subject to change. Subscription subject to acceptance. Dorchester Publishing reserves the right to reject any order or cancel any subscription.

JOIN NOW!

"You've been too soft on him. That's why he mouths off to you so much. What you did was long overdue. It's about time you showed a little backbone, Aaron." The older man put his hands in the pockets of his sweater, and though he didn't look at Aaron, his voice softened a fraction as he added, "Keep up the good work."

Then without another word, Martin Rittinger walked across the front yard and disappeared around the side of the house.

Aaron grinned as he watched his dad depart. As far as Aaron could remember, this was the first time the man had ever given him any encouragement, and it felt damn good. Whistling, he put his hand in his pants pockets in unconscious imitation of his father and started back torward the house, intending to find something to do to pass the time until he left for Penumbra. But as soon as he set foot on the front porch, he paused as the full realization of what had just happened hit him. He'd just spoken with his father— his *dead* father.

Aaron turned and ran across the yard, around the side of the house, and into the backyard. He stopped and looked around, breathing hard, skin slick with sweat. There was no sign of his father, not that he actually expected—or wanted—there to be. The backyard was empty.

He remembered the sensation of the Overshadow's cold tendril penetrating the flesh of his forehead, boring through his skull and burrowing into the soft pulp of his brain. Somehow, the Overshadow had left no mark of its passage. No physical mark, that is. But what if its touch had done something to his mind . . . something bad?

Though it was still hot out, a sudden chill gripped Aaron.

"What the hell is happening to me?" he whispered.

CHAPTER TWELVE

Aaron pulled into the parking lot at 11:20, a full forty minutes before he was due to meet Caroline. He knew he was early, but after what had happened with Colin—not to mention hallucinating his dead father—Aaron had been too worked up to sit around the house any longer. He parked in the same spot he had the night before and sat with the windows rolled down and the radio playing softly. The treacly tones of easy listening music filtered out of the Lexus's speakers, and though Aaron usually didn't listen to this crap outside of a dentist's office, it suited his mood at the moment. After the evening he'd had, he could use a little audio tranquilizer. He sat and stared straight ahead, listening to the banal music and trying not to think about anything. But despite his best efforts, he kept sneaking glances at Penumbra's closed door and wondering who might already be inside and what acts they might be performing on each other's bodies.

At 11:35 Caroline drove up in her white Infiniti and parked next to Aaron. Her windows were down and the booming bass line of some pop song Aaron didn't recognize drowned out his music. Caroline flashed a smile as she turned off her lights and killed the engine, cutting off her music in midthump and leaving Aaron's ears ringing. He put up his widows, punched a button to turn off his radio, then removed his keys from the ignition. Caroline was already standing outside waiting for him by the time he got out of his Lexus.

"You're early," she said. "Mr. Eager Beaver. Or maybe that should be Mr. Eager *for* Beaver." She waggled her eyebrows in mock lasciviousness, and Aaron couldn't keep himself from smiling.

Caroline was dressed more casually than last night, but she was no less sexy for it. Her jeans were so tight they might have been painted on, and they rode low on her hips, leaving several inches of her taut abdomen visible. Her short-sleeved green blouse was unbuttoned almost all the way to her navel, providing a more than generous view of her cleavage, and the fabric was sheer enough to reveal that she wore no bra. Her nipples jutted forth, stiff in the night air. Her shoes were black fuck-me pumps, and she stood in them as easily and comfortably as if they were old sneakers. Her makeup was understated, and her only accessories were a pair of diamond-stud earrings. Her perfume was subtle as well, and as Aaron breathed it in, he felt his cock begin to harden.

I'm no better than Pavlov's dog, he thought.

Caroline took a good look at his face and frowned. "Something's wrong."

He didn't bother trying to deny it. "Yeah, something

strange happened to me tonight." On the way over here, Aaron had mentally rehearsed what he was going to tell Caroline, but now that the moment had come, he found himself reluctant to speak. Not so much because he was concerned with how she would react—though that was part of it—but because despite everything, he still wanted to go to Penumbra tonight. More than wanted: *needed.*

But before he could say anything, Caroline glanced at the watch encircling her slender wrist. "We've got some time. Why don't we have a drink before tonight's festivities begin?"

"Okay." That sounded good to Aaron. Maybe a little alcohol would help him to get out what he wanted to say. Caroline took his hand and started leading him toward the shops. He expected her to take him to Penumbra, but once they reached the sidewalk in front of the video store, she headed in the opposite direction. Aaron realized then that she intended for them to have their drinks at the bar located at the end of the shopping center—the oh-so-cleverly named Deja Brew. Aaron had never been there before. He didn't go out to bars much, and when he did he tended to patronize more upscale establishments. But he wasn't so much of a snob to prevent him from having a drink or two in a strip mall dive. What did make him reluctant to go was the chance that one of the other customers might recognize him. He wasn't the only vet in Ptolemy, but there weren't many, and it wasn't inconceivable that one or more of his clients might be there. And if they saw him walk into the bar with a woman other than his wife—and holding hands with her yet—

it wouldn't be good. Especially if the news somehow made its way back to Kristen.

"Uh, I don't want to be a jerk about this . . ." he began.

Caroline stopped and turned to look at him. "About what?"

He lifted their hands to shoulder height.

"Oh, right. We're going into a public place. Sorry, I wasn't thinking. Since I have a spouse that plays with me, I usually don't have to worry about being discreet." Caroline released his hand, then turned back around and continued down the sidewalk toward the bar. Aaron was still hesitant about going inside, but he couldn't see any way around it now, and besides, after the night he'd had, he really could use a drink.

The parking spaces in front of the bar were filled even though it was a weeknight. No Lexuses or Infinitis here. Instead, the clientele of Deja Brew drove dented and rusted-out pickup trucks, Fords, and Chevys, many with Nascar decals in the windows and SUPPORT OUR TROOPS stickers on their bumpers. The bar itself was nothing special to look at. Plain brick facade, weathered wooden door, front window with neon signs advertising Budweiser and Coors. Above the window DEJA BREW was spelled out on a wooden sign in crudely painted green letters against a white background. Whatever the owner did with the bar's profits, investing them in remodeling obviously wasn't high on his list of priorities.

Caroline stepped up to the door, opened it, and gestured for Aaron to enter.

"Age before beauty," she said, smiling.

The situation was so similar to how Caroline had introduced him to Penumbra that it gave him a chill. *Deja Brew*, indeed. He took hold of the door and said, "Pearls before swine. Why don't you go first tonight?"

Laughing, Caroline did as he suggested and Aaron followed her inside.

He expected to have his ears assaulted by the twang of country music and his lungs clogged with cigarette smoke. But to his surprise, seventies soft rock was playing on the speakers—America's "Sister Golden Hair"—and while the place smelled faintly of smoke, there wasn't a thick cloud hovering over the tables as he'd feared. The place was crowded with a fairly even mix of men and women, though most were middle-aged or older and shared a similar beaten-down-by-life look.

"I think there are a couple of seats at the bar," Caroline said. Without waiting to see if Aaron wanted to take them, she began threading her way between tables. Aaron followed, trying not to look at the people they passed just in case any of them might be clients. He felt their gazes on him, though, as if they sensed that Caroline and he didn't belong there and were trying to decide whether it was worth doing anything about.

Aaron told himself that he was just been paranoid—and perhaps indulging in more than a bit of class prejudice—but that didn't make him feel any less uncomfortable as he joined Caroline at the bar. A TV was mounted to the wall near where they sat, and Fox News was playing with the sound muted and closed captioning turned on.

The bartender was a man in his late twenties, with a

round face and a neatly trimmed reddish blond beard. He came over, took their drink orders: vodka on the rocks for Aaron, a glass of Merlot for Caroline. While they waited for their drinks, Aaron had the sense that someone was staring at them. He scanned the faces of the other patrons seated at the bar—half afraid that he was going to see Scab-Head sitting there, compulsively rubbing his scalp. Instead, Aaron saw a tall, broad-shouldered man in his early thirties with a black goatee and thick black hair bound in a ponytail that reached down to the middle of his back. He wore a black muscle shirt, jeans, and brown work boots. He was no bodybuilder, but he had more muscle than flab, and the knuckles of his large, hairy hands were scraped, red, and swollen, as if he had recently been in a fight. Mr. Muscle Shirt didn't notice Aaron looking at him, though. He was too enthralled by Caroline and stared at her with undisguised lust. Aaron felt a surge of jealousy, and though he knew it was ridiculous— Caroline wasn't his in any meaningful sense—he couldn't help it. She'd come in here with him, and to the primitive side of his male ego, that was what mattered. If Caroline knew or cared that Mr. Muscle Shirt was staring at her, she gave no sign.

After several minutes, the bartender brought their drinks over, collected their money, then moved off to serve other customers. Mr. Muscle Shirt was still staring at Caroline, and Aaron told himself to just ignore the asshole.

As Caroline took a sip of her wine, Aaron said, "I hope for your sake that didn't come out of a cardboard box."

Caroline grimaced, then set the glass back down on the counter. "I'm afraid you hope in vain. So . . . what's on your mind tonight, Aaron?"

Aaron took a drink of his vodka to stall one moment more; then he began telling Caroline about what had happened with Colin earlier that evening—and about seeing the hallucination of his father.

"I guess I'm worried that something's wrong with me, that after the—" He didn't want to say *Overshadow* in public. "After *it* touched me, it caused some kind of brain damage."

Up to this point Caroline had listened with silent, sympathetic attention. Now she laid a hand on Aaron's leg and gave him a reassuring squeeze.

"You poor thing! No wonder you seemed preoccupied when I showed up tonight. This might be hard to believe, especially after having such an . . . *intense* reaction, but the sort of experience you had tonight isn't uncommon for those who are new to—to *the touch*. But the more times you visit the club, the more acclimated your system will become until you don't have any more bad experiences like the one you had tonight." Now she took Aaron's hand and gripped it tightly. "You'll be fine, Aaron. Trust me."

Aaron wanted to believe her, but though she sounded sincere, there was a hint of strain in her voice, as if Aaron's revelation had disturbed her more than she was letting on.

"I do trust you," Aaron said, unsure whether or not he was lying. "Even so, I'm considering not going tonight." He smiled and tried to make a joke of it. "I think my addled brain could use the rest—not to mention several other organs of mine." But as soon as he said this, a wave of nausea rolled through his gut, and the first stirrings of cold panic fluttered in his chest. It seemed his body didn't like the idea of not going to Penumbra tonight and was making its preference known.

Caroline looked at him for a moment as if she was trying to decide how best to reply. "I understand how you feel, I really do. During the first few weeks after my initial experience at the club, I thought about quitting too. But I didn't . . . and do you know why? Because the experience kept getting better. Stronger, more intense, beyond anything I'd ever imagined was possible. We're not like the others in here, Aaron. You and I, we're explorers. Adventurers in the realms of sensation. People like us can never be happy settling for bland tapioca lives like them." She gestured to indicate the bar's other patrons. "We need to *live,* Aaron— live *big*. And Penumbra allows us to do that, to transcend mundane day-to-day existence and be more than just walking, eating, sleeping meat bags."

Caroline became increasingly passionate as she spoke, and Aaron found the intensity of her words surprising—and a little disturbing. She sounded almost like a religious fanatic.

"No matter the potential cost, both to our health and to those who love us?" Aaron was thinking of Kristen and Lindsay, of course, but most of all about Colin, of the tears in the boy's eyes and the quaver in his voice just before he'd run out of the yard, fleeing from a father who'd seemed to have suddenly lost his mind. And who maybe had.

Caroine leaned forward and squeezed his hand so hard it hurt.

"No price is too high when it comes to reaching your full potential, Aaron. Never forget that."

Aaron didn't know how to respond, so he changed the subject. "I've been meaning to tell you something, but with everything that's happened in the last day or so, it keeps slipping my mind."

Caroline released his hand and arced an eyebrow. "Oh? I hope it's something dirty."

"I'm afraid not. At least, not in the way you mean." Aaron went on to tell her about his encounter with the filth-encrusted bald-headed lunatic in the parking lot outside his office the previous evening. "While he was plenty strange all by himself, the strangest thing was that he seemed to know about you and the club. He acted as if he wanted me to, well, to *spy* on you, I guess. It's hard to say; he wasn't exactly the most lucid conversationalist."

As Aaron told his story, he watched Caroline closely to see how she'd react. For the most part, she remained expressionless, but as he went on, her eyes narrowed and her lips pursed as if her wine had left a sour aftertaste in her mouth.

"Do you have any idea who he is?" Aaron asked. From her reaction, it was clear Caroline knew *something*. The question was, would she lie to him about it, and if so, how much?

"Not specifically. But at a guess I'd say he was one of the Forsaken. At least, that's what they call themselves." She paused to take another sip of her wine. "Penumbra has been around for over thirty years. My mother and father were two of the original members. It was the seventies, and drugs, sex, and the occult were all in fashion, all part of the self-focus of the Me Generation. Mom and Dad owned the Valley View Shopping Center—among other properties—and they decided to turn the one unleased unit in the building into a personal playground for themselves and a few of their friends. They wanted to create a place where they could explore the limits of experience physically, chemically, and spiritually.

"Things were fine for a while. Penumbra—the word means the shadow zone between light and darkness—served as an outlet for my parents and their friends, a respite from the pressures of jobs and families. And no matter how wild their fun became behind Penumbra's locked door, they managed to lead normal lives outside its walls. Normal enough, anyway. Their families and coworkers never suspected what was going on. I was just a child, and I thought my parents played cards once a week and left me with a babysitter. They played, all right, but not with cards."

Caroline let out a little laugh, then finished off her wine. She signaled the bartender for another, and he brought it over, along with another shot of vodka on the rocks for Aaron, though he still had two-thirds of his first drink left. When the bartender left, Caroline resumed her story.

"After a while Penumbra began to bore my father. He'd always had an interest in magic—not stage illusions but the real thing—and he began voraciously reading occult books, researching various rituals, the more obscure and bizarre, the better. He then convinced the others to incorporate some of these rituals into their playtime at the club. I don't know all the details about what happened next, but somehow my father came in contact with a strange man who wore an old white suit, kind of like the stereotypical image of a southern preacher. But there was nothing holy about this man. I never saw him myself, but my mother described him to me once. She said he had the coldest smile and the darkest eyes she'd ever seen." Despite the bar's stuffy atmosphere, Caroline shivered. "My mother said that one night this man stopped by Penumbra and brought them a present: a tiny shapeless black thing that fit in the palm of his hand."

"The Overshadow," Aaron said.

Caroline nodded. "How he could touch it without being harmed, I don't know, but he did. The man had previously instructed my father to pour concrete in the back room of the club and draw a circle into the floor while the concrete was still wet. Then the man in the white suit carried the small dark creature into the back room and gently placed it in the middle of the circle. He told Dad and the others what the creature was, what it could do, and warned them never to cross the circle no matter what. And then with a last cold smile, he left. They never saw him again."

Caroline paused once more to take a drink of wine, and Aaron took the opportunity to down the last of his first shot of vodka and start in on his second. Several days ago, he would've thought Caroline's tale was nothing but insane fantasy. But after having experienced the touch of the Overshadow for himself, it sounded all too believable.

"So the sacrifices began," Caroline said, "and the members of Penumbra were rewarded with pleasure beyond anything they'd ever imagined. And as the years went by, the Overshadow grew from a handful of darkness to what it is today."

Aaron hadn't been able to see the Overshadow last night, but he'd been able to sense it. He figured it was human-sized, if not larger.

Caroline went on. "The membership roster of Penumbra has changed over the years. Some members grew old and passed away, while some . . . made mistakes."

Aaron thought she was referring to the warning about not crossing the circle. He had a pretty good idea what would happen to someone who was careless and got too close to the Overshadow. They'd end up like the rabbit last night.

"New members are carefully chosen for specific qualities. Sexual appetite, a willingness to push past the boundaries of what so-called normal society considers acceptable . . . but perhaps most importantly, a strong mind. Over time, the Overshadow's touch can cause those with weak minds to become . . . unbalanced."

Aaron thought of how he'd hallucinated his father. His alarm must've showed on his face, for Caroline reached out and patted his hand.

"Don't worry. Like we told you, you're still in the initial stages of adjusting to the Overshadow's touch. I'm talking about people who've been touched dozens, maybe even hundreds of times."

"What . . . happens to them?" Aaron asked.

"Some become so unstable that they're asked to

leave Penumbra and never return. These excommunicates call themselves the Forsaken. We refer to them as Dements." She gave Aaron an embarrassed smile. "Not the most complimentary of terms, I'll admit."

"And you think the bald man who assaulted me yesterday is one of them?"

"I do. I don't recognize him from your description, but I'm sure I'd know him if I saw him."

"What did he want? I mean, why bother me? I hadn't even been to Penumbra yet."

Caroline shrugged. "I honestly don't know. But if he's demented, his motivations might not make sense to anyone but himself. My guess is that he's been watching the club and saw you try to open the door the other night." She smiled. "Don't look so surprised. We heard the knob turn, and when I saw you the next morning, I put two and two together. This man must've followed you home and kept you under surveillance. When he saw me visit you at work, he must've guessed I'd invite you to the club and then he approached you. As to why he wanted you to spy on us, I'd guess he simply wants to get back inside Penumbra—they all do—and hearing some juicy details about your visit would be as close as he could get. You haven't seen him again, have you?"

"No, and believe me, I've been keeping an eye out for him." The idea that Scab-Head had been stalking him creeped out Aaron big time. The guy was nuts and could be capable of anything.

"I'll tell the others tonight, and we'll all watch out for him. Try not to worry, though. Dements are usually harmless enough. They just want to be touched by the Overshadow again."

Despite Caroline's words, it didn't sound like she thought Dements were all that benign. Her voice sounded angry . . . and scared.

They finished off their second drinks, and Aaron's head was spinning by the time he put his empty glass down on the counter. Some of it was due to the alcohol, but most of it was caused by everything Caroline had told him. So much information swirled around in his brain, too much to sort out right then. He had so many questions: What had happened to Caroline's parents? How had she eventually learned about the Overshadow and become a member of Penumbra? Was she lying to him about his being fine—was he already dementing? What did Scab-Head really want from him, and were there other Forsaken out there somewhere? But one question rose above all the others, and it was the one he now asked.

"The man I saw you take into Penumbra two nights ago . . . the young guy with the striped shirt. What happened to him?"

Caroline looked at Aaron for several moments without answering. But then there was no need for her to speak; the look in her eyes told Aaron what he wanted to know. He remembered something Caroline had said to him last night when she'd driven him home. *And that was after just a rabbit. If you thought tonight was something, wait until* . . . She'd never finished the thought, but now Aaron had a terrible feeling he knew what she'd almost said.

"You used a rabbit last night only because it was my first time. You were testing me, weren't you? You wanted to see how I'd handle the Overshadow's touch . . . *and* how I'd feel about having to sacrifice a life to the goddamned thing!"

"Please, Aaron, calm down. It's not like you think."

Caroline reached out to take his hand, but Aaron jerked it away. He was about to tell her that he was through with her, with Penumbra, and definitely with the Overshadow. But just thinking this caused a wave of weakness to wash over him and his gut to spasm painfully.

Shit! Just like crack; one hit and I'm already hooked!

"We having a little lovers' quarrel over here?"

Aaron wasn't at all surprised when he looked up and saw Mr. Muscle Shirt standing there. The man wasn't looking at Aaron, though. His gaze was fixed on Caroline. Even so, Aaron couldn't help feeling that it was his place to respond to the man's implied challenge.

"Not that it's any of your business, but we're fine," Aaron said in a tone that he hoped made it clear that he was really saying *Fuck off, asshole*.

Muscle Shirt didn't take his gaze off Caroline as he responded. "Maybe, maybe not. What's the lady got to say about it?"

Caroline gave the loudmouth a cold glare. "The lady says that it's time to go." She got off her stool, and Aaron also rose from his seat. He took a ten out of his wallet to pay for their second round of drinks and dropped it on the bar. Caroline then put her hand in the crook of Aaron's arm and together they walked past the idiot in the muscle shirt. Aaron knew he shouldn't do it, but he couldn't resist giving the man a smug look at they walked away. As Caroline and he drew near the exit, Aaron heard a couple of people laugh and call out taunting remarks to Muscle Shirt.

"Man, Bryan, that was *harsh!*"

"Forget it, man! She's outta your league!"

"*Way* out!"

More laughter, some of it good-natured, most of it not.

Aaron had a bad feeling and he urged Caroline to move a little faster. They reached the door as the laughter was dying down, and Aaron risked a quick glance over his shoulder. Muscle Shirt—whose real name evidently was Bryan—still stood at the bar, hands clenched into fists as his sides, face crimson with fury.

He started toward the door.

Then Aaron and Caroline were outside and heading away from the bar down the strip mall's narrow side-walk. Deja Brew's door slammed open behind them, and Aaron looked back to see Bryan come out. The man stopped and pointed toward them.

"Where do you think you're going?" he shouted. "I'm not through with you yet!"

They weren't that far away from the man, so there was no reason for him to shout. Unless he was doing it so the customers still inside the bar could hear. What was the point of trying to save face if no one knew you were doing it?

"Just ignore him and keep going," Caroline said, not bothering to keep her voice low, as if she didn't care if Bryan heard. No, as if she *wanted* him to hear.

"Let's head for our cars," Aaron said. "We can't lead him to . . . you know."

"Goddamnit, I am *talking* to you two!"

Before Aaron could react, he heard the sound of boots pounding concrete, then felt Bryan's hand clamp down on his left shoulder. Aaron tried to shrug off the man's grip, but he was too strong and too pissed, and he swung Aaron around to face him. Caroline lost hold of Aaron's arm, but she also turned around and stood next to him, so close their shoulders touched.

Bryan leaned forward until his face was only inches away from Aaron's. "What is your fucking problem? You think you're too good to talk to someone like me, someone who actually works for a living? I've seen your type before, yuppie trash out slumming in a blue-collar bar, whispering snide comments about all the troglodytes around you and laughing your asses off after you leave."

Aaron had assumed that the man was drunk, but though his breath was redolent with beer—not to mention the Mexican food he must've had for dinner— Bryan's words were crisp and clear, with no slurring. Either he was one of those drunks who never sound like they're wasted, or he was stone-cold sober. Aaron would've preferred Bryan to be a roaring, stumbling drunk. The two shots of vodka Aaron had downed had given him a pleasant buzz, which he knew meant he was at least tipsy. If it came down to a fight—and Aaron was afraid that's exactly what was going to happen—he'd much rather go up against someone more drunk than he was, preferably someone on the verge of losing consciousness altogether.

"We just stopped in for drinks, that's all," Caroline said. "We have as much right to drink in there as you do."

"That's not how I see it, darlin'," Bryan said. "I've been going to Deja Brew a few times a week for over three years now. That makes it *my* place. And you don't come into *my* place and disrespect me in front of *my* friends."

"Don't be so melodramatic," Caroline said. "You hit on me, and I wasn't interested. What's the big deal?"

For a moment, Bryan looked confused, as if he hadn't counted on Caroline using logic against him. But he quickly recovered. "The big deal is that if you're going to turn a man down—and why'd you pass up a stud like me for a weasel dick like him is beyond me—you do it with *respect*." He paused then, and a sly look came over his face. "I've seen you around, darlin'. That's why I came over to talk to you. You drive that white Infinti over there, don't you?" He pointed in the direction of Caroline's car. "Like I said, Deja Brew's my hangout spot, and I've seen you pull into the parking lot—sometimes when I'm sitting at the table by the window, sometimes when I've stepped outside for a smoke. A couple times I've seen you go into a door down there." He nodded in the direction of Penumbra. "I don't know what you do in there, but I've seen others go in, so I know that whatever it is, you don't do it alone."

Bryan's mouth stretched into a grin, and the anger left his eyes to be replaced by lust. "How about you invite me to your private party tonight, princess? If you do, I promise to forget all about what happened in the bar. Hell, I'll even take back everything bad I said about no-nuts here." He gave Aaron a wink. "Course, if you insist on being antisocial and *don't* invite me, maybe I'll start spreading the word about your secret playground. All sorts of folks will come knocking at your door then, too many for you to ignore. A secret's not much use when everybody knows it. So what do you say? Do I get to tag along tonight?"

Aaron heard the Dad Voice say, *Are you going to let the fucker get away with this? He's trying to blackmail you!* Aaron even thought he saw a hazy outline of his father's form standing close by, scowling. Then, as if a switch had been thrown somewhere within Aaron, cold fury took hold of him, and he stepped toward Bryan.

"Respect *this*, asshole!"

Aaron reached out and grabbed Bryan's neck, squeezed, and then with all his strength shoved the man toward the building's brick wall. The move took Bryan by surprise and the side of his head struck the brick with a sickening hollow sound, like an overripe melon being dropped on concrete. His eyes sprang open wide, then rolled white as his body went limp. Aaron released his grip, and Bryan collapsed to the sidewalk and didn't get up. Aaron looked at the spot where Bryan's head had hit the brick and saw a bloody smear the size of a half-dollar. As if seeing the blood was a trigger, the fury instantly drained out of Aaron, leaving him feeling sickened by what he'd done.

Don't be a pussy. He deserved it.

Aaron didn't look in the direction of the Dad Voice because he was afraid that doing so would cause the hallucination to fully manifest. If that happened, he feared he wouldn't be able to make it go away again.

He was a vet, not an MD, but he knew how to take a pulse. He knelt next to Bryan. The man looked so much smaller lying there, more like a child masquerading as a man. Aaron placed two fingers against Bryan's carotid artery and was relieved to find a pulse. It seemed strong enough, but Bryan was out cold and the side of his head was bleeding. Aaron figured some damage had been done, but he had no way to tell how severe it was.

He looked up at Caroline. "I left my cell phone in my car. Do you have yours?"

She shook her head, her expression unreadable. She didn't seem upset, but otherwise Aaron couldn't tell what she was feeling. He stood.

"You stay with him, then. I'll go back into the bar and use their phone."

Before he could take a step, Caroline grabbed hold of his arm. "What for?"

"Are you kidding? He's hurt! We have to call an ambulance!"

"Let me go get Phillip. He'll know what to do."

"We don't have time! For all we know, he might be dying right now!"

Aaron heard the edge of hysteria in his voice, but he couldn't help it. Never in his life had he committed an act of violence like this, and it horrified and sickened him. But more than that, despite Caroline's assurances in the bar, he was afraid that what he'd done was another sign that he was starting to dement.

"Please, let me go get Phillip. He'll be at the club by now, I'm sure of it. Promise me you won't do anything until I get back." She tightened her grip on his arm. "Promise!"

Before Aaron could answer, she let go of his arm, slipped off her pumps, and left them lying on the sidewalk as she turned and started running toward Penumbra.

CHAPTER THIRTEEN

Aaron remained crouching next to Bryan's unconscious form, hoping no one would choose this moment to walk out of the bar or drive into the parking lot. He had the feeling that someone was standing close by, but when he looked around, he saw no one. Still, he sensed a presence—his *father's* presence—and he wondered if it was possible to have an emotional hallucination instead of a visual or auditory one. He tried to get a read on how his father was feeling, whether he approved or disapproved of what his son had done to the bastard who'd just tried to blackmail Caroline, but he couldn't tell.

Stop thinking like that, he chided himself. *Dad's dead, remember? Whatever you think you sense, it's just another aftereffect of the Overshadow's touch. It's not real.*

"That's a fine thing to say about your own father."

The words seemed to come from right next to Aaron, so close he could've sworn he felt the speaker's breath on his ear. But when he turned to look, no one was there. Aaron heard the sound of someone approaching. He turned, half expecting to see his father, but it was Caroline and Phillip. They ran up to him—Caroline still in bare feet—and Phillip lost no time in crouching down next to Bryan's other side.

"Help me get him up, Aaron."

Phillip grabbed hold of Bryan's right arm, Aaron took the left, and together they managed to hoist the man up.

"We're going to carry him to Penumbra," Phillip said. "If anyone sees us, hopefully it'll look like we're just helping out a drunk buddy."

Caroline bent down to pick up her shoes, but she didn't put them back on. "Better if no one sees us at all. Let's get going."

With Caroline leading the way, Aaron and Phillip began half carrying, half dragging Bryan down the sidewalk toward Penumbra. The man's feet slid on the concrete and his head lolled forward, giving Aaron his first good look at Bryan's injury. His hair on that side was a blood-sodden mess, and there was a concave depression in his skull, as if his head were a partially deflated beach ball.

As they moved past doors and windows of businesses that had been deserted for the night, Aaron's attention was caught by the darting and diving of insects clustered around the fluorescent lights in the parking lot. He looked up and saw moths the size of owls circling the lights, wings a blur as they beat furiously to keep the large insects aloft. Each of the gigantic creatures had misshapen, dented heads and blood dripped from their wounds, pattering softly to the ground like crimson-black rain.

Aaron started to ask Caroline and Phillip if they saw it too, but he kept his mouth shut. Of course they didn't see it since it wasn't really there. It was just another hallucination, and Aaron didn't want Caroline and Phillip to think that he was dementing, especially if he really was. He took his gaze off the oversized insects and concentrated on holding up his side of Bryan.

As they reached Penumbra, the fuckle door opened and Wyatt stepped out. The cop held the door open for them as they carried Bryan inside, and then—after a quick scan of the parking lot to make sure no one was watching—Wyatt shut and locked the door.

Someone *was* watching, though. From his chosen vantage point in the Speedy Lube parking lot across the street, Gerald had witnessed everything through the lenses of his binoculars. This was an unexpected development, but one Gerald thought he could turn to his advantage. All he had to do was remain patient and wait for his chance.

The back of his Beetle was empty tonight. Depending on how things went, he might need the space. He'd just have to see.

He trained his binoculars on the fuckle door, watched, and waited.

"I'm not sure this is a good idea," Spencer said. "We can't make an offering of him. He's injured, and you know the rules . . ."

"The rules were made up by *my* father," Caroline

snapped. "I know them better than anyone. Besides, you can see for yourself that this man is in the prime of his life."

"Except for the divot in the side of his skull," Gillian said. She knelt next to Bryan, who now lay on the black Naugahyde couch, still unconscious, a folded towel tucked beneath his head more to soak up any blood than to provide comfort. "It's been a few years since I was in med school, and I'm an ophthalmologist, not a head-trauma specialist. But it's my professional judgment that he's not going to make it."

Gillian wiped her bloodstained hands on Bryan's muscle shirt and stood. She exchanged looks with Phillip, and though Aaron couldn't be certain, he had the sense that Gillian was lying, or at least overstating the severity of Bryan's injuries. The others stood in a half circle around the couch. Everyone was clothed; Aaron assumed they hadn't had enough time for any of them to get undressed before they'd brought Bryan inside.

"It's a shame, too," Gillian continued. "I really would've liked a chance to play with him a little before we serve him up as tonight's main course."

Aaron glared at the others. "I can't believe you're actually contemplating feeding the poor bastard to the Overshadow. A rabbit is one thing, but a *person* . . ."

Caroline walked over to Aaron and took his hands. "We don't have a choice. You heard what he said. He knows about Penumbra . . . at least, he knows *something's* here. If we let him go, he'll start telling people about us, and once that happens—"

"It's over," Phillip said. "Penumbra will be exposed and the Overshadow will be revealed to the world." He scowled at Caroline. "And while I can't say my dear wife used her best judgment in taking you to Deja Brew, Aaron, I have to agree with her. This man must be dealt with."

"Dealt with?" Aaron repeated, incredulous. "Jesus, you sound like a B-movie villain!" He took his hands away from Caroline, and she made no move to take them again.

"Lighten up," Gillian said. "After all, you're the one who went psycho and caved the guy's head in. Besides, it's not like he'll be the first."

Phillip spun around to face Gillian. "That's enough!"

"Well, it's true, isn't it?" she said. "Why bother playing games at this point?"

Trevor quickly stepped between the two of them. "We don't have time for bickering. If we're going to take him into the back room, then we'd better do it before he weakens any further."

"What difference could that make?" Aaron asked.

"The Overshadow won't accept a dead sacrifice," Caroline said in such a matter-of-fact tone that it gave Aaron a chill. "And while it will accept one that's weak or injured—"

"If a sacrifice is too damaged, the Overshadow doesn't give pleasure then," Shari said. "It . . . punishes you, makes you feel sick and miserable. It's so awful you'd give anything for the Overshadow to take it away—including your own life." She shuddered at the thought.

"For that reason we're very careful about who we

take in back," Wyatt said. "They have to be strong and in good health."

"Sometimes we make mistakes," Spencer added. "Why, just last month one of us brought in a woman who was a heroin addict and . . ." Spencer locked gazes with Aaron then and paused, eyes widening as if he realized he'd been about to say too much. He glanced at the others who, Aaron noted, were all frowning at the overweight insurance agent.

Spencer licked at the perpetual trickle of blood dripping from his nose. "But that's not important right now. In fact"—he gave Aaron a weak smile—"forget I said anything."

"I'm not about to forget any of this!" Aaron said. "Caroline told me Penumbra's been in existence for thirty years. How many people have been *offered* to the Overshadow in that time? Dozens? Hundreds?"

No one spoke for a moment, but then Spencer said, "I'm afraid the members of Caroline's parents' generation didn't keep accurate records. So it's impossible to say. If I were to estimate, however—"

"Shut up, Spencer," Caroline said. "You've said more than enough for one evening."

Spencer's mouth closed with an audible click of his teeth. Embarrassed, he lowered his gaze. Tiny drops of blood pooled on his upper lip before falling to the tile floor.

Caroline went on. "Gillian's right. It's time to stop playing games." She turned toward Aaron and put her arms around his neck. He wanted to pull away from her touch—a murderer's touch—but he remained where he was.

"You were originally attracted to Penumbra, and to *me* because you have a need deep inside you, Aaron. A need that's gone unfulfilled for far too long. Last night, when we sacrificed a rabbit to the Overshadow, you had a taste of the pleasure that you've been missing in your life, and unless I'm very much mistaken, you liked it." She began lightly stroking the sides of his neck with her fingers.

Despite himself, Aaron said, "I did."

"What you experienced last night at the Overshadow's touch was nothing compared to what you'll experience tonight if you choose to go into the back room with us. The sensations you felt, while intense, are as a sputtering candle flame compared to a blazing inferno. You're so close to finding what you've been looking for all these years. You *can't* turn away now."

Aaron could feel the need Caroline spoke of quivering inside him. Extreme hunger, intense thirst, raging lust, absolute loneliness . . . it was all of these combined and more, ratcheted up to a level that he hadn't thought possible. Simply put, he *needed*, and only the Overshadow could provide.

He glanced over at Bryan lying on the couch, eyes closed, face pale, breathing shallow . . . How could Aaron condone purchasing his relief with the life of another human being?

The fucker attacked you, the Dad Voice said. *He deserved what he got. And you heard what Gillian said: He's going to die no matter what you do. So why not allow his pathetic excuse of a life to be redeemed in death?*

Aaron understood what the Dad Voice was saying and found himself tempted to agree. But was that what he *really* felt or what the hunger inside him *wanted* him to feel?

"It's your choice, Aaron," Caroline said gently. "Stay or go."

Aaron wanted to believe he had a choice, but from the grim expressions on the others' faces, he knew that if he didn't willingly go into the back room with them, he'd end up going *un*-willingly. And if that happened, Aaron didn't think he'd ever leave the back room again, at least not alive.

There's an upside to this you haven't considered, the Dad Voice said. *After tonight, neither Mr. Muscle Shirt nor any of his relatives will be able to press any charges against you for caving in his skull.*

Aaron was ashamed to find himself feeling relieved by this notion.

What's to feel bad about? They're going to feed him to their pet monster anyway. It's not like you could stop them even if you wanted to.

Maybe not, Aaron thought, but that didn't mean he shouldn't try.

He took a step toward Phillip and got as far as grabbing his arm before nausea twisted his gut and vertigo spiraled through his brain. He let go of Phillip's arm and stumbled backward, feeling so weak that it was a struggle to stay on his feet.

Phillip smirked. "A noble effort, but you've been touched by the Overshadow. There's nothing you can do to harm it now, including denying it a meal."

215

"You're one of us now, lover," Gillian said. The crimson portion of her odd eye seemed to pulse with a baleful red light. "Whether you like it or not."

"Oh, he likes it just fine," Caroline said. "He's just having a bit of difficulty admitting it to himself." She cupped Aaron's cheek with her hand. "But he'll adjust soon enough. Won't you, sweetie?"

The weakness and nausea began to subside, and Aaron stood straight, shaky, but in control of his body once more. He looked at Caroline but he didn't say anything. He feared that any response he might make could bring on another near-crippling wave of discomfort. It seemed he was along for the ride tonight, whether he liked it or not.

"Enough foreplay," Gillian said. "Let's get this hunk into the back room before he croaks."

Phillip frowned at Gillian. "If anyone ever accused you of having too much class, they were lying."

Gillian stuck her tongue out at Phillip, but he ignored her and motioned to Wyatt to join him at the couch. Phillip took Bryan's arms and Wyatt his legs, and the two men lifted Bryan off the couch and carried him toward the door to the back room. Caroline removed a key from her jeans pocket, unlocked the door, then stepped aside to hold it open for the others. Phillip and Wyatt carried in Bryan first, followed by Trevor, Shari, Spencer, and Gillian. Aaron hung back as long as he could, but he felt pulled toward the open doorway and the darkness that waited beyond. The sensation grew with each passing second, until it had become so strong that Aaron thought nothing could prevent him from joining the others. Still, as if to make sure he came, Caroline took hold of his hand and led him inside.

As soon as they were across the threshold, Caroline released Aaron's hand and closed the door, cutting off the light from the outer room. At first the Overshadow's chamber was just as dark as it had been last night, but Aaron's vision quickly began to adjust. It seemed his eyes had changed, just as Caroline had promised they would. Another blessing bestowed by the Overshadow's cold touch. The room looked more gray than black now, and Aaron could make out the forms of the others as distinct dark silhouettes that held only a suggestion of individual features. He also had a sense of the chamber's basic dimensions—the distance from one wall to another, from the ceiling to the floor. But the object that drew his attention the most was in the exact center of the room, surrounded by a circle etched into the concrete floor.

The shape was seven, maybe eight feet tall and three feet wide. Its inky black substance seemed to rise and fall slowly, as if it were a column of dark water held in some invisible container. It was wider at the base than the top, and its surface was smooth and featureless. The way the thing pulsed made Aaron think of a huge, throbbingly erect penis. His first sight of the creature called the Overshadow filled him with a confused mixture of conflicting emotions: revulsion, fear, hatred, wonder, lust, reverence, and love.

Just as she had last night, Caroline led him to the edge of the circle. Aaron again felt waves of cold emanating from the Overshadow, but instead of making him uncomfortable, the cold was soothing, welcoming. It washed away his doubts until he felt as if he were standing in the one place in the universe where he truly belonged, ready to perform the single task that he had been born to do—feeding his god.

Aaron watched with calm detachment as Wyatt and Phillip carried Bryan's unconscious form to the edge of the circle. They laid him down gently on the concrete floor and then rolled him into the circle until his body rested on its side only a foot away from the Overshadow's thick base. Phillip and Wyatt then stood and took their places outside the circle. Wyatt—the policeman—stood on Aaron's right side as if he were determined to ensure that the group's newest member didn't do something foolish to disrupt the ceremony. Wyatt needn't have bothered, though. Aaon's reluctance and confusion had vanished, and he was looking forward to what was to come as much as any of the others.

At first the Overshadow didn't seem to be aware that a new sacrifice had been laid before it, and Aaron began to fear that Bryan had died in the time it had taken them to carry him in from the outer room. He remembered what Shari had said the Overshadow would do to them, how awful it would make them feel if they brought it an unsuitable sacrifice. But then a groan escape from Bryan's lips and the man struggled to sit up. By this time Aaron's vision had adjusted even more, and he could now discern Bryan's facial features as the man reached up and gingerly touched his head wound.

Bryan winced in pain. "Christ Almighty, what the hell happened? The last thing I remember was sitting at the bar and having a drink—"

Whether the man's memory would ever return completely was destined to remain unknown. A pseudopod emerged from the Overshadow's side and quickly lengthened into a tentacle. The dark appendage lunged toward Bryan's open mouth with the speed of a striking snake and flowed between his teeth and down his throat. Bryan's eyes went wide and he clawed frantically at the ebon tendril that had penetrated his body. But though he could grab hold of the pseudopod, could hit it, squeeze it, scratch it, yank on it, he couldn't dislodge it. Though it was difficult to tell given the Overshadow's black substance, it appeared that the tentacle continued to lengthen, burrowing into Bryan's body and filling him with its darkness. Small tendrils emerged from his nostrils and ears, poked through the corners of his eyes, tips writhing as they wormed their way outward. Bryan stopped trying to pull the main tentacle out of his mouth and his body began convulsing violently, as if millions of volts of electricity surged through him. What Aaron first took to be black hair began to grow from Bryan's face and hands, but as the tiny "hairs" began to lengthen, Aaron realized that what he was seeing was thousands of whisker-thin tendrils of the Overshadow's black substance oozing forth from the pores in Bryan's skin. The tendrils—large and small—began to flow together and merge, covering Bryan's spasming body in a coating of darkness. When the covering was complete, Bryan's exertions began to lessen until he lay still within the shadowy cocoon created by the Overshadow. A moment passed, then two, and then the darkness began to recede, flowing off Bryan's body and back into the main pseudopod extruding from the Overshadow's side. The tentacle then retracted and rejoined the column of blackness, leaving no sign that it had ever existed.

Aaron looked at Bryan's body, or rather what was left of it. His clothing was intact, but his form had shrunken in on itself, skin parchment dry and leathery, hair and beard bleached white, desiccated lips drawn back to expose yellowed teeth, eyes sunken into the skull, leaving behind twin dark hollows. The skin of his hands had become so dry and tight that the tips of the finger bones had broken through, making it appear as if Bryan had grown two sets of ivory claws.

Aaron had no doubt the man was dead, his life force having been leeched away by the dark creature undulating within the circle. A small voice deep within Aaron that belonged to the rational portion of his mind cried out in horror at the sight of the mummified corpse. But the rest of Aaron barely heard it. He was anticipating the reward he was about to receive. Eight pseudopods emerged from the center of the Overshadow and extended toward the humans who stood at the edge of the circle that bound it. The tentacles then gently touched each of the eight on the forehead and slid past skin and bone and into their brains.

The cold touch of the Overshadow's tentacle made Aaron gasp, and he took in a deep breath as the tentacle dug into his mind. He didn't worry about what damage the Overshadow might be doing to his brain this time. He was completely focused on receiving the great gift the Overshadow was about to bestow on him. Yesterday the Overshadow had been given a rabbit, and the pleasure that it had in turn granted its worshippers had been beyond anything Aaron had ever experienced or imagined. Despite what the others had hinted at, Aaron hadn't been able to conceive of the Overshadow being able to make him feel any better than he had last night. But tonight the creature had feasted on a human being, and as it began manipulating the pleasure centers of its worshippers' brains to show its gratitude, Aaron realized how wrong he'd been. Every cell, every atom, every subatomic particle of his being was awash in ecstasy beyond human comprehension. He felt as if he had become One with all existence, that he was fucking and being fucked by all creation. He was both God and God's lover. He was all, he was nothing, he was everything. Life and death, good and evil, pleasure and pain . . . he was all these things and so much more. He was the most unstable particle that winks out of existence nanoseconds after its creation, and he was eternal. And though the immensity of the experience threatened to obliterate his individual self, somehow he still remained Aaron Rittinger.

Once again, Aaron felt the Overshadow reaching outward, trying to connect to him mind to mind, soul to soul . . . Strange, alien concepts flashed though his consciousness. Twisted shapes, distorted sounds, dark hungers for which humanity had no words . . . It hurt to experience them, as if the hardware of his brain wasn't designed to process these inhuman thoughts. In his mind's eye, he saw himself standing inside the Overshadow's circle, though there was no sign of the shadow creature itself. He saw himself take a step toward the circle's perimeter, pause, and then step over the line etched into the concrete floor. It seemed so real, *felt* so real, as if he were that Aaron instead of the one whose body he currently inhabited.

And then the vision ended.

Aaron feel to his knees, heart pounding, lungs heaving, sweat pouring off his body. He looked at the others, saw that Spencer was lying on his back gasping for air, saw Gillian with her hand shoved down her pants, frantically masturbating. Trevor and Shari sat on the floor, Shari sitting in her husband's lap, Trevor with his arms around her, both with their eyes closed and content, dreamy smiles on their faces. Wyatt stood with his hands clenched at his sides, legs trembling, taking deep breaths as if he were trying to ride out the last of the sensations granted by the Overshadow. Caroline and Phillip stood as well, holding hands and smiling contentedly at one another.

Caroline turned to Aaron.

"Now you truly are one of us," she said.

Aaron looked at the dried husk that had once been a loudmouthed asshole named Bryan, and his mouth slowly stretched into a lopsided smile.

"Great."

CHAPTER FOURTEEN

Aaron sat behind the wheel of his Lexus, engine idling, the motor's vibrations sending tiny ripples of pleasure throughout his body. He hated to admit it but the others had been right: The sensations the Overshadow provided in thanks for a rabbit's life were nothing compared to what he had experienced—was *still* experiencing—tonight.

Aaron stared through his windshield, still not used to the change that had occurred to his vision. Instead of blacks and dark blues, the night world was painted in varying shades of gray. He couldn't see as well as he could in full daylight, but it was damned close. He wondered if this was what it was like to be a cat or an owl . . . a creature more at home in the darkness than the light.

He'd parked behind the strip mall, outside a featureless door that, according to Caroline, led to the Overshadow's chamber. Aaron hoped he'd parked by the right one. He was still buzzing from the Overshadow's touch and had a bit of trouble maneuvering his car back here, and it didn't help that this door didn't have *fuckle* or its equivalent scratched into the paint to identify it. Now that Aaron was alone and in his car, he knew he could take off if he wanted to. But he had several reasons for sticking around. The most important was that he was still awash in the afterglow of the Overshadow's touch, and he didn't trust himself to operate his vehicle safely over any distance—not without someone riding shotgun, anyway.

"So what's wrong with me? I'll watch the road for you."

Aaron looked at the rearview mirror and saw his father's face reflected in the glass. As usual, Martin Rittinger was scowling.

"I appreciate the offer, Dad, but you're just a hallucination. You can't really navigate for me."

Martin sniffed. "Maybe you just *think* I'm not real. Maybe the Overshadow's touch has done something to your brain, widened your range of perception, and now you're able to see me."

Aaron let out a snorting laugh. "So you're telling me that I can see dead people now? Nothing personal, but I don't think so."

Martin shrugged, then crossed his arms and looked out the side window. "Fine, have it your way."

Normally, fighting with his father—whether the man was real or not—would've depressed Aaron. But he felt too damned good right now to care. There was another reason he hadn't driven off; he had the sense that the others were testing him by giving him some time alone. Had his second experience with the Overshadow removed his earlier misgivings about sacrificing humans to it? The truth was he hadn't thought too much about this last part. His thoughts were sluggish and fuzzy, drifting this way and that like a fat lazy bee in an endless field of succulent flowers. He knew that sooner or later he'd have to come to terms with what he'd allowed himself to be part of, but that would have to wait for his mind to clear. Assuming it ever did.

Penumbra's back door opened then, and the most important reason Aaron hadn't left walked out into the night. Caroline crossed over to the driver's side of Aaron's Lexus and motioned for him to roll down the window. He did so, and all at once he was over-whelmed by sensations—the near-deafening sounds of night birds and insects, the moist cool humidity of the summer night air, the acrid-sweet musk drifting forth from between Caroline's legs, thick and strong despite the jeans she wore. The sudden deluge of sensory input was so intense that Aaron thought he might pass out, but then the feeling passed and he was able to focus on Caroline's face.

"You all right?" she asked.

Aaron gave her a smile that he hoped didn't look as dopey as it felt. "Fantastic. A-OK. Peachy keen."

She frowned slightly but said, "Go ahead and pop the trunk. Phillip's ready to bring him out."

For an instant, Aaron didn't understand what Caroline wanted. It was as if she was speaking a foreign language, and it took him a moment to translate in his head.

"Right. Got it."

He reached out and pulled a plastic lever and was rewarded with a hollow *chunk!* sound as the trunk sprang open. Caroline crouched down and leaned partly through the open window. She gave Aaron an appraising look, then said, "I think it might be better if I drove. You look like you're still pretty wrecked."

"Who, me?"

"She's right, kid," Martin said from the backseat. "You try to drive you'll end up wrapping your prized Lexus around a telephone pole. Won't hurt me since I'm not real—at least as far as you're concerned—but it'd sure cramp your style."

"All right, you win." Aaron undid his seat belt. Caroline stepped back as he opened the door and climbed out of the car. He nearly pitched forward into her arms, but he grabbed hold of the car door and kept his balance.

"Let me guess," Aaron said. "This is where you tell me that I'll recover more quickly from the Overshadow's touch as time goes by." He said this to Caroline, but it was Phillip who answered.

"Maybe. But Spencer still quivers like a jellyfish for an hour or so after being touched, and he's been a member for years."

Aaron turned to see Phillip walking toward the Lexus's trunk. In his arms he carried a large object wrapped in an old dirty sheet. Bryan's remains, and from the relaxed way Phillip carried them, they obviously didn't weigh much anymore. Phillip stopped when he reached the car, and he gently lowered the cloth-wrapped corpse into the trunk. Aaron was surprised to see this unexpected touch of tenderness from Phillip, but then the man said, "Can't just throw him in there. Wouldn't want any pieces to break off." He then closed the trunk and walked around to the driver's side to join Aaron and Caroline.

"This is it, Aaron," Phillip said. "The last step in your orientation to our little family. The rule in Penumbra is that whoever brings a playmate is responsible for disposing of the . . . leftovers at the end of the evening. Caroline will go with you tonight, but after this you'll do it on your own whenever necessary. There's little risk of our getting caught. Wyatt helps with that by making sure no other police officers patrol around here late at night. But just in case, we usually handle the job solo. Understand?"

Aaron wasn't sure if he did or not. Phillip had used so many words . . . But he figured that if he hadn't caught everything now, Caroline would fill him in on the rest later.

"Sure thing," Aaron said, grinning.

Phillip looked at Aaron for a moment, then laughed and clapped him on the shoulder. "Man, you are still so wasted!" He turned to Caroline. "Was I that bad after my first touch?"

She smiled lovingly at him. "Even worse." She moved into his arms and gave him a lingering kiss. Aaron watched, not thinking or feeling much of anything at seeing his new lover kiss her husband.

"See you later, lover," Caroline said to Phillip as they parted.

Phillip nodded. "Good luck, you two. And don't have *too* much fun."

Caroline gave her husband a mock-innocent look. "Why, whatever could you possibly mean?"

Phillip laughed, then stuck out his hand for Aaron to shake. It took Aaron a couple of tries to get hold of it, but then the men shook.

"See you soon, Aaron." Then Phillip released his hand, gave Caroline a last wink, and headed back toward Penumbra's rear door. Once inside he closed and locked it.

Caroline smiled at Aaron. "Let's go, sweetie. It's not far away, but the sooner we get there, the better." She came toward him and cupped his cock and balls through his pants. "Once we're done with our chore, then you and I can play. Won't that be nice?" She slid her tongue out between her lips, then slowly licked Aaron's face, starting at his chin and moving over his lips, nose, between the eyes, then over his forehead, kneading his genitals the entire time. She pulled her hand away then and stepped back.

"Let's go," Aaron said, voice thick with lust. As Caroline climbed into the driver's seat and Aaron headed around the front of the car to the passenger's side, he almost forgot that there was a dried husk of a dead body wrapped in a dirty sheet in his trunk.

Across the street in Speedy Lube's parking lot, Gerald watched Aaron's Lexus come around from behind the strip mall and pull out onto the street.

He grinned as he put his VW in gear and began to back out of his parking space. He didn't have to hurry; there was no need to keep up with them. He knew where they were going, and when he got there, that's when the fun would truly begin.

Gerald flipped on his headlights and then, rubbing his scabby bald head in glee, he pulled onto the road and followed the red glow of the Lexus's taillights.

The world outside the Lexus was a swirling, dancing interplay of gray-black shadows. Aaron had the impression the shadows were alive, or nearly so, and he wondered if the entire planet, perhaps even the whole universe, was nothing more than a gigantic version of the Overshadow, greedily draining the life force of the tiny beings that inhabited it.

He laughed. "I feel like a kid who's just gotten high for the first time." He turned to look at Caroline. "You know, the one who suddenly has the dazzlingly banal insight that an atom inside his thumbnail could contain an entire universe of its own?"

Caroline smiled and nodded. "Yeah, I know what you mean. I really *was* a teenager the first time—" She broke off, frowning. The glow of the dashboard lights colored her skin a pale aquamarine, making her look like a statue carved out of some kind of bluish jade. Aaron didn't know if the effect was natural or caused by his altered perceptions, but he didn't care. Either way, she was breathtakingly beautiful. He tried to reach over and embrace her, but his seat belt held him back.

"Easy, boy," Caroline said, smiling once more. "We'll get there soon. And after we've finished our chore, we'll have plenty of time to play."

Chore? For a moment, Aaron didn't know what she meant, but then he remembered the mummy in the trunk. Caroline was driving them to a place where they could dispose of him. No, *it*. Aaron had the feeling this trip would be a whole lot easier if he thought of Bryan's remains as *it* instead of *him*.

"Don't be such a wimp," Martin said from the backseat. "If you're going to do this, you might as well be a man about it."

Aaron glanced sideways at Caroline to see if she would react to his father's words. Aaron was confident that Martin was his hallucination and his alone, but he couldn't help checking. Being confident was not the same as being certain.

But Caroline continued driving, her attention fully on the road. If she perceived Martin Rittinger, she was doing a damned good job of hiding it.

Aaron looked out the window again. He wasn't sure how long they'd been traveling, though he doubted it was more than a handful of minutes. And he wasn't sure exactly where they were, though he knew they were no longer in town. The sinuous gray-black shapes that writhed and intertwined alongside the road he guessed were trees, temporarily transfigured by his altered perceptions. If so, that meant they were out in the country somewhere, which made sense. You wouldn't want to dispose of a body by simply tossing it into a Dumpster. You'd want to go somewhere secluded, somewhere private.

"Maybe she isn't intending on just getting rid of your dried-up friend in the trunk," Martin said. "Maybe she's planning on getting rid of you, too."

Aaron started to turn around and answer, but then he remembered that Caroline couldn't see his father because he wasn't there to *be* seen. So he answered in his thoughts, hoping his dad could hear them.

Why would she want to do that?

"Who knows? Maybe because she's tired of you already. Maybe you don't measure up in the sex department, not compared to the kind of kink she's used to getting. Maybe because she's a killer and it's in her nature."

Aaron was about to protest this last bit, but then he remembered seeing Caroline escort her stripe-shirted young lover into Penumbra a couple of nights ago.

I don't think Caroline wants to harm me, Aaron thought. *But even if she did, she wouldn't take me out to the woods to do it. She wouldn't waste my life force like that. She'd give me to the Overshadow.*

Martin had no reply to that, and Aaron felt a sense of smug satisfaction that he'd finally scored a point against his father. He glanced over his shoulder, hoping to get a look at his dad's expression, but the backseat was empty. He turned around and looked out the window once more. While the shapes on the side of the road were still undulating, they were recognizably trees now, if slightly blurry, distorted ones. It appeared his perceptions were beginning to return to normal. Or whatever normal might be for him from now on.

Images flashed through his mind. A thick dark tentacle squirming down Bryan's throat. The man being covered with darkness as the Overshadow's substance oozed out of his pores. The contorted, withered husk that remained once the Overshadow had finished with its grisly meal.

Don't think about it, Aaron told himself. *There's nothing you can do to change it now, and he was going to die anyway. Gillian said so.* Giving Bryan to the Overshadow might've been more merciful than letting him suffer through a slow, lingering death.

Aaron remembered how Bryan had fought to pull the black tentacle out of his mouth, how he'd thrashed as the darkness covered him entirely. Whatever else Bryan's death had been, it hadn't been a mercy.

To take his mind off these thoughts, Aaron looked at Caroline and said, "A minute ago you started to talk about your first experience with Penumbra. Tell me about it."

The road they were now on was narrow and wound through a wooded area. Caroline eased her foot off the accelerator, and the Lexus slowed to a more manageable speed. Caroline didn't answer right away, and Aaron thought that perhaps she wouldn't. But after a moment she took a deep breath and began to speak in a calm, toneless voice.

"Like I told you before, my mother and father founded Penumbra, and throughout my childhood, I had no idea it even existed, let alone what my parents did there. But that didn't mean I wasn't aware something was going on. As the years went by, Mom and Dad began spending more nights away from home, and they began changing. In small ways, at first. Dad would break off in the middle of a sentence and stare off into the distance, sometimes for minutes at a time, and Mom started chewing her nails so badly that her fingers constantly bled. They stopped talking to each other—at least, when they were home—and after a while they stopped talking to me, too. I tried to ask them what was going on, tried to offer my help, but they refused to listen, acting as if I wasn't even there. By this time I was seventeen, and I figured that it didn't matter what was wrong with my parents. One more year and I'd be an adult. I could move out and start my own life and leave them to each other."

Caroline slowed down as they approached a narrow gravel path on the right. She stopped, turned, and drove slowly down the path, gravel crunching softly beneath the tires. The trees and undergrowth were thick here, and it was like the Lexus traveled between walls of solid green. Caroline drove only a few yards on the gravel path before a chain-link fence blocked their way. She stopped, put the Lexus in park, and got out. The fence was old, the rusted metal so brown it seemed like it had grown here, organically blending with the woods around it. The section that stretched across the path was chained and padlocked, and Caroline removed a single key from her pants pocket—how did she keep all those keys straight without a ring to hold them?—and undid the chain. She pushed the fence door inward until there was enough room for the Lexus to get through. She then got back into the car, put the transmission in gear, and eased forward once more.

When they were past the fence, Aaron said, "Shouldn't we close and lock it again?"

"Don't worry about it," Caroline said. "We're way out in the boonies here. No one's going to drive by the path entrance, and even if someone does, they'll go right on past without noticing it."

Aaron wasn't so sure, but then this was his first time coming here. Caroline had made this trip many times before and knew what she was doing.

As they continued down the path, Caroline resumed telling her story. "One day Mom was at the dining table waiting for me when I came home from school. For the first time in months she seemed like her old self, talkative and sweet. She said she was sorry for the way things had been lately, that she and Dad had been having problems, and they hadn't wanted to involve me. But things would be better from then on, she promised. And then she asked if I wanted to take a little drive with her. She had something she wanted to show me, she said. Something important. Something amazing. I had no idea what she was talking about, but I didn't care. Right then I would've gone anywhere with her. I was just so thrilled to have my mom back."

Aaron knew where this story was leading. "She took you to Penumbra."

Caroline nodded. The trees and underbrush began to thin out, and the gravel path widened slightly.

"She took me around the rear of the strip mall and through the back door. She didn't quite close it all the way; I'm not sure why. Maybe it was because she had demented too far and wasn't thinking straight. Or maybe—and I admit this is probably just wishful thinking on my part—on some level she wanted me to be able to see, to be able to defend myself. Whatever the reason, I could see her well enough when she came at me. We fell to the ground and fought for several moments, rolling back and forth, screaming, slapping, scratching, hitting . . . Finally I shoved her off me, and she rolled into the Overshadow's circle.

"I'd been distantly aware of the Overshadow from the moment I'd first set foot in the room, but I'd been so busy struggling with my mother that I hadn't *really* noticed it, you know? I watched as it fed on my mother. It's funny, but even though she fought and thrashed around like anyone else as she died, I thought I saw a look of relief in her eyes just before the darkness engulfed her. When it was over . . . well, she was like Bryan. And then the Overshadow stretched a tentacle toward me. I thought it was going to do the same thing to me that it had done to Mother, but I was too scared, too grief-stricken to do anything but stay there and let the tentacle penetrate my forehead."

The trees gave way to a field of waist-high grass. Caroline braked, parked the car, and turned off the ignition. She then turned to face Aaron.

"I don't know how my father ever figured out where we were, but when I began to recover from the aftereffects of the Overshadow's touch, he was there. Without a word, he took me to his car, then went back into Penumbra to get Mom's body. He drove me here and showed me how they disposed of their sacrifices when the Overshadow was finished with them." She sighed. "And that was my introduction to Penumbra."

They sat in silence for several moments, the only sound the ticking of the Lexus's cooling engine. Eventually, Aaron asked, "What happened to your father?"

"He continued going to Penumbra for a few more years. I started going too, bringing companions, both male and female, when it was my turn to do so. Then one day I stopped by the house to visit Dad—I'd gotten an apartment of my own by this time—and he was very excited to see me. He told me he had a neat trick to show me. He led me into the kitchen, where he'd put on a large pot of water to boil. As I watched, he walked over to the stove and submerged his entire head in the boiling water. Sometimes, late at night, I can still hear his screams."

She pushed the button to activate the trunk release.

"C'mon, we've got work to do."

She opened the driver's-side door and got out of the Lexus. Aaron sat in the passenger seat for several more seconds before finally opening his door and joining her at the rear of the Lexus. He looked into the open trunk and saw that the sheet had come partially unwrapped during the drive, revealing Bryan's withered remains. Aaron wasn't certain, but the husk looked even smaller, as if it had continued to shrink in upon itself as they'd driven.

Caroline gave him a look that was half expectant, half sheepish. "You brought him tonight, Aaron. Or at least, you were the reason he ended up at Penumbra. That means—"

"It's my responsibility to dispose of him," Aaron finished.

"Would you mind? I know I sound all girly for saying this, but I hate touching them when they're like . . . *that*." She nodded toward Bryan's contorted, desiccated form, her nose wrinkling as if there was a foul odor in the air, though as far as Aaron could tell, the corpse didn't smell at all.

Awfully thoughtful of the Overshadow to process its waste in such a way that it doesn't stink.

Aaron couldn't tell if this thought was his or if it had been something his father said. He glanced through the Lexus's rear window and saw the backseat was empty. Good. He had enough to deal with right now without having to put up with the overly critical hallucination of his dad.

He reached into the trunk and did his best to rewrap Bryan. Then he got a grip on the corpse and lifted it out. He knew the body would be light, but he was surprised by just how little it weighed. If you straightened out the arms and legs and tied a string to it, you could probably fly the damned thing like a kite. The resultant image that passed through Aaron's mind nearly made him giggle, and he wasn't sure whether that was due to his still being somewhat intoxicated from the Overshadow's touch, or from mounting hysteria over what he was about to do. Maybe a little of both, he decided. He managed to repress the giggle and cradled the sheet-wrapped thing to his chest as if it were a sleeping infant and not the remains of a man who had been alive only a short while ago.

"Now what?" Aaron asked.

Caroline closed the trunk hard, and its loud *chunk!* echoed through the night.

"Follow me," she said, and started walking. Aaron trailed her as she made her way through a grassy field. There seemed to be a path, but the grass was so high here it was hard to tell. The night breeze was cool, and the sky above was cloudless, and out here, away from the artificial lights of town, the stars shone clear and bright. Birds sang and insects chirped in the darkness around them, and Aaron was struck by how beautiful and perfect the night was. Given the grim errand they were on, coiling wisps of fog and eerie silence would've been more appropriate. It seemed almost obscene that the setting should be so pleasant considering what they were here to do.

The ground sloped downward from where Caroline had parked, and Aaron walked carefully, not wishing to trip and fall. The idea of losing his footing and dropping Bryan—or worse, actually *landing* on the dry, brittle remains—made him queasy.

What's wrong, boy? The happy-happy of the Overshadow's touch starting to wear off?

Maybe. Or maybe even the ecstasy granted by the Overshadow could only emotionally insulate a person so much.

A thought occurred to him then. "Does everyone who's touched by the Overshadow dement?"

Caroline, who'd been walking slightly ahead of him, glanced back over her shoulder, but she didn't slow down. "I've been going to Penumbra since I was seventeen, and I brought Phillip in a few years after that. Do either of us seem demented to you?" She faced forward again before Aaron could answer. He wondered if she did this because she thought the answer was a foregone conclusion, or because she preferred not to explore the issue too deeply.

As they continued down the sloping hill, Aaron saw

two rows of parked vehicles not far ahead: four cars, two SUVs, a van, and a pickup. Engine and lights off, silent and dark.

Before he could ask, Caroline said, "This is where we keep the vehicles that belonged to our . . . temporary guests. Whenever possible, we try to drive our guests to Penumbra ourselves. But when that doesn't work out, when the Overshadow is finished with them, we take their keys and drive their cars here." She looked back at Aaron and smiled. "We can't have the Valley View Shopping Center's parking lot filled with abandoned vehicles, can we?"

"What about Bryan's car?"

"Assuming he didn't get a ride with someone else or walk to the bar, Wyatt will use the man's ID to check on his vehicle registration. In fact, Wyatt's probably doing that right now. Once he's identified Bryan's car, we'll bring it here."

"I only see eight vehicles," Aaron said. "I'd think there would be a hell of a lot more considering how long Penumbra's been around."

"Oh, we don't keep vehicles here long," Caroline said. "Wyatt has connections to several chop shops around the state. We sell the cars to them cheap, but we're careful not to get rid of too many at a time so we don't arouse too much suspicion. We usually have only a couple of cars here at a time. Wyatt's gotten a bit behind in his work, I suppose."

"You've really got this down to a science, don't you?"

"Well, we *have* been at this a long time."

They reached the parked vehicles and walked between their rows. A dozen yards on the other side was an opening in the ground, a pit ten feet across. Caroline walked up to the edge and stopped.

"This is it," she said.

Aaron joined her and gazed down into the pit. It looked to be about ten feet deep with sloping sides. At the bottom, resting in a shallow pool of muddy rainwater, lay two cloth-wrapped bundles. Aaron couldn't see any identifying features beyond one withered clawhand sticking out, but he assumed one of bodies belonged to the stripe-shirted young man Caroline had taken to Penumbra the other night. But Aaron didn't need to know *who* they were for certain to know *what* they were: the Overshadow's leftovers.

"You just throw the bodies in there?" Aaron asked. "After everything I've seen about how Penumbra operates, this seems a bit . . . primitive. Not to mention risky. What if someone runs across the pit and discovers the bodies?"

"I'll admit it's a minor risk," Caroline said. "But like I told you earlier, we're in the boondocks here. My folks used to own this land; now I do. And it's fenced off all around, with NO TREPASSING signs posted everywhere. And on the off chance someone did find this place and went to the police, Wyatt would deal with them."

Aaron wondered just what Wyatt would do. He had the feeling that whatever it was, it would end with several more bodies at the bottom of this pit.

"There's a practical reason why we do it this way," Caroline said. "Once the Overshadow has finished draining the life force from someone, their body is changed. Not just physically, but chemically. After a few days' exposure to the elements, they basically turn to slime. The bones, too. I don't fully understand the process, but Wyatt assures me that after seventy-two hours, what's left can't be identified as human, let alone as the remains of a specific person."

"What about their clothes and the sheets they're wrapped in?"

"It takes a bit longer, but the slime the bodies turn into eventually dissolves their clothes and wrappings, too." She smiled. "Another of the Overshadow's blessings."

Aaron looked down into the pit once more and realized that though it had rained some in the last few days, the muck in the bottom of the pit wasn't mud. Or at least, not only mud.

"Go ahead," Caroline said. "Toss him in."

Aaron hadn't known Bryan as anything other than a drunken, belligerent asshole. But even so, he'd been a human being, and he deserved something better than being thrown into a pit like he was nothing more than garbage to be disposed of. But Aaron couldn't think of anything else to do with him, and the thought of saying a few words of farewell before throwing him into the pit—not that Aaron had any idea what to say—somehow seemed as if it would only make the situation worse. So he did as Caroline suggested, and tossed Bryan's cloth-wrapped remains into the pit. They landed in the slime next to the other two with a thick, wet splat that reminded Aaron of the sound vomit makes when it strikes a hard surface.

Bryan's head hit only inches away from another

body, and the impact caused a flap of sheet covering it to roll back, revealing a woman's black low-heeled shoe. Aaron stared. There was something almost familiar about that shoe, but he couldn't—

Caroline took hold of Aaron's shoulders, turned him away from the pit, and then kissed him. Her lips felts cold at first—cold as the Overshadow's touch, cold as he imagined the slime in the pit must feel—but they quickly warmed as they moved over his. He didn't want to respond to her, not after he'd learned the final harsh truths of Penumbra, but he couldn't help himself. Warmth flooded his body, and blood rushed into his penis, bringing him instantly and painfully erect. Caroline reached down to rub his cock through his pants, and a soft moan escaped from the back of his throat. Their tongues met, circled, probed, jousted, and then Caroline drew back, breaking their embrace. She stood looking at him for a moment, her expression unreadable. Then her mouth curved into a half smile, and she raised her hand and wiggled her index finger in a "come here" gesture. Aaron took a step forward, and then Caroline—like a deer that's suddenly been startled—whirled around and dashed toward the cars. Grinning, Aaron took off in pursuit.

Caroline ran toward the closest vehicle in the bunch, an Accord. Blue, Aaron thought, though the night made the car look black, as if it had been formed from shadow. Caroline stopped as she reached the car, turned around, and leaned back on the hood, breathing hard, sweat trailing down her face and neck. Aaron half expected pseudopods to emerge from the Accord's dark surface and reach for her, but of course they didn't. The Overshadow was confined to the back room of Penumbra, and this car was nothing more than a simple machine.

Caroline had already removed her top by the time Aaron caught up with her, and she started undoing her jeans. Aaron pulled off his shirt and tossed it to the ground, shivering as the night air caressed his bare skin. He then yanked down his pants and underwear in a single motion, setting his erection free. Caroline, completely naked now, grabbed hold of his stiff penis and pulled him toward her as he stepped the rest of the way out of his pants. Caroline leaned back against the hood of the Accord once more, her bare ass flattening against the metal. The hood must've been cool, for she took in a hissing breath as her flesh came in contact with it.

Diane drove an Accord just like this, Aaron realized. No big deal; it was a common enough car, and lots of folks in Ptolemy had them. Yet a warning signal went off somewhere deep in his subconscious, telling him that something was wrong here. Seriously wrong. But before he could tease the thought to the surface of his mind, Caroline spread her legs wide, tightened her grip on his cock, and yanked him forward hard, as if she didn't care whether he came along with the organ or not. He stumbled forward and nearly fell on top of Caroline as she vigorously rubbed the head of his penis back and forth against her wet clitoris. Then she moved his cock into position, reached around to grab hold of his ass, and pushed him inside her cunt. She was warm and slick as honey inside, and after experiencing the full force of the Overshadow's gratitude this evening, Aaron's nerve-endings were still so stimulated that he nearly came at once. He might have, too, if at that moment they hadn't heard the sound of gravel crunching beneath car tires and hadn't seen the harsh glare of approaching headlights.

CHAPTER FIFTEEN

Aaron pulled out of Caroline, his dick making a soft squelching sound as it withdrew. He was already beginning to soften, like a cock-shaped balloon with a serious leak.

"Who's that?" he said, unable to keep an edge of panic out of his voice.

Of course you're panicking, the Dad Voice said. *You're standing there naked, in the process of fucking a woman that you just helped get rid of a dead body, and you're screwing her on top of a car that used to belong to yet another dead person. Talk about getting caught in a compromising position!*

Caroline sounded more frustrated than concerned as she replied. "It's probably just Wyatt bringing Bryan's car. He no doubt wanted to give us a scare before getting a chance to fuck me too. He's a dear, but he can be a little greedy at times."

Aaron relaxed a bit, though Caroline's words didn't completely reassure him. "From the sound of it, Bryan's car must be a real junker. The engine's rattling so hard that . . ." He trailed off as he remembered where he'd heard that half-dead engine before. "That's not Wyatt! It's that bald guy I told you about, the one that attacked me in the parking lot outside my office the other day!"

"What? You can't be serious!" Caroline pushed Aaron away from her, then bent down to snatch her clothes off the ground. The car came to a rattling, chuffing stop next to where they'd parked the Lexus. From where they stood, Aaron couldn't get a good look at the vehicle, but he had no doubt it was a powder-blue Volkswagen Beetle.

The Bug's headlights went out and the engine burbled as it died. For several seconds there was only silence, and then came the creaking sound of an ancient car door opening. The door *chunked* closed, followed by a raspy voice calling out, "Caroline! It's Gerald! Did you miss me?"

Caroline had her top back on and was pulling up her panties when the bald man's words echoed through the night. Even with the enhanced nocturnal vision granted by the Overshadow's touch, Aaron couldn't tell for certain, but it seemed to him that Caroline went pale.

"Oh God," she whispered.

"What's wrong?" Aaron grabbed his pants off the ground and started putting them back on. "Do you know this guy?"

"He used to be one of us, a member of Penumbra. But he demented about a year ago, and we haven't seen him since. I'd hoped he'd killed himself by now, but I guess not. More's the pity."

Aaron saw Scab-Head—Gerald—start to make his

way down the hill toward them. The man moved clumsily, his bulk a hindrance when it came to maneuvering the slope, and he was forced to go slowly.

"Is he dangerous?" Aaron asked.

"*All* Dements are dangerous in some way," Caroline answered. She hadn't bothered putting her pants on yet, just left them sitting on top of the Accord's hood. From the fearful tone in her voice, Aaron expected her to crouch down and attempt to hide behind the car. But instead she said, "Stay here. I'll go see what he wants. Don't worry, he won't hurt me. I was the one who originally brought him into Penumbra; he has a thing for me." She gave Aaron a quick wink and then stepped around the Accord and started walking toward Gerald, moving with a languid grace that was as calculated as it was sexy.

Aaron—still barefoot and bare-chested—stood and watched her go, torn as to what he should do. The protective male part of him wanted to rush forward and interpose himself between Gerald and Caroline, to guard her from this potentially dangerous lunatic. But the dispassionate, rational part of him understood that Caroline knew far more about Dements in general, and Gerald in particular, than he did. He might well make things worse by confronting the man, might set him off into a maniacal rage.

"Whatever you do, you'd better decide quick. He's almost reached her."

Aaron turned to see his father leaning against the Accord, hand resting on the side panel.

"And you *do* realize this is Diane's car, right?" Martin Rittinger asked. "I mean, you may be kind of slow on the uptake sometimes, but surely you've figured that out by now."

Aaron stared at his father, unable to fully process what he was saying. But before he could reply, he heard Caroline speak.

"It's been a while, Gerald. What have you been up to?"

Aaron pushed the matter of Diane's car from his mind and turned to watch Caroline and Gerald. They stood a dozen yards from the parked cars, only an arm's length between them.

"Nothing much," Gerald said. "Making sure you and the other Insiders don't catch me and feed me to the Overshadow, spying on you with the help of my good buddy Aaron over there . . ." Gerald nodded in Aaron's direction.

Caroline looked back at Aaron, surprise and suspicion mingling on her face.

Aaron felt a sudden need to defend himself. "I don't know what this crazy son of a bitch is talking about! I'm not spying for him or anyone else!" He started toward the two of them.

"Watch yourself," his father warned as Aaron walked away from the Accord. "That fucker looks fruitier than a nutcake."

"It's all right," Gerald said. "The time for secrecy has passed. The knowledge you've acquired will allow me and the other Forsaken to plan our final assault and retake Penumbra once and for all." He turned to Caroline. "And there's nothing you or any of the others can do about it." He stuck his tongue out at her, and Aaron was close enough now to see that the tip was bifurcated, as if it had been cut.

Caroline took a step back as Aaron drew closer. "I thought it was luck that brought us together . . . that you just happened to see me go into the club the other night and got curious. I never imagined that you were working with Gerald and the other Dements."

Aaron stopped when he was within five feet of the two. "That's because it's not true! It *was* coincidence that I saw you the other night, and I approached you because I've been attracted to you for years. The first time I ever met Gerald was in the parking lot outside my office the other day. I told you about that, remember? For Christ's sake, you said it yourself—the man's a Dement. This is just some sick fantasy on his part, a delusion conjured up in his diseased mind!"

"You're a fine one to talk about diseased minds!" his father called out.

Aaron almost whirled around and told the old man to shut up, but he didn't. That was the sort of thing a crazy person would do, and he wasn't crazy.

He turned to Caroline and took a step toward her. "Please . . . you have to believe me!"

Caroline didn't retreat this time, but her eyes widened and her body tensed, as if she were preparing to either defend herself against him or flee. He remembered what she'd said only a short while ago.

I've been going to Penumbra since I was seventeen, and I brought Phillip in a few years after that. Do either of us seem demented to you?

Maybe Caroline wasn't as obviously crazy as Gerald, but that didn't mean her mind hadn't been scarred by her encounters with the Overshadow throughout the years. Gerald's words were insane, but that didn't mean Caroline wouldn't believe them—especially if she was insane as well.

His father's words returned to him then.

You do *realize this is Diane's car, right?*

Aaron frowned as he looked at Caroline. "What did you do to Diane?"

Caroline's eyes narrowed. "What makes you think I did anything to her?"

"That was her car we were about to fuck on," Aaron accused. "What the hell is it doing here?"

Caroline sneered. "What do you think? The old bitch listened in while we were talking on the phone—talking about Penumbra. I couldn't allow her to live with that knowledge, so I took her for a little ride to see the Overshadow."

Gerald's eyes gleamed in the starlight. "Alone? Did you receive the full force of the Overshadow's gratitude? What was it like? Tell me, and don't leave out a single detail!"

Caroline stepped toward Gerald and spoke in a voice that was almost a purr. She ran her hands over her breasts, and her nipples grew erect beneath the thin fabric of her shirt. Gerald's gaze fastened on her nipples as if they exuded irresistible hypnotic power.

At this point, Aaron was only paying partial attention to Caroline and Gerald. He was too stunned by the revelation that Diane—his office manager and friend of so many years—was dead. And the way she'd died . . . food for a creature of living shadow. Diane's only crime was that she cared about Aaron enough to want to look out for him, to keep him from making the same mistake in his marriage that she'd made in hers.

Caroline continued to speak as she inched closer to Gerald. "You wouldn't believe how horny I was after feeding that old bitch to the Overshadow . . . my cunt was so wet that my panties were drenched and juice was running down my legs . . ."

Gerald licked his lips with his forked tongue and nervously rubbed his scabby scalp. The front of his pants swelled as his cock became erect, and still Caroline edged closer. Aaron wondered how she could bring herself to go near Gerald as filthy as the man was. Maybe his dirt and stink turned her on, Aaron thought. He doubted any sort of deviance was beyond her.

As she reached Gerald, she put her hands on his shoulders, looked him in the eye, smiled, and slammed her knee into his crotch. Gerald's eyes bulged and his mouth opened as if he was going to cry out in pain, but no sound escaped his throat. Caroline removed her hands from his shoulders and stepped back. Gerald put his hand to his groin as if to hold his wounded genitals together before falling to his knees and collapsing onto his side.

"Come on!" Caroline ran toward Aaron, grabbed his hand, and pulled him away from where Gerald lay moaning softly. Confused, Aaron allowed her to lead him, and they ran hand in hand.

"Where are we going?" he asked.

"We have to get out of here before he recovers," Caroline answered.

They ran past the parked vehicles, and Aaron's dad—who now sat on the roof of Diane's Accord—waved as they went by.

Aaron realized that something was wrong. They were running in the opposite direction from where they'd left his Lexus. They were, in fact, running toward—

Caroline let go of his hand and rammed her shoulder into his. Aaron lost his footing and tumbled down into the pit. He rolled, slid, then hit the muck in the bottom in a splash of viscous goo. He felt more than heard something break beneath him as he landed, and he realized with sick horror that he had fallen on top of one of the three sheet-wrapped bodies in the pit. He raised his head to look—face and hair smeared with rank, foul-smelling slime—and saw that he'd decapitated one of the corpses, and its head had popped out from underneath its crude burial shroud.

Aaron stared into Diane's withered, mummified face.

He tried to crawl away from the grisly thing, but all he managed to do was thrash about in the slime and damage Diane's brittle, desiccated corpse even more. He forced himself to stop moving and reflexively licked at a glob of slime on his lip. As he swallowed, from off in the distance he heard his dad shout, "Congratulations! On top of everything else, you're now officially a cannibal!"

Aaron's stomach rebelled, threatening to eject its contents in a single violent eruption. But Aaron fought to keep from throwing up, for the idea of vomiting all over Diane's remains made him feel even worse than the notion that he might've just ingested part of her. Besides, his dad was wrong. He hadn't just become a cannibal; he'd been one the moment the Overshadow touched him after feeding on Bryan. Like a mother bird regurgitating half-digested food for her babies, the Overshadow used a small portion of its meal's life force to reward its servants.

He heard the sound of a car engine starting and recognized the vehicle as his Lexus. A moment later the engine roared and he heard gravel crunching. The noise faded as quickly as it had come, and he knew that Caroline was gone. It seemed that she had bought Gerald's story that Aaron was in league with him and had decided that her latest recruit to Penumbra could no longer be trusted.

He was almost completely covered with slime. He tried wiping it off his chest, face, and arms with his fingers, but he succeeded only in smearing the horrid gunk around. He took one last look at Diane's head. He felt as if he should try to take her remains out of here with him—to give her a decent burial, if nothing else—but covered in slime as he was, he wasn't sure he could get himself out of the pit, let alone do so while carrying Diane's body.

Diane's head stared back at him, eyes sunken so deep into the hollow of her skull that they were barely visible, even to Aaron's enhanced night vision. He told himself that he imagined the look of sad rebuke Diane's head seemed to be giving him; then he turned and began trying to claw his way out of the pit. It wasn't easy, for the sides sloped sharply downward and the slime coating his body turned the ground to mud beneath him as he went. But yesterday's rain had softened the earth enough for him to dig his fingers into the soil, and slowly, torturously, he managed to make his way toward the rim of the pit. As he reached the top and was about to put his hand over the side, the ground beneath his feet started to give way and he began sliding back downward. He flailed about, trying to find some purchase to halt his descent, but he continued sliding.

Then a fleshy hand reached over the edge of the pit and latched on to his wrist. It was followed by another hand that grabbed hold of his hair. Their grips held and Aaron stopped sliding.

Gerald crouched at the pit's edge, looking down at him and grinning with twisted yellow teeth.

"Looks like your new girlfriend ditched you, huh? But don't worry; *I'm* not going to abandon you. We've got work to do, you and me. Serious work. And it's high time we got to it."

Gerald began hauling Aaron out of the pit.

Headlights illuminated the asphalt surface of the road and spilled over to glaze the trees on either side as the Lexus flashed by. Caroline gripped the steering wheel so tight it felt as if the skin over her knuckles might tear. Her bare legs felt cold, and she realized she'd left her jeans behind. She flicked on the car's heater and adjusted it to direct the warm air onto her legs. Better. The gas pedal was rough beneath her bare foot, but she'd left her shoes with her jeans, so there was nothing she could do about it now. She did ease off the accelerator, though. While Gerald's balls might have recovered enough for him to be capable of getting into his car, there was no way his piece-of-shit Beetle could catch Aaron's Lexus. She had no need for speed, and as upset as she was, she might get into an accident by driving too fast.

"Slow and easy, girl. That's the way to take it."

Caroline sighed. "Yes, thank you, Mama. I know."

She glanced in the rearview mirror and saw a gray-skinned, skull-faced creature with sunken eyes and white wisps of hair clinging to her parchment-dry scalp. This was exactly the way Caroline's mother had looked when the Overshadow finished with her. Caroline believed her mom chose this appearance to make her feel guilty. If so, it wasn't going to work; it never did.

"So Aaron turned out to be a jerk," Caroline's mother said, her words distorted by her tight, leathery lips. "All men do eventually."

Caroline considered turning on the radio and cranking the volume all the way up in an attempt to drown out her mother's voice. But she knew from experience that it wouldn't work. Mama would just shriek her words over the music.

"He's more than a jerk, Mama. He's a fucking spy for the Forsaken!" But as soon as she'd spoken the words, she wondered if they were really true. She only had Gerald's word for it, after all, and he was a god-damned Dement, just like all the other Forsaken. Maybe she was overreacting, being too impulsive . . . She'd always been the sort of person who acted first and thought later—if she thought at all. But it seemed that she'd been getting worse over the last few years.

"Of course you have, darling," her mother said in a voice that rattled like ancient bones. "You're a Dement, too, you know. All the Insiders are. The only difference between you and the Forsaken is that they've descended to greater depths of madness. But don't worry—you and the other Insiders will catch up to them soon enough."

"*You're* the crazy one," Caroline said. "*You* tried to sacrifice *me* to the Overshadow when I was seventeen, remember? Why should I listen to anything you have to say?"

"No reason . . . other than I'm right." It was difficult for Caroline's mother to communicate expressions given the condition of her face, but she managed to achieve a look of smugness now.

Caroline knew better than to argue with her mama. The rot-faced bitch could be so stubborn sometimes. She decided to turn the subject back to Aaron and his betrayal. "Aaron was working with the Forsaken all along. He wants to help them take over Penumbra. But I don't understand why he would want to do that. He's already a member, and he has *me*—not to mention Gillian and Shari. What could the Forsaken promise him that he doesn't already have?"

"They could've promised him anything, dear," her mother said. "Money, power, you as his eternal sex slave . . . What do the specifics matter? The point is he did it, so what are *you* going to do now?"

Caroline drove on in silence for several moments while she contemplated her options. She'd been so shocked by the revelation of Aaron's betrayal that all she'd wanted to do was get away from him and Gerald. But now that she was free, alone, and safe she realized she had no clear idea what step to take next.

It was one of the most important rules in Penumbra: When a member dements, he or she is given to the Overshadow. No exceptions. But over the years several

Dements had escaped their former friends in Penumbra, banded together, and started calling themselves the Forsaken. Caroline knew little about them. Not where they lived or even how many of them there were, exactly. She knew only that they were crazy and dangerous. Wyatt and Phillip tried to hunt the Forsaken down from time to time, but while they'd managed to find and take out a few, they had yet to discover where the Dements nested.

Maybe Aaron's betrayal could turn out to be a blessing in disguise. If she and the others could capture Aaron, maybe they could force him to reveal the Forsaken's hidden lair . . . maybe even use him to draw them out into the open so they could be destroyed once and for all.

But before any of that could happen, she had to find a way to bring Aaron back to her. She couldn't simply turn around and go get him. He wouldn't trust her now, and she didn't have the strength to force him to come with her. Plus, she'd have Gerald to contend with. She needed some kind of lure, and sex wouldn't be enough. Not this time.

"When I was alive, the most important things to me were always my husband and daughter." The dead thing in the backseat bared its dingy teeth in a hideous grin. "Family is everything, dear."

Caroline's lips stretched into a smile that mirrored her mother's. "Thanks, Mama. I know *exactly* what I need to do now."

Caroline pressed down on the gas pedal once more, and the Lexus sped toward town.

* * *

Aaron sat in the passenger seat of Gerald's VW. The stench inside the tiny car was so thick it was almost a physical thing—and the slime that coated Aaron's body didn't freshen the air any. But he barely registered the stink. He couldn't stop thinking about Diane's head, and the accusing look on her dead face that had to have been his imagination but which didn't hurt any the less for that.

He remembered what Caroline had said to him in Deja Brew before Bryan had come over to hassle them.

You and I are explorers. Adventures in the realms of sensation . . . We need to live, *Aaron, live* big. *And Penumbra allows us to do that, to transcend mundane day-to-day existence and be more than just walking, sleeping, eating meat bags . . . No price is too high when it comes to reaching your full potential, Aaron. Never forget that.*

In his mind, he saw again the look of accusation on Diane's dry, withered face, and he knew that Caroline was wrong. Some prices were much too high.

"It won't be long now." Gerald reached up and rubbed his scalp. He performed this action at least once every couple of minutes or so, more often when he was excited, and Aaron was beginning to get used to it. "We'll be at the Homestead soon, and I'll introduce you to the others. Then you can tell us everything you've learned."

The dome light flickered on and off erratically, like a firefly caught in the throes of a grand mal seizure. Normally the malfunctioning light would've annoyed Aaron to the point of distraction, but it seemed appropriate for Gerald, as if it were wired directly into the man's misfiring nervous system.

After Gerald had helped Aaron out of the pit, he'd followed the lunatic back to his Beetle and climbed into the car without thinking twice. He supposed he'd been in shock or something. But though his mind still felt sluggish, he was starting to think straight once more. He wasn't sure where they were—he didn't have a clear memory of getting back on the road or what route they'd taken after that. He looked out the window now and saw that it was still night, though he didn't know the time. Maybe 3:00 A.M. or thereabout. He glanced at the clock set into Gerald's dashboard, the old-fashioned kind with slim red hands and white hash marks indicating minutes on a black background. It said 9:20, but the second hand wasn't moving, and Aaron knew the clock was broken. He looked out the window again and saw there were few trees around; instead they drove past fields of tall cornstalks. So they were out in the country. A suitable location for a place called the Homestead, Aaron thought.

"What makes you think I know anything that will help you?" These were the first words Aaron had spoken since Gerald had helped him get free of the pit. And once they were out of his mouth, more followed. "You and the other Dements—I mean, the *Forsaken*—all used to be members of Penumbra, right?"

"Yes," Gerald said. "Some of them for quite a few years before being forced out."

Before they went crazy, you mean, Aaron thought. "That means you and the others know the place inside out. Far better than I could after only going there twice. What possible help can I be to you?"

Gerald slowed as the VW drew near a gravel driveway. A rusty mailbox sat atop a weathered wooden post at the road's edge, the door hanging open as if eagerly awaiting a delivery that would never come. Gerald pressed the brake pedal and was rewarded by the squealing groan of worn brakes struggling to do their job. He turned into the driveway and accelerated, leaving clouds of gravel dust in the Beetle's wake.

"You've interacted with the Insiders more recently than any of us," Gerald said. "You'll know if they've made any changes to Penumbra's layout, if they've set any traps to stop us, stockpiled any weapons . . ."

Aaron snorted a laugh. "You make it sound as if Penumbra's a military bunker instead of a place to get drunk and get laid."

Gerald turned to glare at Aaron, bloodshot eyes seeming to spark in the flickering illumination cast by the dome light.

"It's much more than that, and you know it." Gerald sounded almost sane as he said this.

"All right, I'll concede that point, but I didn't see any signs of traps or weapons. You're just being paranoid, Gerald."

Gerald's lips tightened and his jaw clenched. "We'll just have to see about that, won't we?" He turned to look forward once more, and Aaron decided it would be best not to press the issue any further.

Fields of waist-high grass rose on either side of the driveway, waving in the night breeze like undersea plants caught in a slow, steady tide. Not far off he could see a farmhouse and a barn, both illuminated by a fluorescent light mounted on top of a telephone pole. He had no doubt that this was the Homestead to which Gerald had referred. Now that his mind was reasonably clear again, Aaron realized that he had made a huge mistake allowing this nutcase to bring him here. Caroline had said that all Dements were dangerous, and she'd implied that the Forsaken were the worst. Just because Gerald said all they wanted with Aaron was to glean whatever information about Penumbra he had to share didn't make it so. Or didn't provide any guarantee as to what else they might do to him when they were satisfied he had told them all he knew. And since he didn't know much, it might well be a short and extremely unpleasant interrogation. It looked like he would have to go along with Gerald for now and keep both eyes out for opportunities to escape. And if no opportunities presented themselves, he would just have to make them himself.

The spot behind Aaron's left ear itched, and without thinking he reached up to scratch it. When he lowered his hand, he saw that it was full of his hair. Clumps of it, all smeared with goo from the bottom of the slim pit. Caroline had said the shit could dissolve clothing in a short time. What effect might the gunk have on living flesh? He glanced over at Gerald's scab-dotted head and wondered if the man might've lost his hair in a similar fashion. The thought made Aaron shiver, and he dropped his hair to floor of the car, watching the strands drift down to settled amid crumpled fast-food sandwich wrappers and bags.

Gerald turned to Aaron and grinned. At first, Aaron

thought the lunatic was going to comment on his sudden hair loss, but instead he said, "We're here." He brought the Beetle to a stop midway between the house and the barn, parked, and killed the engine.

"Ready to meet the others?" Gerald asked.

"As ready as I'll ever be, I suppose." The itching had grown worse, and now Aaron's scalp felt as if it were being nibbled on by thousands of fire ants. He started to reach up to scratch, thought of Gerald's nervous gesture, then put his hand back down on the seat beside him.

"Before we go meet your friends, do you have a hose or something you can use to wash this crap off me?"

"Sure," Gerald said. "I'll be glad to help—provided you let me save as much as I can in a bucket."

Aaron's stomach did a flip at the thought of what use Gerald and his fellow Dements might put the salvaged slime to. But he wanted to get the crud off him before he lost a nose, an ear, his eyes, his lips . . .

"Sure, whatever."

True to Gerald's words, there was a hose coiled on the ground at the side of the farmhouse. The house itself was in a terrible state of disrepair—paint flaking, porch subsiding, windows cracked if they still had panes at all. Aaron doubted anyone had lived there in the last thirty years. But then, maybe that's the way the Forsaken wanted it to look so they could remain hidden.

The house still had running water, though, for when Gerald turned the valve, spray blasted out of the hose's nozzle. Gerald quickly showered him off, the water cold and sharp as ice-needles, and then turned the water off.

"Better?" Gerald asked before peering into the metal bucket he'd placed by Aaron's right leg to catch some of the slime.

Aaron gritted his teeth to keep them from chattering. "I might be if I hadn't been so dazed that I left my shirt back at the pit."

"You'll dry soon enough. Let's go. The others are waiting." Gerald left the bucket of slime and water where it was and started walking toward the barn.

Ignoring the bucket—and doing his best not to imagine what Gerald might do with the leftover slime—Aaron reached up to probe the matted hair plastered to his scalp. He wasn't certain, but he thought he'd lost a bit more hair thanks to the hose's water pressure. Then he realized something—this was it! Gerald had left him alone. He could make a break for it. His muscles tensed as he prepared to run.

"Don't bother," Gerald called back over his shoulder as he rubbed his scalp yet again. "We'll just track you down."

Aaron hesitated for a moment. Then, still shivering, he crossed his arms over his chest in a futile attempt to seek warmth and followed Gerald to the barn. The building was just as worn and battered as the farmhouse. It might've been red once, but time and the elements had leeched all color from the wood, leaving it an almost white gray. The structure leaned slightly to the left, as if it were being pushed by silent winds. The ground in front of the large sliding door was bare, as if it had been tainted by some blight and vegetation now refused to grow there.

Gerald walked up to the door, gripped a rusted metal handle bolted to the gray wood, and pulled. Aaron expected it to make a grinding-groaning sound, but the door moved smoothly along its track, as if it were the only object on the farm that was regularly maintained. Before the door was even halfway open, the smell rolled out like a wall of rancid fog. Aaron's nasal passages burned and his eyes watered, and he found himself stepping backward in a vain attempt to escape the olfactory assault. It was almost a living vapor wafting outward from the interior of the barn, reaching toward him, hoping to enter his body through nostrils, mouth, pores . . .

When the door was open all the way, Gerald walked over to Aaron, gripped him by the elbow, and steered him toward the barn. Aaron wanted to resist, but he allowed Gerald to lead him forward. Maybe he had slipped back into a state of shock, or maybe he'd experienced so many strange and awful things in the last few days that he was beginning to become numb to them. Whatever the reason, he accompanied Gerald through the large open doorway and into the barn—and immediately wished he hadn't.

The inside of the barn was illuminated by harsh bright work lights set atop metal poles. Three people were present, one woman and two men, all of them obviously Dements like Gerald. They were filthy and dressed in stained, tattered clothes. The woman's gray hair was twisted into long braids with sharp bits of what looked like bone threaded into them. One man had thick black hair, no eyebrows, and a toothless grin, while the second was older, perhaps in his sixties, his face a ruined, puckered mask of scar tissue. None of the three looked in Aaron's and Gerald's direction, for they were too focused on their work. The toothless man held a severed arm—a young woman's from the look of it—while Bone-Braids ran a needle and thread through the ragged stump where the limb had once been attached to its owner's body. Scar-Face stood back several paces, watching as they worked, offering critiques and suggestions as needed. But as awful as that scene was, it might as well have been a tableau of three preschoolers collaborating on a construction-paper-and-paste craft compared to the gigantic patchwork grotesquerie that rose into the air behind them. It nearly filled the entire barn, wall to wall, ceiling to floor, held in place by a crisscrossing network of chains and hooks.

"Isn't it marvelous?" Gerald spoke in a hushed, reverent voice. "We call it the Tapestry."

CHAPTER SIXTEEN

It appeared black at first, but then Aaron became aware of a low buzzing noise, and he realized that the black was moving, rippling like an ebon wave. The Dements' creation was covered with flies. And the reason for this became clear once Aaron's traumatized mind finally allowed him to comprehend the full reality of what he was seeing. The Forsaken had used severed body parts—hands, feet, torsos, heads—to make their Tapestry. The pieces were sewed, lashed, and wired together in seemingly random fashion, an ear stapled to the back of a hand, four heads sewed to the stumps where a torso's limbs had once been, a foot emerging from a ragged neck stump . . . Not all of the body parts were fresh. Many were in various states of decomposition, flesh mottled, gray green, bloated and maggot-infested. Quite a few were little more than bone, testifying to how long the Dements had been assembling their grisly work of art.

"It's an offering," Gerald said. "To prove to the

Overshadow that we're worthy of standing in its presence once more."

Aaron tried to estimate how many people had been killed to provide the raw material to build the reeking, fly-covered abomination that hung in the barn. A hundred? More? It was impossible to tell simply by looking. Maybe if he tried counting the heads . . .

Toothless and Bone-Braids continued working to attach the latest addition to the Tapestry, but Scar-Face turned to look at Aaron and Gerald and he came shuffling over to them. He looked Aaron over, then said, "So you're my daughter's latest toy." His puffy, distorted lips twisted into a shape that might have been a smile.

Aaron stared at the ruined face of the old man standing before him, feeling as if a cold sliver of steel had been rammed into his sternum. He remembered what Caroline had told him on the drive to the pit.

He told me he had a neat trick to show me. He led me into the kitchen, where he'd put on a large pot of water to boil. As I watched, he walked over to the stove and submerged his entire head in the boiling water. Sometimes, late at night, I can still hear his screams.

Aaron had assumed that Caroline's father—the man who'd founded Penumbra—had died. But he realized that Caroline had never said her father was dead. The man was here and very much alive. And judging from the number of body parts that had gone into the creation of the Tapestry, he'd been keeping quite busy over the years since sticking his face into a pot of boiling water.

"What do you think of it, boy?" Caroline's father made a sweeping gesture toward the Tapestry. And though he didn't touch it, the breeze stirred up by his hand's passage through the air disturbed the flies crawling on the nearest portion of the Tapestry. They took to the air, buzzing furiously, their movement setting off still more groups of flies, one after the other, like a chain of tumbling dominos. Within seconds all the flies had taken flight and were circling the Tapestry, filling the barn with their angry, confused droning.

Aaron's knees threatened to buckle, and swirls of darkness appeared before his eyes, obscuring his vision. He knew he was on the verge of losing consciousness, and the only thing that kept him from doing so was the fear that once he'd blacked out, the Dements might vivisect him and add his parts to the Tapestry.

A cry of disgust tore its way out of his throat, and he turned and fled the barn. He ran wildly, blindly, without thought of direction or destination. But as he passed directly beneath the fluorescent light in the yard, he remembered: the farmhouse. Maybe he could barricade himself inside, hide, maybe even find a weapon to protect himself. He didn't care, just as long as he could put some solid walls between himself and those lunatics with their obscene sculpture of dead flesh.

Aaron started running toward the house, doing his best to ignore the sounds of pursuit that followed him.

Kristen opened her eyes. Only half awake, she looked at the digital clock radio. It was 4:10 in the morning.

She rolled in the opposite direction and reached out for Aaron, but her hand found only covers that hadn't been disturbed. Aaron wasn't there, and it seemed he hadn't been to bed at all.

Kristen sat up, fully awake now. She had a bad feeling that something was wrong, but she wasn't sure what. She often had a nightmare that some unknown person was trying to break into their house, and when she woke up, she always made Aaron go check to make sure everything was okay. She knew it was a just a dream, most likely caused by simple anxiety, but she still couldn't get back to sleep unless Aaron make a quick patrol of the house. She didn't remember having that dream tonight, but she knew she would have difficulty returning to sleep. Maybe some soothing Sleepytime Tea would help. Besides, she wanted to find Aaron and reassure herself that everything was all right between them.

She got out of bed, put on her robe and slippers, and walked out into the hallway. She made her way quietly toward the stairs, not wishing to disturb Colin or Lindsay. Just because both of their parents were having trouble sleeping was no reason why their rest should be interrupted.

As Kristen descended the stairs, she expected to hear the sound of the TV playing at low volume. It wasn't uncommon for Aaron to fall asleep in front of the television, and he'd remain on the couch the entire night if she didn't come down to wake him. But the house was silent, and when she went into the living room, she found it dark, the TV off, the couch unoccupied. Kristen felt the first faint stirrings of worry upon seeing the empty couch, but she told herself not to get worked up yet. Maybe Aaron was in the kitchen. When she couldn't sleep, she drank tea, but Aaron preferred a mug of warm milk to help him get drowsy again.

She passed through the living room and the dining room, then into the kitchen. The light above the sink was on, the only illumination. But it was enough for her to see that Aaron wasn't here either.

Now she began to worry in earnest. She couldn't imagine where else in the house Aaron might be at this time of night. He didn't have a home office, and though he sometimes puttered in the basement, it wasn't like he had a workbench down there or anything. Aaron wasn't the hobby type.

Her worry began edging over into fear.

She was aware of Aaron's . . . *restlessness* was as good a word for it as any, she supposed. After all, she was his wife. How could she not know? She felt confident that part of it was simply due to his age. There was a reason why the cliché of the middle-aged man suffering through a midlife crisis had become a cliché in the first place. Everything she'd read about it—and all of the friends she'd talked to who were dealing with husbands displaying similar symptoms—advised being understanding, tolerant, sympathetic, and patient. Most male midlife crises ran their course without doing any serious damage to a marriage, provided there were no other problems in the relationship. But if there were other problems, the midlife crisis could make them worse until the marriage was beyond repair.

Her and Aaron's relationship had such a problem: They weren't sexually compatible. She loved Aaron and believed he loved her as well, but their sex drives were almost diametrically opposed. She enjoyed sex and had no trouble climaxing, but she didn't *need* sex very often. The urge came over her once a month, if that often. She wasn't averse to sex at other times, though, but while she did her best to respond to Aaron's overtures, it wasn't always possible for her to accommodate his stronger sexual desires. She was often too busy, too stressed, too tired. Take this morning, for example. She'd meant what she'd said when she told Aaron that they could make love tonight, but when the evening rolled around and the chores were done and the kids in bed, she'd felt drained of energy. She'd hoped Aaron wouldn't remind her of her earlier promise—though she felt guilty for feeling that way. He'd seemed to be tired too, and he hadn't said anything. Kristen had told herself that they could try again tomorrow.

For some time now, she'd been concerned that Aaron was getting tired of her putting him off, though she tried her best not to. He'd become more emotionally distant and short on patience, especially when it came to dealing with Colin. She was afraid he was coming to resent her and that he might end up turning to another woman to get what Kristen wasn't giving him. A *younger* woman who, besides giving him sex, could also make Aaron feel young again. Someone like Patti, who worked in Aaron's office as his vet tech. Kristen was glad that Diane was there to keep on eye on the two of them. Or maybe that little tramp Caroline Langdon down the street. Kristen had seen how Aaron looked at Caroline sometimes when he thought she wasn't paying attention to him.

Though the thought of Aaron sleeping with another woman tore her up inside, she might be able to look the other way *if* the affair didn't last too long, and *if* it was a onetime thing. In the end, it might even be good for their marriage. Aaron could sow a few wild oats, get a last taste of his lost youth, and then they could go on together afterward, their relationship all the stronger for having been tested. But what scared her more than the thought of Aaron straying was the possibility of his leaving her for good. What if he found someone who satisfied him both sexually *and* emotionally? What if he decided to divorce her? What would she do? What would the kids do?

Kristen stood in the kitchen and thought. She wanted to go back upstairs, crawl in bed, pull the cover up to her chin, and cry until she fell asleep once more. But she knew she should go take a look in the garage and see if Aaron's prized Lexus was there. If it was, then that could mean he went for a walk. When they'd first moved here, he'd sometimes gone out on a night walk, especially when the weather was nice, though admittedly he'd never gone out this late. Still, the possibility would give her at least a little hope to cling to. But if his car was gone . . .

She thought of another cliché, that of the husband who says he's going out for cigarettes one night and never comes home. Aaron didn't smoke, but he might well have decided he'd had enough of not getting enough and left her and the kids.

Even if the Lexus isn't there, that doesn't necessarily mean he's gone forever, she told himself.

She looked at the door that led to the garage and

stood there debating for a good five minutes. In the end, she made her choice and started toward the door. She unlocked and opened it, turned on the light, then stepped into the garage. Their Ford Sierra van was there—what Aaron sometimes derisively referred to as their kiddie-mover—but the Lexus was gone. Now she couldn't even pretend that he'd gone out for a walk. She stood there, not wanting to go back inside, because if she did she'd have to admit that something was seriously wrong and try to think of what she should do next. She wasn't ready for that yet. She didn't think she'd ever be ready.

Oh, Aaron . . .

She jumped when the garage-door opener activated. She almost ran inside so Aaron wouldn't see her when he pulled in, wouldn't know that she was aware he'd left and was worried about him. But she needed to see him so badly, and while she wasn't a big believer in fate, perhaps she'd come out here now, when Aaron was returning home, because she was meant to. Whatever was threatening their marriage, it would only get worse if she continued to act as if it wasn't happening. For better or worse, she and Aaron needed to deal with the situation.

So Kristen stood with her arms crossed as the garage door slowly rose, revealing the Lexus's bright headlight beams. She grimaced and put a hand to her face to shield her eyes from the light as the Lexus rolled into the garage. The sound of its finely tuned engine rose in volume, amplified in the garage's confined space. When the car had pulled all the way in the engine cut out, though the headlights remained on. Several seconds passed, and then the garage door began lowering.

Kristen continued to stand by the open kitchen door, shielding her eyes and trying her best to keep a neutral expression on her face. She didn't want to appear either scared or angry, at least not until she had a chance to gauge Aaron's mood. But she couldn't do that until he got out of the damned car. Why was he taking so long? Was he afraid to confront her or maybe working furiously on coming up with a believable lie? She tried to see past the headlights' glare, but all she could make out was a dim silhouette behind the driver's wheel . . . and another in the front passenger seat.

There were two people in the car.

The headlights flicked off, the driver's door opened, and Caroline Langdon got out of the Lexus.

"Hi, Kristen. It's good to see you again." The words were friendly, but the tone was ice-cold.

The passenger door opened and Caroline's husband, Phillip, stepped out. "Howdy, neighbor. Long time, no see."

Kristen was trying to figure out what the hell was going on when she discovered that her earlier assumption was wrong. There weren't just two people in the car; there were four. Two others emerged from the back of the Lexus, a board-shouldered man with a facial tic and a woman with one bloodred eye. Kristen had never seen either of them before. The four started toward her, Caroline and Phillip in the lead.

"We'd hoped to surprise you when you were sleeping," Caroline said.

"But that's okay," Phillip added. "This way will be more fun."

Kristen's instincts screamed a warning and she made a dash for the kitchen door. Unfortunately, she didn't move fast enough. Phillip caught hold of her easily, spun her around, grabbed hold of her wrists with one hand, and then shoved them against the small of her back. The pain made her draw in a hiss of breath, but before she could let it out, Phillip's other hand clamped over her mouth. She struggled, trying to break free of his grip, but Phillip was too strong.

Caroline stepped close to Kristen, leaned forward, and spoke softly in her ear. "I've always thought you were attractive, Kristen. I can't wait to taste you." She slid her tongue into Kristen's ear and slowly circled it around. Kristen shuddered in revulsion and Phillip laughed.

The other man, the one with the facial tic, said, "You two stay here. Gillian and I will go inside and get the kids." The man and the woman stepped around the three of them and entered Kristen's house through the open door.

Kristen fought harder to get away from Phillip. Whatever these people wanted, whatever they might have done to her husband, she couldn't let them harm her children. But as she struggled, Caroline reached out with both hands, pinched her nipples through the fabric of her robe, and twisted hard. Phillip's hand muffled Kristen's cry of pain.

"Don't resist," Caroline said.

"Unless it turns you on," Phillip amended. "Then by all means, go ahead. I know *I* like it."

Caroline continued. "We're not going to hurt you. We're just going to use you as bait." Caroline still had hold of Kristen's nipples, and now she began to roll them roughly between her forefingers and thumbs. "Your husband has been a very naughty boy, Kristen. Now, normally we like naughty . . ."

"We do indeed," Phillip said. He pressed his crotch against the back of Kristen's leg and she could feel his erection through his pants.

"But Aaron's been *especially* naughty," Caroline said. "He needs to be punished, but we don't know where he is. We need something to make him come back to us."

Phillip began grinding his cock against her leg. "Something like you and your kids."

Caroline smiled, then went back to work on Kristen's ear while her husband continued dry-humping their captive's leg. Unable to do anything else, Kristen began to cry.

Aaron stumbled and nearly fell as he negotiated the house's sunken front porch. But he managed to maintain his footing, open the front door—which wasn't locked, thank God—and run inside. He immediately shut the door behind him and threw the dead bolt. A second later, something heavy slammed into the door, and Aaron knew his pursuers had caught up with him.

"Come out of there, Aaron!" Gerald yelled. He pounded his fist on the door three times in rapid succession, almost as if he were knocking. "You need to tell us what you know!"

"Fuck off, you sick son of a bitch!" Aaron shouted.

"I don't care about you, Penumbra, or the goddamned Overshadow! Just leave me the fuck alone!"

Gerald started pounding on the door again, harder this time. Aaron backed away, wishing he had a cell phone so he could call the police, but he hated carrying his cell around and usually left it in the glove box of his Lexus. No 911 calls for him. Unless . . .

A much louder crash came from the door, and Aaron guessed Gerald had thrown the full weight of his considerable bulk at it. He knew a simple dead bolt wouldn't hold out against Gerald for long, and there was an excellent chance the man's fellow Dements were right now searching for other ways into the house. Aaron knew he couldn't afford to stand around. He turned and started making his way through the house. It was dark and precious little light filtered in from outside. But Aaron's enhanced night vision was enough to allow him to discern the basic layout of the house. Even so, he kept his hand on the wall to guide himself as he moved forward.

The house appeared to have been deserted for some time. Most of the furniture had been draped with sheets, while other pieces had been overturned or were in sorry states of disrepair. The floors were littered with trash, and Aaron had to move carefully. Most of it appeared to be fast-food wrappers from a variety of restaurants, but there were occasional pieces of bone and bits of meat—rotting meat from the smell and the flies. Aaron wanted to believe the meat and bones weren't human, but he saw no reason to delude himself at this point. He assumed this house, the barn, and the surrounding property were part of Caroline's parents' real estate holdings, as were the Valley View Shopping Center and the land where the pit was located. And judging from the condition of the interior, Aaron guessed this was where the Dements came to kick back and take a load off after a hard day of making collage art out of dead bodies. Aaron wondered if Caroline was aware this place existed. Probably not, he decided, or else she and the other Insiders would've come here by now, captured the Dements, and given them to the Overshadow.

Aaron was heading toward what he hoped was the kitchen. Since the house had running water and electricity—witness both the fluorescent light pole and the work lights in the barn—then there was a chance that there might be a working phone, too. Not much of a chance: The water probably came from a well and the electricity from a portable generator. The Dements were crazy, but they were also cunning. They'd avoided being caught by Caroline and the others, not to mention the police, while they went about creating their obscene "offering" to the Overshadow. It was possible they'd found a way to keep a working phone line out here. Maybe not likely, but possible. And right now that possibility was all he had.

He found the kitchen at the back of the house. The air was thick with a truly horrendous stink, but after smelling the hellish stench of the Tapestry, this was like inhaling the aroma of prize roses. The trash was piled up in mounds on the floor here, and the sink was filled with a foul-smelling brackish liquid that, if it ever was water, wasn't anymore. Roaches scuttled away at his approach, along with more than a few mice and rats. But Aaron was a vet, and vermin didn't bother him. Hell, after what he'd seen tonight, he wondered if anything would ever truly bother him again.

There was a back door. Aaron checked and found it unlocked; a situation he quickly remedied. No dead bolt here, just an ordinary lock built into the doorknob. He hoped it would hold long enough. He looked around the kitchen then, hoping to find a phone mounted on a wall. That was where his family had kept their phone when he'd been a kid, and the house seemed old enough to be the same way. There'd be no wireless phones or cells here.

"And just who do you think you're going to call?"

There—mounted on the wall next to the refrigerator—was an old-style black rotary dial phone.

Aaron started toward it, but his father said, "At least get some kind of weapon first in case those lunatics manage to get in before your fingers are finished doing the walking."

Aaron glanced in his father's direction. The old man was sitting at the kitchen table. The surface was piled with soiled paper plates. Numerous tiny scavengers skittered across the plates as they searched for even the smallest scrap of deliciously rotten nourishment. Martin seemed not to notice them.

"Good idea," Aaron acknowledged. He hurried to the counter near the stove and began rummaging through drawers. It only took him a moment to find a large, wicked-looking butcher knife. The blade was stained—with what, Aaron didn't want to know—but it looked sharp enough to do the job. Aaron gripped the handle tight in his right hand and walked over to the phone. He took the receiver off the hook, put it to his ear, and was equally surprised and relieved to hear a dial tone. He tucked the receiver into the crook of his neck and started dealing with his free hand, 911.

"You're wasting your time," the apparition of Martin Rittinger said. "You should be outside where you can run and hide."

"They have to be stopped, Dad. Didn't you see that damned thing in the barn? Don't you realize how many people they killed to make it? And don't think they'll ever stop, because they won't. They can't." Aaron might've said more, but someone on the other end picked up and asked him to state the nature of his emergency.

"People have been murdered and their bodies left in a barn. The address is 1783 Hoke Road. Please hurry." Aaron hung up before the police dispatcher could ask him any questions.

"So you caught the address when Gerald pulled into the driveway," Martin said.

Aaron nodded. "I saw a road sign along the way, and the number was painted on the mailbox. It was faint, but I could read it."

"So now what are you going to do?"

Before Aaron could answer his father, someone started pounding on the back door. The blows weren't as loud as Gerald's, so Aaron knew it was one of the other Dements. Maybe Bone-Braids or Caroline's dad.

"Now I try to avoid the Dements while I wait for the cops to get here. After I make one more call." He turned back to the phone, picked up the receiver once more, and began dialing again.

"Don't be an idiot, son. You've been lucky so far, but these old doors won't keep them out forever."

"I know, but there's a good chance I may not live through the night. I need to talk to Kristen one last time, just in case I don't make it."

Aaron thought his father might protest again, tell him that he was allowing sentiment to override his common sense. But all his father said was, "I understand." And when Aaron glanced over at the kitchen table, Martin Rittinger was no longer there.

Aaron finished dialing and listened for the ringing of his home phone. More pounding on the door then, louder this time, and Aaron—still holding the butcher knife—pressed the heel of his left hand over his other ear to shut out the noise.

One ring . . . two . . . three . . .

They kept a phone on the nightstand next to their bed, and though Aaron wasn't sure of the exact time, he was confident Kristen would still be asleep.

Four rings . . . five . . .

He mentally urged her to pick up, as if he could send thought waves to his wife over the phone line and wake her. He just wanted to hear the sound of her voice once more, tell her that he loved her and the kids, tell her how very sorry he was.

Five rings, six, followed by a click.

"Hello, Kristen? It's me, I—" He broke off as he realized the answering machine had kicked in. He expected to hear the sound of his voice since he was the one who'd recorded the outgoing message. Kristen got performance anxiety whenever she tried to make one. But the voice he heard was a woman's, and it didn't belong to Kristen.

"—paid a visit to your darling family. They were surprised to see us but were gracious enough to forgive the lateness of the hour. They also did us the honor of accepting an invitation to our favorite playground. We'll all be waiting for you there. Hope you can join us. Oh, and by the way, don't bother stopping here to check if I'm telling the truth. All you'll find is a note saying the same thing I've just told you. I have faith that you *will* join us, love. You aren't real good with the delayed gratification thing. It's one of your most delightful qualities. See you soon." Then came the sound of smacking lips, as if Caroline were giving him a kiss, followed by a beep. Aaron paused for a moment and then hung up.

It was all his fault. Kristen, Colin, and Lindsay had been abducted by Caroline and the others, all because he'd been foolish enough—and selfish enough—to become involved with that group of lunatics. The question before him now was what, if anything, he could do to save his family. If he did as Caroline said and went to Penumbra, he was certain they'd kill him, probably by sacrificing him to the Overshadow, and they'd do the same to Kristen and the kids. He had to come up with an alternative plan, and he had to do it fast before—

He heard a crash as the front door gave way, followed by the pounding of feet as people ran through the house toward the kitchen. Before they could reach him, the back door exploded inward, and Caroline's father stepped inside, holding the sledgehammer he'd used to break in. Bone-Braids followed him inside. Aaron turned and saw Gerald and Toothless enter from the outer hall. He was trapped. He gripped the handle of the butcher knife tight. Aside from Caroline's dad, none of the Dements carried any weapons. He considered fighting his way out, and he almost gave it a shot, but a simple realization stopped him. If he wanted to save Kristen and the kids, he was going to need help—and if Caroline and the other Insiders believed that he was working with the Dements, then maybe he should go ahead and do so.

He turned to face Gerald, hoping the man was so insane he'd forget Aaron's earlier protests that he knew nothing of value to them. "You brought me here to tell you what I know about Penumbra, but that's not why I came. I bring you a message from the Overshadow itself."

Aaron paused to see if the Dements were buying it. They were frowning, but none advanced toward him. He'd gotten their attention.

"The Overshadow is aware of your great offering. You have not only proven yourself worthy of returning to Penumbra, you've proven yourselves *more* worthy of being its caretakers than those who cast you out. The Overshadow wishes you to reclaim Penumbra for yourselves. The time for war has come, and the Overshadow has sent me to lead you into battle. Are you prepared to follow me?"

Aaron held his breath while he waited to see whether the Dements would believe his bullshit or would come rushing at him to tear him to shreds with their hands and teeth. Several moments went by, and then finally Caroline's father grinned.

"We are," he said.

CHAPTER SEVENTEEN

"It'll be morning soon."

Aaron glanced over at Gerald. The man rubbed his bald head with one hand while he steered the Volkswagen with the other. The Beetle didn't have a functioning dashboard clock, and the Dement didn't wear a watch. Aaron looked out the windshield, but he detected no trace of the coming dawn: Clouds had rolled in and the sky appeared black as pitch. Maybe Gerald reckoned time using some sort of primitive instinct. If so, Aaron wished he possessed a similar faculty. Right now, he wasn't confident the dawn would ever come.

They were driving on Route 8, heading for town. Behind them, riding in an ancient beat-up green Oldsmobile, followed the rest of the Dements. Caroline's father was driving, and though the man—whose name was Hayden—was insane, he handled the vehicle well enough. Which was a good thing because the car was so old that ever since they'd left the Homestead, Aaron had been waiting for the death trap to blow a tire, throw a rod, or drop its transmission.

Maybe all three. But so far the Olds had kept up with the Beetle, and with some luck it might make it all the way to the Valley View Shopping Center. Aaron hoped so. They could never fit everyone inside Gerald's VW if the Olds broke down.

"At least you had room for me," Martin Rittinger said from the backseat.

Aaron gave Gerald a quick look. He wouldn't have been surprised if the man was crazy enough to somehow perceive Martin. But the Dement kept driving, his gaze focused on the road ahead as he continued rubbing his raw scalp. He'd started rubbing it the moment they drove away from the farm and hadn't stopped since. Obviously, he was both excited and nervous about the battle to come. Aaron wondered that if Gerald kept rubbing, would he finally wear away the last of his scalp and reveal the white bone of the skull underneath?

Not that Aaron could blame Gerald. He was pretty nervous himself. And his head still itched from having been smeared with the viscous goo in the pit. Watching Gerald rub his scalp just made Aaron's itch all the more. It took a huge effort of will to keep from scratching. He guessed he'd already lost half his own hair, and he'd rather not lose anymore if he could avoid it. He decided not to worry about it; he had slightly more important things to concern him, like whether he'd survive the night.

The interior of the VW was dark. A few moments after getting into the car, Aaron had rammed his fist into the flickering dome light and broken its plastic cover, along with the tiny lightbulb inside. They couldn't afford to have the malfunctioning dome light draw attention to them as they approached Penumbra. Besides, the goddamned flickering thing annoyed the piss out of Aaron.

He reached up and brushed some stray strands of fallen hair off his shoulder. He was no longer shirtless or shoeless. The Dements had provided him with a filthy flannel shirt and a pair of worn sneakers with holes in them. Nasty, but serviceable. The cloth—which had likely once belonged to one of the Dements' victims—stank and the shirt made his chest and back itch almost as bad as his scalp. But he didn't pay much attention to this sensation, and he avoided scratching, afraid that once he got started, he wouldn't stop until he'd clawed deep furrows in his flesh.

He tried not to think about Kristen and the kids, but it was impossible, like when someone tells you to do your best not to think of a polar bear. The act of trying not to think about a specific thing only focuses your mind on that thing even more. He wondered how Kristen, Colin, and Lindsay were doing right now. Were they scared or injured? Were they even still alive? Aaron closed his eyes and tried reaching out to them mentally. He'd never experienced any kind of psychic communication before, didn't know if such a thing was even possible. But when people had strong, deep connections, it seemed only logical that those connections would remain no matter how far apart the people should be. But though Aaron groped about in the darkness of his own mind, he felt not the slightest psychic trace of his family.

"Please, God, I have to know if they're okay," he whispered.

But God—assuming there were any gods besides the dark thing in the back room of Penumbra—must not have been listening because Aaron still sensed nothing. He knew that didn't mean his family had been killed, but it gave him no reason to suspect they still lived, either. Caroline and the other Insiders could be damned cold-blooded when the occasion demanded it. His family might already be dead, and he might be joining them soon.

The VW rolled past the NOW ENTERING PTOLEMY sign, and as the car continued shortening the distance between the city limits and the shopping center, it began to rain. Not very hard, but steady, the kind of soaking rain that comes as a blessing to dry, browning lawns during summer months in southwest Ohio. Gerald activated the Beetle's windshield wipers. Only the one on the driver's side worked; the other flopped uselessly, merely smearing water around on Aaron's side of the windshield. As Aaron viewed the world through a rippling distortion of water, he reached up and—without realizing it—rubbed the top of his itchy head, sending strands of dead hair drifting down around him.

Several moments later, they approached the Valley View Shopping Center from the north. Penumbra's front door faced south, and there was a high wooden fence around the back of the strip mall, blocking the view from the rear door. As further insurance that they wouldn't be seen, Gerald killed the VW's headlights before pulling into the parking lot. Behind them, Caroline's father did the same as he followed the Beetle into the lot. The drivers pulled over to the side of the strip mall, which happened to be the east-facing outer wall of Deja Brew. They parked side by side and cut their engines. Aaron released a nervous breath of air. If everything had gone well, the Insiders were unaware of their arrival.

"*If* is a mighty small word that can cause mighty big problems," Martin said from the VW's backseat.

I'm well aware that our attempts at stealth might prove useless—after all, this is *a trap and the Insiders know I'm coming—but we need any advantage we can get, even if all we achieve is momentary surprise.*

Martin was silent, and Aaron smiled. It seemed like he'd managed to shut up the old man for a change.

Aaron and his lunatic allies climbed out of their vehicles and gathered on the sidewalk beneath the building's overhang to get out of the rain. Not that a shower would hurt his aromatic new friends, Aaron thought. Each of them was armed. Aaron gripped the butcher knife he'd found in the ruined farmhouse; Caroline's father held the sledgehammer he'd used to break into the farmhouse's kitchen; Toothless carried a double-barreled shotgun; and Bone-Braids had a rusty, blood-encrusted hand scythe. Gerald won the award for nastiest weapon, though: a baseball bat with razor blades embedded in its wooden surface. Aaron assumed Gerald had made it himself; it wasn't exactly the sort of thing one could buy simply by logging onto Psychos-R-us.com. The razor blades were stained with dried blood, attesting to the weapon's long use. Normally Aaron would've been sickened by seeing the blood, but now the sight made him smile grimly. He hoped Gerald would get the opportunity to add many fresh stains to his nasty little toy tonight.

"Everyone remember the plan?" Aaron asked.

All four Dements nodded, and Aaron said, "All right, let's get to it, then."

Toothless and Bone-Braids headed toward the back of the strip mall, while Aaron, Gerald, and Hayden walked around to the front of Deja Brew. The bar was dark inside, and the parking spaces in front were empty, its patrons long departed. Empty, that is, except for one space where a red Chevy pickup truck with a dented left front quarter panel was parked. Aaron realized that the truck most likely belonged to the not-so-dearly-departed Bryan. Evidently Wyatt hadn't had time to dispose of the dead man's vehicle yet.

Aaron expected to feel something upon seeing Bryan's truck—guilt, sorrow, disgust—but he felt nothing. Maybe he was so focused on saving Kristen and the kids that he didn't have the emotional energy to feel anything else. Maybe he'd experienced so many terrible things tonight that his mind had created an emotional buffer to shield his psyche from further damage.

"Or maybe you're starting to go bug-fuck just like all the others," Martin pointed out.

Aaron glanced over his shoulder and saw his father trailing behind them. Martin was unarmed, but then since he wasn't real, it hardly mattered whether he carried a weapon or not.

Aaron looked forward again. Maybe he *was* dementing. If so, he hoped he'd be able to hold on to his sanity long enough to save his family.

The three of them (four if you counted Martin's apparition) walked slowly and silently, watching the door to Penumbra, waiting for it to swing open and the Insiders to come running out to meet their assault. But the door remained closed. Aaron swept his gaze across the mostly deserted parking lot, checking to see if any of the Insiders were hiding inside cars, waiting to ambush them. But he saw nothing.

As they reached Starbrite Movie and Game Rentals, Aaron examined several vehicles parked nearby. He recognized Caroline's Infiniti and his Lexus—obviously Caroline had driven his car back from the Insiders' dumping ground. But his breath caught in his throat when he saw the copper-colored Ford Sierra van parked next to his car.

"Don't get too excited," his father warned. "They would've needed a vehicle big enough to haul Kristen and the kids back here. It doesn't mean they're all right, any more than Bryan's pickup still being here means he's at the peak of his health."

"I know, I know," Aaron muttered.

"What?" Gerald asked.

"Never mind. I wasn't talking to you."

Gerald and Hayden exchanged glances.

"Congratulations," Martin said. "Two lunatics now think *you're* crazy."

Aaron stared at the van. The parking lot's fluorescent lights lit the vehicle well enough, but the tinted windows made it impossible to see if anyone was inside. Aaron doubted his family was in there—why would they be? They were prisoners of Penumbra, not guests permitted to come and go as they pleased. But he knew he couldn't go on without checking the van.

"Wait here," Aaron told his two companions and

stepped out from underneath the overhang and into the rain. He felt raindrops patter on the newly bald patches on his head, and his borrowed shirt began to get wet. Good. Maybe the water would diminish the stink. He kept his gaze fixed on the van as he drew near it, alert for any sign that it wasn't empty. Several yards before he reached the vehicle, he imagined gripping the side door handle, sliding the door back, and seeing his family's mutilated corpses spill out onto the rain-slick asphalt at his feet. He imagined Caroline and the other Insiders standing in Penumbra's open doorway, laughing at him.

He shot a quick glance back over his shoulder at the fuckle door and saw that it remained closed. He looked back to the van; still no sign of life.

His father called out to him from the sidewalk in front of the video store.

"This doesn't rank very high on the good-idea scale!"

Maybe not, Aaron thought. But he had to do this, had to know whether his family—alive or dead—was inside the van. He ignored his father and continued walking until he reached the Ford Sierra. He looked up and saw the tiny silhouettes of falling raindrops hurtling toward the ground like shadow-rain, their paths backlit by one of the parking lot lights. Even raining as it was, insects clustered around the glowing blue-white bulb atop the gray metal parking light pole. Darting, dipping, they continued giving in to their eternal compulsion to flirt with the death light regardless of the weather.

Aaron hoped the van wasn't locked. Caroline had

taken his keys when she'd driven off in his Lexus. He reached the van and stood before the side door. This was the side where Lindsay usually sat, and though she was a big enough girl to open and close the door herself, she sometimes had trouble closing it all the way. Aaron still opened and closed it for her most of the time. If he opened it now, what would he find? An empty seat with graham cracker crumb residue scattered on the upholstery? Or would he find himself looking into the dead, empty-eyed face of his little girl's corpse?

There was only one way to find out.

He reached out, gripped the door handle with his right hand, and—vision blurring from the rainwater running off his forehead and into his eyes—threw the door open.

"Peekaboo, we see you!"

Trevor and Shari chanted this together in a child's singsong voice. They sat in the middle seats usually occupied by Aaron's kids. The dentist and his wife were both completely naked, giving Aaron another look at Shari's strange puckered-flesh nipples. Trevor bared his silver teeth in a feral smile and held up a wicked-looking stainless steel instrument that was at least nine inches long and which ended in a sharp curved hook.

"How long has it been since your last checkup, Aaron?" Trevor asked. His cock jutted from between his legs, erect and quivering.

Shari giggled. She held a similarly nasty tool, though hers ended in a three-pronged fork, making it look like a miniature trident with tips sharp as needles. "My guess is way too long, hon," she said.

Trevor was closest to Aaron, and he lunged out of his seat and swiped his steel-hooked weapon at Aaron's throat. Aaron jumped backward and nearly slipped on the wet asphalt, but he maintained his balance. Flashing his silver teeth, Trevor climbed out of the van, cock bobbling, and advanced on Aaron, slashing his hooked tool through the air in vicious arcs. Aaron imagined the curved needle tip of the weapon puncturing the skin of his neck, sliding beneath the carotid artery, and tearing it loose in a gushing spray of blood.

Screw this, he thought.

Aaron stopped retreating and as Trevor stepped in for the kill, Aaron brought up his butcher knife to block the man's strike. The dentist howled in pain as his unprotected wrist met the cutting edge of Aaron's blade. Trevor's flesh peeled back like paper and blood jetted from the newly created wound. His fingers sprang open and his hook tool clattered to the asphalt. He pulled his wrist away from the knife in a trailing arc of blood and cradled the wound against his abdomen in an attempt to stanch the bleeding.

He glared at Aaron with eyes full of blazing hatred. "We never should have let you in," he snarled.

"I wish you hadn't." Aaron stepped forward and with a single swift motion slashed his butcher knife across Trevor's throat.

The man's eyes widened in almost comical surprise, and a thick gurgling sound came from his mouth as blood poured out of the throat wound, splashed onto his chest, and ran down to trickle off the tip of his rapidly deflating cock. Trevor took several stagger-steps to his right and then collapsed to the ground. Blood mixed with rainwater pooled around his head, his eyes still wide but now unblinking.

Aaron looked down at Trevor's body. While he'd contributed to Bryan's death, perhaps even was ultimately responsible for it, Aaron hadn't actually killed the man. But Trevor had literally died by Aaron's hand, and self-defense or not, that made Aaron a killer. He thought he should feel something. Self-loathing, guilt, satisfaction, anything. But he felt nothing.

A scream tore through the night, and Aaron whirled around in time to see Shari running toward him, mini-trident raised to strike, face contorted with rage, breasts bouncing. As she ran, her puckered nipples opened and closed like tiny mouths eager to be fed. Aaron knew he should do something to protect himself, but all he did was stand there and watch Shari's nipple mouths gawp open and closed as she ran toward him to avenge her husband.

A flash of motion, and a razor-blade-studded baseball bat smashed into Shari's face. Her body jerked as if an electric current surged through it, and twin high-pitched sounds like the cries of injured birds erupted from her nipple mouths. Shari then fell to the ground and twitched, her face a shredded, pulped ruin. Her breasts continued keening their song of pain.

Gerald held the bat at his side as he looked down upon Shari's spasming form. Blood dripped from the razor blades embedded in his bat, and several of the woman's teeth were stuck in the wood.

"I guess I'll never get to fuck her again," Gerald said sadly. Then he turned to Aaron and put on a brave smile. "But you can't make an egg without breaking a few omelets, right?"

The pain song of the nipple mouths continued, high and mournful. Caroline's father stepped up, raised his sledgehammer, and brought it down on Shari's forehead. There was a hollow, wet sound like a melon imploding, and the nipples fell silent.

Hayden shuddered. "That noise goes right up and down your spine, doesn't it?"

Aaron swallowed to keep his gorge from rising and turned to look in Penumbra's direction. He expected to see that the fuckle door was wide open and the surviving Insiders were running toward them, weapons in their hands and death in their eyes. But the door remained closed.

Aaron frowned. Why lay a trap and not take advantage of it once it was sprung? While Trevor and Shari had failed to kill Aaron, they'd managed to distract him long enough for the other Insiders to attack.

"They're crazy, remember?" Martin Rittinger stood at his son's side. Despite the rain coming down, he appeared perfectly dry. That was one of the benefits to being a hallucination, Aaron supposed. You didn't have to worry about minor inconveniences such as getting wet in the rain. "You can't expect them to use strategy . . . at least, not a sane one."

Point taken, Aaron thought. Out loud, he said, "If

the Insiders didn't know we were coming before, they certainly do now. I guess that means we don't have to bother trying to be sneaky anymore."

Gerald raised his gore-smeared bat in the air and let out a whoop.

"All right! Let's go break that fucking door down!" He started running toward Penumbra's entrance as fast his bulk allowed.

Caroline's father grinned, rainwater trickling through the cracks and fissures of his scarred face like tiny rivers. "Sounds like a plan to me!" Hayden gripped the hand of his sledgehammer tight and headed off after Gerald, his thinner frame allowing him to move faster than the much fatter man, despite his advanced age.

Aaron reached up to scratch his head and took a deep breath. "Well, Dad, I guess this is it."

"Guess so."

Father and son started across the rain-splashed parking lot toward the fuckle door.

"Is this the right door? I mean, it *looks* like the right one, but it's been a long time since either of us has been back here. If we were looking for the front door, no problem, right? But here all the doors look the same."

Meredith didn't respond, for she knew Ned didn't really expect her to. He had a tendency to babble whenever he was nervous or excited. It was simply his way of relieving stress. Still, if he kept it up much longer, she just might jam the tip of her hand scythe up his ass and with a few precise cuts, release his intestines to fall to the asphalt in a mound of steaming coils.

The mental image made her smile, and with her free hand she reached up to caress one of the bone shards woven into her braids. She had seventeen shards in all—eight on her left side, nine on her right. Each was taken from a particularly interesting guest they'd brought to the Homestead. This shard—left braid, fourth from the bottom—had once been the tailbone of a child she'd snatched from a grocery store parking lot after the girl's mother had left her in their unlocked car while she ran inside for a pack of cigarettes. Stupid cow. What Meredith had found so intriguing about the girl was that she hadn't cried, hadn't uttered a single sound. Not even when they began to make the first cut. A strong child, a precious one, and Meredith was proud to honor her by wearing a piece of the girl in one of her braids. Sometimes, if she listened closely enough, she thought she could hear the sweetmeat, along with the others whose bones she wore, whispering to her. But try as she might, she'd never been able to make out what they were saying.

Funny. For so many years, she'd thought of little save returning to Penumbra. She wasn't one of the founders like Hayden was, but she'd joined not long after he and his wife had established their club. But now that she was closer to Penumbra than she'd been since the day she'd been cast out, she found herself thinking about the many dark delights she'd found at the Homestead over the years. Would it really be worth giving all that up just to experience the cold blessing of the Overshadow's touch once more?

A shudder of pleasure ran through her body, and her vagina quivered in excitement.

Yes, she decided. *Yes, it would.*

"This is it," Ned pronounced. "I'm sure of it!"

They'd stopped at a gray metal door that looked exactly the same as the others they'd already passed, lit by a small fluorescent light bolted to the wall above. But though there was nothing to mark it visually as Penumbra's rear door, Meredith felt a tingling deep within her uterus and her nipples became painfully erect. Ned was right; this *was* it.

They stood in the rain, weapons held ready, and looked at the door for a number of seconds before Ned the nervous talker broke the brief silence.

"Okay, we're here. What it is again that we're supposed to do?"

Meredith started to berate Ned for his abysmal memory, but she stopped herself. Her memory was hardly much better than his. Oh, there were some things she recalled with absolute crystal clarity. Like the little sweetmeat whose tailbone adorned her left braid. But many other things were so difficult to recall, and it seemed that she too couldn't remember what they were supposed to do now. Still, she felt confident they could puzzle it out. Before being recruited for Penumbra by Hayden and the others who'd been members at the time, Meredith had worked as an elementary school librarian. She'd prided herself on her sensible, logical mind back then, and while it had been far too long since she'd used these qualities, she felt certain they were still there, somewhere in the chaotic soup that served as her brain.

"There are only two reasons for us to be back here," she said. "Either we're supposed to try and get in and surprise the Insiders by attacking from the rear, or we're here to make sure that when the others do their thing out front, none of the Insiders escape by this route."

Ned looked her blankly for a moment, and she knew he was struggling to process what she'd just said. Finally, he nodded. "Sounds reasonable to me. But which do we choose? Break and enter or stand guard?"

Meredith hoped some instinct would pull her in the proper direction, but it didn't happen. She had no more idea what to do now than she'd had a moment ago. Perhaps even less.

"You forgot a third choice," said a female voice from the closest Dumpster. "You can die."

Meredith spun around as the woman stepped out from behind the Dumpster where she'd been hiding. She was followed by a short, potbellied man who waved sheepishly as he stepped into view. Both were dressed in casual clothes, and the woman had one eye that was half red, while the man's nose trickled a constant thin stream of blood. But the detail that stuck out most strongly to Meredith was the stainless steel mixing bowl the red-eyed woman held in her hands. The bowl was filled almost to the rim with a fluid that Meredith was certain couldn't be water. She raised her hand scythe at the same instant that Ned cocked his shotgun.

"Here," the red-eyed woman said as she stepped forward. "I made this special for you." She flung the contents of the bowl into the faces of the two Dements.

The liquid struck Meredith in the face and burned her eyes like chemical flame. The pain was so intense that it drove all other thoughts from her mind. Instinctively, she reached up to touch her eyes, but unfortunately for her she still held the small scythe in her right hand. The blade's pointed tip plunged into her right eye, causing it to pop like a tiny white flesh balloon filled with viscous jelly.

Meredith's scream of agony was so loud that she almost didn't hear the sound of Ned's shotgun firing. If his eyes had been splashed with even half the amount of chemicals she'd been hit with, he was hurting bad. She didn't expect the shotgun blast to hit either of the two Insiders, not as poor as Ned's aim had surely been. But one of the two—the chubby man—cried out in shock as much as pain. She then heard the sound of Ned's shotgun hitting the ground, followed by hitching breaths as he began sobbing.

"God, it *burns!*"

"Of course it does," the red-eyed woman said. "One of the good thing about being an ophthamologist is that you know all sorts of nasty chemicals that can damage eyes."

With one eye seared by chemicals and the other a bloody mess, Meredith couldn't see but she heard the woman approach. She'd released her grip on the hand scythe when she'd accidentally plunged the blade into her eye, and it protruded from the socket like some nightmarish prosthesis. Now she took hold of the handle once again, not because she needed a weapon to defend herself against Red-Eye, but simply because it hurt so damned much that she wanted the fucking thing out *now*.

Overshadow, give me strength.

She started to pull the scythe out, heard the wet sucking sound of metal withdrawing from her bloody eye socket. But it hurt even more than it had going in, and she jerked her hand away.

"Having some trouble? Let me help."

Meredith didn't have to see to know what the woman intended to do. She started to back away, hands raised to fend off her attacker, but her head was yanked forward with a sharp tug, and she screamed even louder than before as fresh agony blazed where her right eye had once been. She sensed more than heard the hiss as the scythe cut through the air, and then the blade sliced through her throat, nearly decapitating her.

Meredith was still alive when she started to collapse, but as the last dregs of her misbegotten life drained away, for the first and last time she heard clearly the whispers coming from the bones braided into her hair. There were variations in word choice and phrasing, but they all communicated the same concept. *Die, bitch!*

And no voice whispered this with more venomous hatred than one that had once belonged to a little girl stolen from a grocery parking lot.

Gillian watched the female Dement fall to the ground and lie still. Blood continued to pour from the second mouth Gillian had carved into the woman's throat, spreading out from her head and surrounding it like a widening black halo.

She smiled. "That was fun." She heard sobbing and saw that the other Dement, the male, had fallen to his knees and covered his chemically seared eyes with his hands. Gillian held the blood-smeared scythe in one hand and the empty mixing bowl in the other. She dropped the bowl and it hit the asphalt with a loud metallic clang. Then she walked over to the male Dement and cut his throat with the hand scythe. It might have been her imagination, but the gasp that escaped his mouth as he fell over onto his side seemed almost like a sigh of gratitude.

She heard moaning then, coming from behind her. Still holding on to the scythe—which was now twice as bloody as before—she turned and walked back to Spencer. He lay on the ground next to the Dumpster, his left arm little more than shredded meat clinging loosely to the bone. She looked down at him and shook her head in disgust.

"Christ, Spencer . . . didn't you ever learn to duck?"

Spencer's breathing was rapid and his eyes wide with terror.

"Please, Gillian . . . call an ambulance. I need to get to a hospital." He reached out toward her with his good hand.

She laughed. "You're kidding, right?"

Spencer continued pleading with her, his voice becoming increasingly shrill as she stepped toward him. She knelt down and with a single swift motion silenced him forever. She paused to wipe the scythe off on Spencer's clothes before heading toward Penumbra's rear entrance. She considered retrieving the shotgun, but decided against it. The hand scythe was more her style. She didn't worry about leaving the bodies behind; they could be disposed of later. Right now there was still more fun to be had inside.

CHAPTER EIGHTEEN

Aaron heard the gunshot before they'd crossed half the distance to the fuckle door. Then he heard the screaming. He felt a twinge of guilt at what might be happening to Bone-Braids and Toothless, but only a twinge. This was the reason he'd convinced the Dements to come with him, right? To serve as diversions and cannon fodder. He knew it was cold-blooded of him: The Dements might be crazy murderous bastards, but they were still human. He didn't care, though. He had to save his family; nothing else mattered.

He continued toward the door at a jog, quickly catching up to Gerald and Hayden. Neither seemed to have heard the screams, or maybe they had and simply weren't bothered by them. Perhaps the Dements had heard so many screams during the creation of their Tapestry that the sound no longer meant anything to them.

They had to move fast. The surviving Insiders would be on high alert now. Hopefully, they'd be too busy dealing with Bone-Braids and Toothless to guard the front door.

"You realize how insane this all is, don't you?"

Aaron's father now stood to the right of the fuckle door. Aaron hadn't seen him move from where he'd last been standing, but Aaron supposed unreal people could move in unreal ways.

"You're not some kind of fucking commando," Martin Rittinger said. "You're just a goddamned vet. You're not going to be able to break in, and even if you do, you won't be able to rescue Kristen and the kids. All you're going to do is get the four of you killed."

Aaron increased his pace until he was running full out. He heard Gerald and Caroline's father struggling to keep up, but he forgot about them.

"You know something, Dad?" Aaron shouted. "I've had more than enough of your bullshit to last a lifetime!"

He ran onto the sidewalk in front of the strip mall, heading for his father, gripping the handle of the butcher knife so tight it hurt. Aaron's dad made no move to protect himself, didn't raise his hands to ward off the blow, didn't step to one side or the other to avoid being stabbed. Martin Rittinger simply stood still and allowed his son to ram the knife blade into his chest.

Aaron looked into his father's eyes, but he saw no emotion in them. No anger, no surprise, no regret and—worst of all—no approval or pride.

A jolt ran through Aaron's hand and up his arm as the butcher knife's blade struck brick and snapped off the wooden handle. The blade clattered to the sidewalk, point blunted and useless. Aaron stared at the chip in the wall where the knife had struck. There was no blood, no sign that Martin Rittinger had ever stood here at all. His father was gone—perhaps for good this time.

As his two companions caught up to Aaron—chests heaving, mouths gulping air—he held out his hand toward Caroline's father.

"Do you mind if I borrow your hammer?"

"Only if you promise not to try to kill the wall with it," Hayden said.

Aaron nodded. As the old man handed over the sledge, Aaron noticed that strands of Shari's hair were stuck in the blood-paste smeared onto the hammer's head. He resisted an impulse to pick the hairs off the hammer before stepping in front of the fuckle door. He took aim, lifted the hammer, and brought it crashing down on the doorknob. The metal knob snapped off, hit the concrete, and bounced away. Aaron paused only a second before swinging the sledge back sideways and then slamming it against the round opening where the knob had been. The fuckle door flew open, and light spilled out from inside. Penumbra had been breached.

Aaron started to go in, but before he could take a step, Caroline's father shoved him aside with surprising strength for a man of his years.

"I'm home!" Hayden shouted and ran through the open doorway. As he passed by, Aaron thought he saw the scars on the man's face pulsing with a deep crimson color, reflecting his excitement.

Some instinct prompted Aaron to make a grab for Hayden, to get hold of his shirt and pull him back. But as Aaron reached out, he heard the explosive crack of a gunshot, and Caroline's father flew backward. The man hit the floor, landing halfway across Penumbra's threshold. The scar tissue covering his forehead had a round bloody hole in it, dead center, and even as Aaron stepped out of the doorway to avoid getting shot, a distant part of his mind couldn't help but be impressed with Wyatt's aim.

"Gotcha, motherfucker!" Wyatt crowed from inside the club. "And it was pretty fuckin' dumb of you to bash in the door like that. We left the damned thing unlocked!"

Aaron tried to think of a way to distract Wyatt so they could get inside and attack. If he stepped into the doorway and hurled the sledgehammer in Wyatt's general direction—

But before Aaron could fully formulate his next move, Gerald let out a bellow of rage and rushed through the doorway, stepping on Hayden's chest as he went. The old man was too dead to protest. Another shot exploded, followed by men shouting. Gerald, Wyatt, and Phillip too, Aaron guessed. He'd only heard the next sound for the first time a few minutes ago, but there was no mistaking it: a baseball bat covered in razor blades being slammed into someone's face.

Aaron decided that was his cue. Holding tight to the sledge, he hurried through the doorway, trying not to think about how it felt to step on a dead body as he made his way inside.

Wyatt was on his hands and knees in the middle of the room, blood streaming from his face and pattering to the floor like thick crimson rain. His breath came in ragged, wet gasps, and there was a soft keening sound, as if he were trying to cry but no longer possessed the anatomical equipment to do so. Wyatt's gun—a 9mm, Aaron guessed, though he was far from a weapons expert—lay on the floor nearby. Gerald stood over Wyatt, his razor bat dripping with fresh gore. The Dement had a maniacal grin on his face as he gazed down upon his bloody handiwork, and he rubbed his bald scalp vigorously with his free hand, almost as if it were the tip of his cock and he were masturbating. The Dement appeared unwounded, and Aaron assumed Wyatt's second shot had missed its target. Phillip stood off to the side, looking back and forth between Gerald and Wyatt, as if he couldn't quite bring himself to believe that everything had gone to shit for the Insiders so fast, and he wasn't sure what to do about it. He saw Aaron then, and the confusion left his face to be replaced by grim determination. His gaze then flicked to Wyatt's gun and he lunged for it.

Aaron ran forward, hoping to beat the other man to the weapon, but Phillip had gotten the jump on him. Before he was halfway to the gun, Aaron knew Phillip would reach it first.

Gerald saw Phillip make his move, and he swung his razor bat one-handed toward the Insider, the motion sending an arc of blood flying from the weapon's blades. But Phillip was moving too fast, and Gerald's aim was off, and the razor bat missed the Insider. Phillip reached the 9mm, snatched it off the ground, and aimed it at Aaron. Without thinking, Aaron hurled the sledgehammer toward the man, and the head struck him in the sternum just as he fired. Aaron expected to feel a bullet penetrate his flesh, but the hammer blow had spoiled Phillip's aim and the bullet went wide. The sledge's impact knocked Phillip onto his back, and the gun flew from his hand and skittered across the floor.

Aaron stepped over Phillip, who now lay on his back staring up at the ceiling, fighting to draw breath into his shattered chest. Aaron bent down and picked up the sledgehammer. He then stood over Phillip and held the hammer upside down by the handle and dangled it over the man's face.

"Where's my family? Are they in the back room? Are they safe? Tell me or I'll drop it."

Phillip's eyes were wide with fear as he looked up at the iron hammer hovering over his face. His mouth opened and closed, like a fish struggling to breathe out of water, but no sound came out.

Aaron released his grip on the hammer and the head smashed Phillip's nose to a bloody pulp. An agonized hiss of air escaped Phillip's throat, the best his damaged chest could do to produce a cry of pain.

Aaron picked up the hammer and held it over Phillip's face once more.

"I'll ask you one more time: Where's my family?"

Gerald stepped to Aaron's side. "He's not going to be able to answer you if he can't talk." The Dement's scalp was smeared with blood, the result of his too-vigorous rubbing. "I've learned a few things about hurting folks at the Homestead over the years. Why don't you let me—"

Gerald didn't get to finish his offer, though. A gunshot roared and the Dement's head jerked to the side as a bullet bored into his skull. The razor bat slid from his limp fingers and fell to the floor, and Gerald followed immediately after, dead.

Aaron turned to see Wyatt on his knees, eyes blazing through a mask of blood, the 9mm gripped with both hands. Wyatt trained the gun on Aaron, but Aaron swung his sledgehammer before the cop could fire. Wyatt slumped to the ground, the top half of his head sheared off by Aaron's hammer blow.

Aaron's pulse thrummed in his ears, and with every breath it felt as if electricity surged through his body. He remembered what it had felt like when he'd slammed Bryan against the wall. He'd felt strong, powerful. He felt the same way now, only ten times more so. He knew the Overshadow's touch had done this to him, awakened a love of violence that he'd never known before. But he didn't care about what had happened to him. All he cared about was saving his family, and if he had to become a monster to help them, then so be it. He dropped the hammer to the floor and pried the 9mm from Wyatt's dead fingers. Aaron had never fired a pistol before, but he figured he could make do.

He turned back toward Phillip. But before he could threaten the man with the 9mm, Phillip pointed toward the rear of the club. Aaron looked in the direction he indicated and saw that the door to the Overshadow's chamber was open, and Caroline stood in the doorway.

"Your family is in here, Aaron."

He trained the 9mm on Caroline, the gun steady in his grip. She stepped forward as if nothing was wrong. She surveyed the carnage around her with a connoisseur's eye. "I'm impressed. I didn't think you had it in you."

She walked over to Phillip and looked down at her husband. He still lived, but his face was gray from lack of oxygen. She knelt at his side and stroked his cheek with the back of her fingers. "Sorry about this, hon, but you fucked up."

She pinched his nostrils closed with a thumb and forefinger, then leaned over and sealed her lips against him. It only took a few moments more for Phillip to die.

Aaron knew he should forget about Caroline, should run into the back room and check on his family, but he couldn't take his gaze off Caroline. Was it because that despite everything that had happened he still wanted her? Or did his new lust for violence keep him rooted to the spot so he didn't miss Phillip's death? Or perhaps now that the way was clear he couldn't bring himself to go in back and look for fear of what he might find. Whichever the case, he stood and watched, but he didn't lower his gun.

"Tell me they're all right, Caroline."

She stood. "Gillian's looking after them, don't worry." She started walking toward Aaron, but then she saw her father lying across the front door's threshold and she stopped.

"Is that . . ." She went over to him, walking at what seemed a deliberately calm pace, but Aaron could see she was trembling. "It is, isn't it? My daddy." She gazed down upon Hayden's body, and Aaron thought she might bend over to touch him, but she didn't.

"After he . . . left Penumbra, I never heard from him again. I'd come to think he'd died, either by his own hand or old age. I never considered that he'd joined the Dements."

"He didn't just join them," Aaron said. He still held the gun on Caroline, and his back was now turned on the door to the Overshadow's chamber. "He was their founder and leader, just as he was here."

A small smile crossed Caroline's lips. "At least he made it back inside, if only partway."

Aaron was about to reply, but then the hair on the back of his neck stood up. He spun around and fired.

Gillian held Bone-Braids's hand scythe. She'd sneaked up on Aaron and had been in the process of raising the weapon to strike. Aaron's shot had struck her crimson-tinted eye, but instead of being reduced to jelly, the organ shattered as if it were made of glass and a shaft of bright red light shone forth. Gillian's body jerked as if she were being electrocuted, and the beam stabbed past Caroline's head—just missing her—through the open doorway, and out into the darkness of the night. Then the beam winked out, and Gillian fell to the floor and lay still.

Aaron spun around to cover Caroline, but she'd made no move to attack him. Instead she was looking at him with smoldering lust in her gaze.

"The others are gone now, Aaron. All of them. There are no more Insiders, no more Dements. Just you and me." She started walking slowly toward him, moving with predatory grace. "But we still have the Overshadow. We could start over, just the two of us.

We wouldn't have to share the Overshadow with anyone else. It would be all ours, its pleasures reserved for us alone."

She came within two feet of Aaron, but he didn't lower the gun.

"You're the one who caused all this." Aaron gestured with his free hand at the bodies surrounding them. "You wanted to kill me because you thought I was allied with the Dements, and now you want to be lovers again?"

Caroline shrugged. "Can't a girl change her mind?"

"What about my family?"

"What about them? We can't let them live, of course. They know too much now. They're already in the back, bound and gagged with duct tape. All we have to do is move them inside the Overshadow's circle and it will all be over with. And then *our* new life can begin, Aaron. Just you and me, together forever."

Aaron looked into Caroline's eyes and saw the madness glittering within them. It called to his own madness, but though it was the hardest thing he'd ever done, he resisted its lure.

"I want to see my family. Let's go. He gestured with the gun to indicate Caroline should precede him.

She bowed her head. "If that's what you want." Then she turned and started walking toward the Overshadow's chamber.

Aaron followed, gun barrel pointed at the space directly between Caroline's shoulder blades. If she so much as twitched, he'd fire.

They entered the back room, and stepped into cold

darkness. Now Aaron could see almost as well as if it were full daylight in here. He saw the black mass of the Overshadow rising forth from within the circle of its concrete prison. And lying before it—well inside the circle's perimeter—lay three withered husks, each bound with duct tape at the wrists and ankles. There was no tape over their mouths, though, despite Caroline's earlier claim. Each mouth was stretched wide in a silent, frozen scream.

Aaron stared at the corpses of his family. He knew he shouldn't be surprised to find them dead, and on one level he wasn't. But the sight nevertheless came as a shock to him. He raised the 9mm to his head, intending to press the barrel to his temple and fire. But before he could, he felt a pair of hands slam into his back and shove him forward. He stumbled, dropping the gun as he crossed over the thin circle carved into the concrete floor.

He fell onto Kristen's body and felt her brittle bones snap to kindling beneath his weight. Horrified, he flung himself off his wife's corpse and fell backward onto Colin's and Lindsay's. More bones broke, and he sobbed as he tried to scuttle away from the desiccated remains of his children. He came close to the circle's edge, but before he could cross back to the other side, a dark pseudopod emerged from the Overshadow's side and shot toward him. The tentacle encircled his left wrist and held him tight, preventing him from escaping. He hissed in pain as he tried without success to pull free. The Overshadow's touch was so cold that it burned. Aaron wasn't afraid to die, though. How could he be when he'd been prepared to end his own life a few moments earlier? He deserved what was about to happen to him, and no matter how much it hurt, it could never be as painful as the knowledge of what had happened to his family as a result of his betrayal.

Caroline laughed. "Well, lover, it looks like I'm going to be the sole member of Penumbra soon. But don't worry; I plan to have a ball starting over." She walked up to the circle's edge and stopped, ready to accept the Overshadow's gratitude after it finished with its latest sacrifice. "Good-bye, Aaron. It's been fun."

Aaron opened his mouth to shout obscenities at her, but a second tendril of darkness slithered inside and wormed its way down his throat. Cold fire eruped through every cell of his being as the Overshadow prepared to begin leeching away his life force on a microscopic level. The agony was far beyond any pain he'd ever known or imagined could exist, and his only comfort came from knowing that it wouldn't last long.

Then Aaron became aware of another presence inside his mind, and he remembered feeling the same sensation the previous two times he'd experienced the Overshadow's touch. He'd felt then as if the Overshadow was trying to communicate with him somehow, but he hadn't been able to tell what it wanted. Now, inside the circle, their contact so much stronger and more intimate than before, Aaron thought he understood what the Overshadow was saying.

You are strong, and you are more than good enough. You are worthy.

And then the Overshadow asked Aaron a question, and Aaron told it yes.

* * *

Caroline was so full of excitement that she could barely stand still. The Insiders hadn't received the Overshadow's blessing after it had drained Aaron's family, and now that it was draining Aaron himself, that meant it would have fed on four lives. Since none of the others survived, that meant she alone would get the full undiluted measure of the Overshadow's gratitude for tonight's four sacrifices. She didn't know if she'd be able to withstand such pleasure. It might well kill her, but if it did, it did. As she'd told Aaron in Deja Brew, ultimate pleasure was worth any price, including her own life.

She watched as the Overshadow reached down Aaron's throat, beginning the process of feeding. She waited to see smaller tendrils emerge from Aaron's ears, nostrils, his pores . . . but none did. She frowned, sensing that something was wrong but unsure what. Then she realized that the Overshadow had grown smaller, perhaps by as much as a foot or more. She looked closer and, though it was difficult to tell from the Overshadow's ebon surface, it appeared that it was continuing to flow into Aaron's mouth, almost as if it were pouring itself into him. The Overshadow wasn't feeding on Aaron; in some strange way, *he* was feeding on *it*.

Caroline watched in horrified fascination as the main body of the Overshadow continued to shrink as it flowed into Aaron's body. Aaron showed no sign that the process alarmed or pained him. He sat still as the Overshadow did its work, and no matter how much of its dark substance entered Aaron, his body didn't increase in size one bit. But then it wouldn't, would it? Caroline thought. Darkness—*true* darkness—had no volume or weight. It simply was.

When it was nearly over and all that remained visible of the Overshadow was a wriggling tentacle hanging out of Aaron's mouth, he stood. The tendril disappeared down his throat as quickly and easily as if he'd slurped up a piece of black spaghetti, and then the Overshadow was gone.

Aaron smiled at her, and she saw that his eyes had become twin pools of swirling darkness. She remembered how her parents had described the nameless man in the yellowed suit who'd given them the infant Overshadow—remembered that he'd had similarly dark eyes—and she shuddered.

"You were all fools," Aaron said. His voice was calm, relaxed, as if he were merely making small talk. "Any one of you might've become the Overshadow's avatar, but your lust and gluttony made you deaf to its voice. Made you unworthy."

Aaron stepped toward her and Caroline instinctively backed away. He crossed the circle's boundary without hesitation, whatever mystic power it held useless against him. Or perhaps the circle had never possessed any power at all, and the Overshadow had merely remained inside while it grew and waited for a suitable host to arrive.

"It's really too bad you missed out on this," Aaron said. He continued to advance, the darkness in his eyes pulsing with each step. "It's the most wondrous feeling . . . like being a god." He cocked his head to the side, as if reconsidering his words. "No, better than that. The concept of *god* is too limited. We are Darkness."

Caroline screamed and turned to run, but Aaron opened his mouth and a vast ebon wave rushed forward to engulf her, and when it receded, she was gone, without even a withered corpse to indicate she'd ever existed at all.

CHAPTER NINETEEN

Aaron sat behind the wheel of the Ford Sierra van. He was driving on Route 70, heading east toward the Ohio state line, Ptolemy left far behind. He wasn't exactly sure yet where he was headed, but that was all right. He'd figure it out—*they'd* figure it out—soon enough.

"Everybody doing okay?" he asked. He caught a glimpse of his face in the rearview mirror. His hair had grown back, and his eyes looked normal, though perhaps the pupils were somewhat larger and darker than before.

"Just fine, sweetheart," Kristen said.

He smiled at his wife, then turned to glance at the backseat. "How about you two? Either of you getting hungry yet?"

"I'm fine, Dad. But thanks for asking," Colin said. He'd found his manners in the last few days, and Aaron was pleased. It looked like his boy was on his way to becoming a man.

"I'm cold," Linsday said. "Can you turn up the heat?"

Though it had to be ninety degrees outside, Aaron said, "Sure thing, pumpkin." A slim tendril of darkness emerged from his right nostril, whipped toward the heating controls, adjusted the temperature higher, then retreated back into Aaron's body as quickly as it had appeared.

"Better?"

"Much. Thanks, Daddy."

"No problem." Aaron settled back into his seat, feeling truly happy for the first time in years. Part of it was because he'd decided to simplify their lives—leave behind his practice, the house, his Lexus . . . It wasn't like they'd be needing these things anymore, not with the work they had to do. The Insiders had misused the dark gift they'd been given. The Overshadow's glory was too great to be hoarded. It should be shared with everyone, everywhere. And that's just what Aaron and his family were going to do.

Still, everything wasn't perfect. Sure, he had his family back, thanks to the Overshadow. What it took, it could restore—to a degree. But it would have been nice if the dark power that now dwelled within him had been able to do something about the smell.

"Any idea where we're going yet?" Kristen asked. The movement of her jaw caused her upper lip to detach on one side, and the gray flap of flesh dangled from the corner of her mouth. Good thing Aaron had done plenty of suturing during his years as a vet. He'd stitch Kristen's lip back on when they stopped for the night.

An image appeared in Aaron's mind then, a vast metropolis of gleaming silver buildings stretching toward a dead black sky, and he felt the Overshadow's hunger stir within him.

"New York." He smiled, and shadows moved behind his teeth. "For starters."

TIM WAGGONER

LIKE DEATH

Scott Raymond is a man haunted by his past and terrorized in the present. As a young boy, he witnessed the brutal murder of his family, but there is so much of the gruesome tragedy that he simply cannot remember. The memories won't come, but the trauma won't go away.

Scott is an adult now, still scarred but learning to deal with it. He has come to Ash Creek to write about another mystery, a missing girl named Miranda. Here, Scott meets another girl named Miranda, who bears an uncanny resemblance to the one who's missing—but she's the wrong age. She will draw Scott into the bizarre hidden world where nightmares are very real...and very deadly.

PANDORA DRIVE

TIM WAGGONER

The small town of Zephyr, Ohio, is home to a very special young woman. Damara is reclusive—and she has the ability to make other people's dreams, fears and fantasies all too real. But this isn't an ability that she can control, as many people in town are beginning to learn. For some, dreams are becoming living nightmares. For others, their deepest fears are suddenly alive and worse than they ever imagined.

As Damara's powers sweep like a wildfire through the town, her neighbors' long-hidden desires are dragged out into the open—and given life. But as the old saying goes, be careful what you wish for, because in this case…it could kill you.

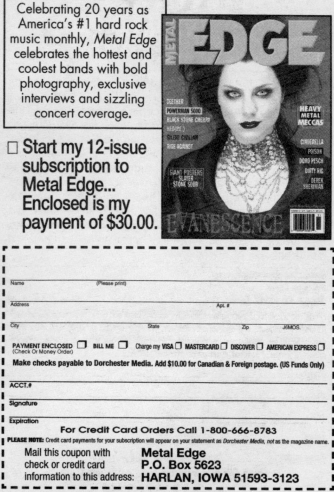

SLITHER

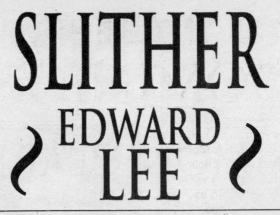

EDWARD LEE

The trichinosis worm is one of nature's most revolting parasites. Luckily, these worms are rarely more than a few millimeters in length. But guess what? Now there's a subspecies that's thirty feet long...

When Nora and her research team arrived on the deserted tropical island, she was expecting a routine zoological expedition. But first they found the dead bodies. Now members of her own team are disappearing, and when they return, they've...changed. And is there any sane explanation for the lurid, perverse dreams she's been having? Indeed, there are other people on the island. But the real danger is something far worse.

DEATH'S
DOMINION

SIMON CLARK

Modern scientists have proven Dr. Frankenstein right. They have discovered a way to raise the dead. Unlike Dr. Frankenstein's monster, these gentle creatures docilely serve their masters, but the living have begun to despise the dead among them. They are disgusted by their creations, and the government has set out to systematically destroy every last one of the "monsters." The monsters cannot fight back—it's not in their nature to defend themselves. That is, until one of the creatures retaliates against humanity with shocking brutality. In the war between the living and the dead, a new leader has arisen.

RICHARD LAYMON

THE
CELLAR

They call it Beast House. Tourists flock to see it, lured by its
history of butchery and sadistic sexual enslavement. They enter,
armed with cameras and camcorders, but many never return.
The men are slaughtered quickly. The women have a far worse
fate in store. But the worst part of the house is what lies beneath
it. Behind the cellar door, down the creaky steps, waits a
creature of pure evil. At night, when the house is dark and all is
quiet...the beast comes out.

- -